TIMBER
CREEK
STATION

Carolrhoda Lab™ is a trademark of Lerner Publishing Group, Inc.

Carolrhoda Lab™
An imprint of Carolrhoda Books
A division of Lerner Publishing Group, Inc.
241 First Avenue North
Minneapolis, MN 55401 U.S.A.

For reading levels and more information, look up this title at www.lernerbooks.com.

Front cover: © Szekely Katalin/Shutterstock.com (shadow); © Lena Pan/Shutterstock.com (cracked desert); © Muamu/Shutterstock.com (tree).

Main body text set in Janson Text LT Std 10.5/15.
Typeface provided by Linotype AG.

Library of Congress Cataloging-in-Publication Data

Lewis, Ali, 1976-
    [Everybody jam.]
    Timber Creek Station / by Ali Lewis.
      pages cm
    First published in 2011 by Andersen Press Ltd, London, under the title, Everybody jam.
    Summary: Thirteen-year-old Danny Dawson lives on a cattle station in the Australian outback, where his family struggles to cope with the accidental death of his older brother a year earlier and his sister's pregnancy by an Aboriginal.
    ISBN 978-1-4677-8117-6 (lb : alk. paper)
    ISBN 978-1-4677-8816-8 (eb pdf)
    [1. Ranch life—Australia—Fiction. 2. Family problems—Fiction. 3. Coming of age—Fiction. 4. Pregnancy—Fiction. 5. Racism—Fiction. 6. Household employees—Fiction. 7. Australia—Fiction.]
    I. Title.
PZ7.L
[Fic]—dc23   2015001620

Manufactured in the United States of America
1 – BP – 7/15/15

TIMBER CREEK STATION

ALI LEWIS

carolrhoda LAB

Minneapolis

For Lucas, Ollie, Megan, Jess,
and Beth, with love

ONE

I'd known for ages how a baby was made. I'd seen enough animals rooting to work it out. But now my older sister, Sissy, was having one and because of that we didn't look at each other —just at her belly. I'd seen everyone doing it. Dad stared at it bulging under the tablecloth at dinner each night, like it was the news.

Sissy was fourteen—just a year older than me—which everyone said was too young, but no one knew who she'd been rooting with. When she came home from boarding school for the Easter holiday, she was throwing up all the time. You couldn't get into the bathroom in the morning to go to the dunny because she'd be in there puking her guts up. I was desperate one morning, so I banged on the door and told her to get a move on, but all I could hear was her heaving and coughing and then something splattering. Eventually she ran out and went straight to her bedroom and slammed the door— like it was my fault.

At first Mum reckoned Sissy'd picked up a nasty bug at school. She gave her crackers and plain toast to try and settle it down. But when Sissy'd been home a couple of weeks and she was still hogging the bathroom each morning, I heard Mum tell Aunty Veronica that the penny dropped—she's up the bloody stick. I didn't know exactly what that meant, but I guess she'd worked out that Sissy wasn't really crook.

Then one night at dinner Sissy was sat in her usual place at the table, but her eyes looked redder than normal. She'd been such a dag since she came home—throwing up, staying in her room and crying all the time, I didn't really think too much about it. But as we all got on with our food, I noticed Sissy pushing hers round the plate. It was steak, so I said that if she didn't want it, I'd eat it. When Dad put his knife and fork down and looked at Mum, I dunno why, but it made me feel a bit like when I found out about Jonny's accident. I thought the steak I'd been shoving into my belly might jump back out again. I looked at Jonny's photo on top of the piano and wished I could run and touch it.

Dad sighed and looked round the table before he took a deep breath and stared at Sissy. As he breathed out he said we might as well all know that Sissy was pregnant. Then he looked back at his plate and ate another mouthful of steak. I nearly choked on my mashed potato, but the farm hands, Lloyd and Elliot, didn't say anything. They just cleared their plates real fast and went outside for a beer. I stared at Sissy, who'd started to cry again.

When Mum asked if anyone wanted more veg, it almost made me jump. No one answered. I guess no one felt hungry any more. That's when Emily, my younger sister, said, "What's prejant?" She is useless. She is seven and can't do anything properly. All she does is talk about the poddy calves, but she never feeds them—she just wants to pet them, and give them stupid names.

Mum sighed and put her arm on Emily's shoulder as she

explained that pregnant meant Sissy was going to have a baby. Emily's eyes got real big and this dumb smile filled her cheeks as she said, "A real one?" Like it was a good thing.

Not long after that we were told to help clear the table and go to our rooms. Then there was a big bluey. I heard it all through the wall between my bedroom and the dining room. It was the first bluey in our house for ages—I reckon it was the first since Jonny's accident. It started with Mum and Dad talking to Sissy in their normal voices, but then they shouted. They wanted to know who she'd been rooting with, but she wouldn't tell them. "Come on, Sissy—who is it?" Mum pleaded. "Just tell us, will you, love?"

Then Dad cut in: "It'll come out in the end—these things always do, so you might as well just save us all the bother and tell us now. Is it one of the boys at school? The little mongrels."

"Why won't you tell us?" Mum asked. "Does he know you're pregnant?"

I reckon Dad got tired of waiting for an answer because that's when he said, "For God's sake, just tell us who it is. WHO IS IT?" I guess he hit the table because there was a loud bang and that's when Sissy started to blub.

Mum said, "Derek, leave it," at the same time as a chair scraped on the wooden floor. I heard footsteps and Sissy's bedroom door banged.

Dad said, "When I find him—God help the little bastard!"

Mum said, "Oh, shut up, Derek!"

Then they really started to row. I pulled the doona over my head and imagined Jonny's picture was in my hand.

After that, Sissy seemed to blub even more than before. She hardly ever came out of her room, and when she did, there was always a row between her and Mum and Dad. Sissy'd always been OK—she wasn't like the girls you see on the TV, all stupid and into dumb stuff like dolls or makeup. She could ride the motorbike better than me, and she could shoot pretty good too. Not as good as Jonny, of course. I dunno, it was like she'd tell me stuff—about things no one else would. She was the one who told me about when the flying doctor came for Jonny—and all the blood.

But then, after she got pregnant, that all changed. She didn't talk to me any more—not really. She didn't really talk to anyone, I guess. All she did was cry. She blubbed after I called her a stupid cow for stealing my wickets. I'd spent ages looking for them and then found she'd used them to wedge the door of the chook pen shut. Before, if I'd called her a name like that, she'd have given me a dead arm.

Once she was up the stick everything changed. I wasn't allowed to hit Sissy—even if she really annoyed me, like when she stole food from my plate. Before I would have whacked her, you know, a dead arm, or something, but because of the baby, I got into trouble just for calling her a name. Dad said I had to be nicer to her because she was going to be a mum. I dunno why the rules suddenly changed just because she was up the stick. I asked Dad about it and he said, "They just do, OK?" Like I was the one in trouble.

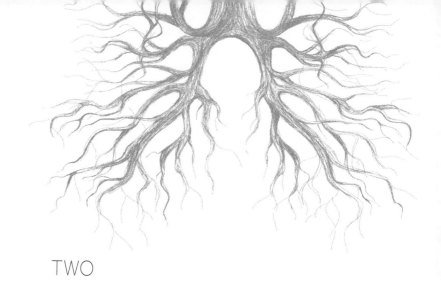

TWO

Sometimes, when everyone annoyed me, I'd go to my bedroom and sit on Jonny's bed. He was fifteen when the accident happened. That was when everything kind of stopped. Well, not stopped exactly. It was a bit like when the ute got three flat tires, or the time when the bank phoned, or something else went wrong. Whenever that happened, we all kept out of the way until Mum and Dad had sorted it. We kind of made ourselves invisible, so we were no trouble to them. With most stuff that would last a few hours, or maybe a day if it was something real serious, like when the generator broke. Only with Jonny's accident, I guess they couldn't fix it, so we'd been invisible for a while.

That's why I liked to keep our room exactly as Jonny'd liked it to be—how he'd left it. No one was allowed to touch his stuff. No one. Mum tried once. She came into our bedroom a few weeks before we found out Sissy was pregnant. She came in to see if I had any laundry, and as she picked up a few things off the floor, she said she reckoned it would be a good idea to start thinking about sorting Jonny's things out. I dunno what she meant by that. There wasn't anything to sort out; his stuff stayed where it was, how he liked it. When I explained that to her, she put down the things she'd picked up and said she didn't mean we should throw anything away, but just change the sheets and tidy a bit. I stood up and shouted "No way" at her. Mum turned to look at me for a moment, then held up her hands and left the room. I guess she knew I was right.

Jonny's accident happened about six months before we found out about Sissy and the baby. Her getting pregnant meant everyone seemed to forget about Jonny, like he'd never been here, or something. Like it gave them an excuse not to think about him any more. So they didn't miss him, I guess. Everything then was about her and that baby. I couldn't stand it. I didn't want Jonny to be invisible. There was a photo of him on top of the piano and I liked to touch it, every day if I could. I think I started doing it to remember what he looked like. I dunno, really, it just made me feel better. Like keeping all his things just how he had them. If I looked at them, I always put them back. I never mixed them up with my stuff. That would have been wrong, like stealing.

A few days after we found out about Sissy, I sneaked into the kitchen, hoping to grab some bickies without Mum catching me. I was stopped in my tracks, though, because she was in there on the phone. She was busy yabbering on to Aunty Ve in Alice Springs. I knew it was her because she was the only person who ever phoned. I hung around wondering if I might be able to sneak into the pantry without Mum noticing. That's when she told Aunty Veronica that Sissy was three months gone, so it must have happened some time around Christmas.

I was getting down on the floor and thinking about crawling into the pantry, so she wouldn't see me. Then Mum said, "I dunno, love, we can't think it would be either Elliot or Lloyd—I mean really? They're decent fellas—Elliot especially." I guess Aunty Ve didn't know Elliot and Lloyd very well, 'cause there's no way they could have been rooting with Sissy. No way. They're loads older than her for a start. Then Mum got mad with Aunty Ve, so I stopped where I was on my belly on the floor and listened. Mum never got mad with Aunty Ve. She said something like, "Over my dead body—we couldn't, we just couldn't! After everything else we've all been through with Jonny. I can't believe you'd suggest that—and the same goes for having the baby adopted." I didn't think having the baby adopted was such a bad idea. I mean it was already causing everyone a whole heap of stress, and it hadn't even been born. I reckoned that was the best idea anyone had had for ages, but I guess Aunty Ve must have apologized for whatever she'd said because Mum calmed down then and said she was sorry for losing her rag. Her voice went kind of quiet when she said she didn't know how we were going to manage after the baby came. She reckoned she was going to see about reducing her hours at work.

I stopped listening then for a bit—I was still trying to work out how to slip along the floor into the pantry where the bickies were without Mum seeing me. I was thinking about just making a dash for it, when Mum said the worst bit. She said Sissy couldn't have chosen a worse time to have a baby. "We've got the muster happening the same month it's due," she said.

The muster is the best part of running a cattle station. It's when we round up all the cattle and decide which will go for slaughter and which will stay on the station for another year. It only happens once a year and this one was going to be my last before I went away to boarding school in Alice. I didn't want Sissy and her baby ruining it. I couldn't help it, I was so mad, I forgot all about the bickies and jumped up and shouted at Mum. I yelled that it wasn't fair—Sissy and that baby were ruining everything. I shouted that I hated Sissy and her dumb baby. Mum shook her head at me and asked Aunty Ve to hold on a minute. She put her hand over the phone as she told me to stop being such a baby and to go to my room, before turning her back to me and carrying on talking to Aunty Ve. I heard her say, "Oh, nothing—just Danny having a fit about nothing, as usual." That made me madder than anything. I stormed off to my room, slammed the door and ripped some pages out of Jonny's cattle book. I dunno why. I was sorry afterward, so I stuck them back in. No one noticed.

––––––––––

Sissy couldn't go back to boarding school in Alice Springs, so she had to go to the schoolroom on the station with Emily and me instead. That's where we learn maths and writing and stuff. The schoolroom is an old shed Dad tidied up when Jonny and Sissy were little. It's pretty basic—wooden with a metal roof, so if it rains it gets so noisy you can't hear the lesson any more. Not that it had rained for a while—not really. When the rains really came the rivers filled up and kind of flooded a bit—but that hadn't happened for ages. We hadn't had enough rain to wet the ground, really—not for a couple of years. We'd had one little shower, but Dad reckoned he could spit and do a better job.

Anyway, we went to the schoolroom every morning at seven o'clock until around lunchtime when it was too hot to concentrate any more. We only went to the schoolroom until we were thirteen, though. That's why after Christmas I was going to go to the boarding school Jonny and Sissy used to go to. I guess that's why Sissy was so unhappy about being in the schoolroom again. She must have felt kind of stupid sitting with us, even though she had her own schoolwork to do. Every day, when we walked over there from the house, she had a face like someone had slapped her. I didn't speak to her, but Emily did—always about the baby and what she was going to call it. They were both so dumb.

Bobbie had been our govvie for more than a year. She helped us learn stuff using this radio program called School of the Air. It is for kids like us who live at places like Timber Creek, too far away from a normal school. Timber Creek Station is two hundred miles west of Alice Springs in the middle of the Tanami Desert in the Northern Territory. The nearest towns are Warlawurru thirty miles south of the station and Marlu Hill, twenty-five miles north. They're towns for Blackfellas though. Mum works in the office at the health clinic at Marlu Hill, so she drives over there each day, and even though there is a school there, it's just for the Blackfellas' kids. Sometimes we call them gins, as in Abori-GIN-al.

Bobbie was twenty-two and came from a farm in Victoria. She lived in one of the old outbuildings on the station. Dad had turned half of it into a bedroom for her, and she had her own shower and everything. We weren't allowed in there. It was out of bounds. Bobbie reckoned she needed some space and privacy. I dunno what for. In the afternoons all she did in there was read or watch TV. In the mornings she was with us in the schoolroom.

We had a few people working for us at Timber Creek. It was sixteen hundred square miles of desert and we had several thousand cattle, so Dad couldn't run it all by himself. That's why we had Elliot and Lloyd. Elliot had been with us the longest and he was real nice, kind of quiet, but a real hard worker. He knew what he was doing. I know Dad liked him a lot, reckoned he was real reliable. Elliot came from just up the road near Tennant Creek. His folks had a station out that way, but he was the youngest of four brothers, and there wasn't enough work for them all. Their station was a bit smaller than ours and because he was the youngest, and his older brothers were already working there, it was up to him to find a job somewhere else. I once said to him I reckoned that wasn't fair: it wasn't his fault he was the youngest. I said they should have pulled straws or tossed a coin or something. But he just smiled and shrugged. That was Elliot for you—he would never make a fuss.

Lloyd was different, he was real big and strong, which made him handy, but Dad reckoned you had to watch him because he wasn't too bright and he had a quick temper. He was newer to Timber Creek. He arrived not long before Jonny's accident and was a Top Ender—that meant his parents lived somewhere up near Darwin. Our neighbors, the Crofts, who have had a station fifty miles east of ours, had heard from a friend of a friend that Lloyd was looking for work and suggested Dad take him on. At the time Dad wasn't sure about it. He didn't like old Dick Croft sticking his beak into our affairs. Dad reckoned we were doing OK, but Mum said she reckoned Dad was working too hard and it would be good for Elliot to have a mate on the station. She reckoned it was lonely for Elliot. Dad agreed and said he didn't want to lose Elliot, he reckoned he was worth his weight in gold. So Dad thought about it a bit, and after he met Lloyd, I guess he reckoned he'd be handy to have around. And then after Jonny's accident, we were kind of a man down, so I reckon Dad was real glad he'd taken Lloyd on.

The Crofts had been my family's friends and neighbors for years and years. They ran a cattle station called Gold River, which was on the eastern side of our land. Emily once asked Dick why his granddad had called it that. He hesitated for a while and said, "Well, I guess my granddad was an optimist." Later Emily said, "Danny, what does an optimist do?"

All the rivers near us had been dry for so long because of the drought, they were all a kind of gold color like the rest of the desert. Maybe there'd been a drought back then too.

My great-granddad bought Timber Creek Station after the last owner, Arthur Simpson, died in 1930. Ever since then, Dad said, there'd been Dawsons and Crofts working side by side to make a living off the desert. Before my granddad, Alex Dawson, died, he'd been good mates with Dick Croft. Dick was real nice, but he'd got lanky now, like someone had dressed a dead tree. He rattled, as though a pea had got stuck in his breath, and when he talked he wheezed like I did if I ran around the yards chasing a steer—only Dick didn't have an inhaler to make it stop. I once asked Dick's son, Greg, what was up with his dad; he just said: "Too many smokes."

Greg smoked. He was a real hoot. Once he told us this joke: What's the difference between a gin and a dog shit? One eventually turns white and loses its smell. We all died. After Jonny's funeral, Greg gave me a hat. It was real smart: leather. He said it was time I started dressing like a proper stockman. He'd picked it up in Alice when he'd met with his mates. They'd had a wild time. There'd been a fight and one of his mates had been banged up.

Aunty Veronica, my mum's sister, once said it was time Greg found himself a good woman. I dunno what for. Greg ran Gold River cattle station with his sister Mary's husband, Ron. Dick was too old and crook to work much. He had a girlfriend called Penny who looked after him. He met her in a roadhouse. She was younger than Dick and had real yellow hair. Mum said it came out of a bottle. I dunno where Dick's old wife Mavis was. No one really talked about her. Mum said

Mavis ran off with some fella from Katherine when Greg and Mary were kids. That meant Dick had to run the station and look after them all by himself. Gold River was bigger than Timber Creek too. I guess Dick was real glad when he met Penny—it meant he didn't have to do everything himself any more. When I said that to Dad, he nodded and said he reckoned Penny would put the smile back on any fella's face.

Greg's sister, Mary, didn't say much, but Mum reckoned she was real nice. And everyone liked her husband Ron. When they got married, the Crofts had a big barbecue. There was loads of food and a band. We all stayed up real late. Even Emily.

The Crofts had been great after what happened with Jonny and everything, but they had their own cattle station to run, and we couldn't rely on them to help us all the time. I heard Mum saying to Dad how she was worried about how we were going to cope. She was talking about the future and how things were going to be different with the baby coming and no Jonny. I guess everyone had been waiting for Jonny to finish school and start work on the station. He was going to be Dad's right-hand man. I felt sore about that—I knew I was younger and with me going to school in Alice, it meant I wouldn't be around as much, but I still knew a lot about running the station. Part of me wanted to scream at them so they remembered I was there, and the other part of me wanted to never speak to them ever again. But then Mum said something that made me feel even worse. She said she needed an extra pair of hands to look after the house and the young ones. She never called Jonny or Sissy young when they were thirteen. She told Dad she needed a house girl and he said OK.

THREE

HOUSE GIRL NEEDED. That's what it said in big red letters on the piece of card Mum was writing. Underneath, she put: "Job includes: cooking, cleaning, feeding chooks, pigs and calves, and looking after three children aged seven to fourteen on a Tanami Desert Cattle Station. Board and lodging provided. Fair rate of pay. If you're interested, give us a call."

Dad had said she should put a position vacant in the backpackers' hostel at Alice Springs. He said, "One of those young Pommies might just be dumb enough to want to work for us." There are a lot of Pommies in Australia traveling round, looking for work, and Dad reckoned you could pay them peanuts.

I reckoned it was a dumb idea. If Sissy couldn't go back to school, I thought she should help out more, then we wouldn't have to hire a Pommie house girl. I didn't want some Pommie living at the station, working for us. I didn't want anyone new there, making everything feel strange. It was bad enough all the baby stuff without someone new as well.

Mum had to take Sissy to the hospital in Alice because of the baby. She said Sissy needed to have a scan, so while she was there, she was going to put the job advert up on the notice board at a couple of backpackers' hostels—they were the places where the Pommies stayed. She reckoned one of them might read it and phone up.

Because Timber Creek is a fair way from Alice, whenever anyone needs to go into town, they always have a list of things to get, and we always phone the Crofts to see if they need anything too. The list can include just about anything you can think of. There's always food on it—fresh stuff we run out of first, like fruits and veggies, but there are other things, like spare tires, parts for the generator, feed for the calves, worming tablets, or bullets for the rifles. You name it.

Normally me and Emily wouldn't have had to go, but this time Mum reckoned we needed new shoes. I didn't want to go shopping; I wanted to stay at the station with Dad and the fellas. Usually I'd have been given one of Jonny's old pairs of boots to wear, but I dunno where his last pair went. I didn't want to ask anyone about that. I told Mum my boots were OK. A shopping trip to Alice with a bunch of girls was the last thing I wanted. I said she could just bring me a pair back, but she reckoned they were too expensive to risk getting the wrong size. The only good thing about it was it meant we'd get a couple of days off school.

While we were away, Bobbie had agreed to look after the house and the animals at the station. We had chooks, so we always had eggs; a few pigs for bacon; and the poddy calves that had been orphaned in the desert, we hand reared. They were all kept in sties, coops, and pens around the edge of the station. The house was in the middle, with the yard at the back. At the front there was Mum's garden. It was pretty big—you could play cricket in it. It had a lawn, which was a bit bald and burned by the sun and round the edge there were a few plants. Mum was real proud of them. She called them survivors on account of how they were still living despite the drought. We'd had hardly any rain for ages, so we couldn't afford to use the hose to water the garden any more. Instead Mum tipped the dirty water from the washing-up bowl onto the ground.

Mum had put the trailer on the back because we knew we would get too much stuff to fit it all inside the car. Driving all the way to town with a trailer on the back meant it'd take even longer than normal—at least four hours. Most of the journey was on the desert roads, which were just dirt tracks really. You don't get onto the Stuart Highway until you're just a few miles from town.

Sissy was oldest, so she got to ride in the front with Mum. I reckoned we should toss a coin, but before I could even get into an argument about it, Mum shouted at me, "Just be quiet and get in the back, will you?" I tried to explain I hadn't even done anything wrong, but Mum didn't let me get my words out. "Didn't you hear what I said?" she asked.

Mum wasn't like that before Jonny's accident. We used to go places and do things. Sometimes we all went to Clear Water Dam to swim, or we all watched the TV together. Mum would wheel the TV into the dining room on a trolley so it sat at the opposite end of the table to Dad, like another person. It was something we always did on Sundays so we could watch this Pommie show called *Last of the Summer Wine*—it was one of our favorites. But after the accident, that didn't happen any more. I guess no one wanted to laugh at the TV if Jonny couldn't join in too.

As we bounced along the dirt roads I watched the desert change from sandy ground, covered in tufts of spinifex grass, to rocky outcrops where everything was brown and orange and dry. After a while it changed again to patches of yellow earth between scruffy-looking witchetty bushes and gum trees. The sun was high as we overtook a big red kangaroo. It was all on its own and I wondered where it was going.

Sissy had hardly said a word for what felt like weeks, but Emily made up for it. As we drove along, she must have asked a million questions about what the doctor would do to Sissy in the hospital, what a scan was, how long it would take, if she'd have to have an operation, and if she'd die. When she asked that, Mum stopped the car and turned round to talk to Emily. I thought about opening the door, jumping out and running away from them all, back to the station. I dunno what stopped me. As I kept my eyes fixed on the desert outside I listened to Mum telling Emily no one was going to die. "Sissy's having a baby—the doctors just want to have a look and make sure the baby's growing properly. That's all."

I was sat behind Sissy and I watched a tear fall off her cheek and run down the seat belt. Crying again. My heart thumped and I thought my chest was going to explode, but I waited until the car started moving before I took my inhaler out of my pocket and sucked on it.

As we hit the Stuart Highway, the sound of the tires changed. They sounded lighter. I felt my chest loosen—like I could breathe again. As we cruised into Alice, it felt a bit like we were somewhere completely new. I've never been overseas, but I reckon it felt a bit like we were in another country. There were tourists everywhere. They were easy to spot with their shiny sunnies. They all seemed to be wearing white shorts, vests, and thongs. There was the odd Blackfella bumming around too, begging or getting into the grog. As we drove out of town, past the creek, where the Blackfellas camped, I felt a bit excited. It'd been a while since we'd seen Aunty Ve—only once or maybe twice since the funeral.

I liked Aunty Ve, but she looked kind of bad. Her head was the only normal bit of her body, it poked out like a cherry on top of the rest of her. Her body made a shape like a big tear. When she opened the door and walked down to the car, it looked like there were parts of her body that had a life of their own. They were moving in a different direction to the one she was going in. The thin dress she had on looked too weak for everything she had underneath it. She had swollen, flabby, scabby ankles, which overflowed from her shoes, as though her legs were melting into them like candle wax. As her breath heaved and sucked at the air, she pulled a hanky out from her dress sleeve and dabbed at the sweat on her face, like it was only in small patches. "Thank God for air con," she giggled in between gasps. It was like she hadn't a care in the world.

Aunty Ve reckoned we had perfect timing because she had just taken some cakes out of the oven. It was funny because I don't think I'd ever arrived at Aunty Ve's when there wasn't something real tasty just about to come out of the oven. She smiled and put her hand on Sissy's face as she asked how she was. I reckoned Sissy would start to blub again, but she didn't. She just shrugged. That's when Aunty Ve said, "It'll all be OK, you know?"

When Mum and Sissy came back from the hospital they had a little black-and-white picture that was meant to be of the baby—but it was rubbish. Sissy showed it to Aunty Ve who said she thought it was marvelous—the first glimpse of the next generation. Mum showed it to me and Emily. She kept pointing to where she said the baby's head was—but I reckoned she'd got it wrong. It was just a load of black and grey blobs—there was no way that was a picture of a baby. I told her I reckoned there must have been something wrong with the camera or they'd printed it wrong. They all laughed, but I knew Dad would agree with me when he saw it.

After we had dinner, Mum, Sissy, and Emily went to the supermarket to get all the food we needed, while Aunty Ve and me went to the backpackers' to put the job advert on the notice board.

Inside the backpackers' there was a big mob of people coming and going with these big bags on their backs. There were some more watching TV in the next room and a few playing cards outside while they drank beer. I reckoned they were the Pommies Dad talked about. He said most of them were lazy bastards. I guess he was right, so it made me wonder why we wanted one to work for us.

Aunty Ve stuck the job advert in the middle of the board, between an advert for a car someone was trying to sell and a notice asking for people to share a trip to Uluru—that's what the Blackfellas call Ayers Rock.

The next day, after we'd been to buy new shoes and stock up on a load of vehicle parts Dad had ordered, we said good-bye to Aunty Ve. She packed us off with enough cakes and food to keep us going for weeks, which was just as well because Sissy was hungry all the time. Mum reckoned it was because she was eating for two. Two big elephants, I guess.

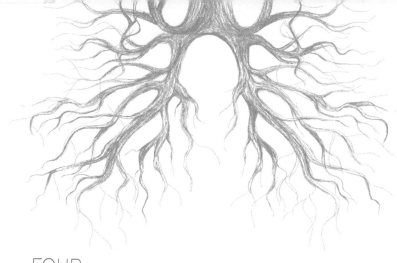

FOUR

We were all eating dinner one night a few weeks later, when the phone rang. It was the cops. They'd found a baby camel and didn't know what to do with it, so they'd phoned Dad to see if he had any ideas. Dad said he'd think about it and call them back. I dunno why, but as soon as I heard that, I shouted out that I'd have it. Dad raised his eyebrows and I thought I might be in trouble, but then he shrugged, looked at Mum, and said, "Well, it might be good for him—a new pet." Mum shook her head and said, "No way—we have enough calves as it is. It's a camel, not a toy."

Dad followed her into the kitchen and they had what sounded a bit like a row about it. When Dad came back on his own, he sat down at the table and looked straight at me. He said that if we did get the camel, it would be my responsibility, so I had to think hard about it. I said I wanted the camel. He shook his head and said I hadn't really thought about it, not properly. He reckoned it was a big commitment. Much bigger than the poddies. He said that if I didn't train the camel it'd be dangerous and it would have to be shot. He said we would talk again in the morning.

As I lay in bed, I could hardly breathe. I was scared and excited all at once. I thought about what Jonny would do and wondered if he'd been watching from heaven—or maybe that's just a story, like with the tooth fairy or Father Christmas. I dunno. The house creaked against the quiet. There was no one around, they were all in bed. I sat up and looked out of the window. It was real dark. There was no moon. I heard a cow somewhere in the distance as I threw off the doona and went into the dining room to touch Jonny's picture. It was so late. As I looked at him I felt kind of happy, I guess. It had been ages since I'd felt happy about anything much. It was like I knew I was going to get the camel. Like it was already mine.

As we ate breakfast I waited for Dad to ask me about the camel. I waited and waited. He talked to Elliot about a borehole that needed checking, he told Mum to take his ute to work so he could fix the oil pipe on the Ford, he asked Lloyd if he would go to Gum Tree Dam and look at the water level. The whole time I sat and waited. Dad tipped what I knew would be his last mouthful of coffee down his throat. That meant he was about to leave the table and go to work. I wanted to say something, but before I could, Emily shouted out, "What about Danny's camel?" I didn't know whether to hit her or smile at her. Dad looked at Mum and then at me. He said it depended on what I thought and if I wanted the responsibility. I looked him in the eye and said I reckoned I could handle it.

Two days later, Bobbie let us all out of school early because the cops showed up with a horse trailer with that little camel inside. We knew they were coming, so all morning we'd been listening out for them. I reckon Bobbie had got real sick of it. She knew none of us really had our minds on her lesson.

Dad came out from one of the sheds and shook the cop's hand. Then the cop lowered the tailgate and there was this gangly-looking thing inside. Its head was way too big for the rest of its body and its legs were too long and too thin—I dunno how it managed to stand up. Its eyes were enormous and when it opened its mouth I was surprised by the noise it made, it was more like a sheep. I heard the cop say to Dad, "It's only a baby, but it kicks like a bastard." I wasn't scared. I took the rope, which was tied around its neck and fastened to a hook on the side. I unhooked it and carefully led him down the ramp. The cop said, "Be careful, son." I reckoned he didn't know what he was talking about, until the little camel reared up and nearly knocked my head off.

Dad grabbed the camel from me and kicked him real hard. He said I had to get a stick and flog him each time he reared up until I'd knocked it out of him. "You have to remember he's real feral. You've got to show him who's boss—you understand?" I nodded.

I was worried about putting the camel in with the poddies. I didn't want him to hurt them. But Dad reckoned they'd be fine. Dad said he'd hold the camel while I went to get a bottle of milk to feed him. We gave him the same milk the calves had, except he drank it from an old pop bottle with a rubber teat on the end. It took a few goes to get him used to it, but I guess he was hungry, so he got the hang of it pretty fast.

The cop stayed for lunch. I didn't want any food. I just wanted to stay at the calf pen with the camel, but Bobbie said I had to have something. While we ate, the cop told us how a road train had hit the baby camel's mother on the Tanami Road. The camel had made a mess of the road train, and was in a pretty bad way. The driver had shot the camel and radioed the cops to report the accident. The cop said that when he got out there a baby camel had come out of the bush and was laid next to its mother's carcass. The road-train driver said he hadn't the heart to shoot it. Between then they managed to catch it. The cop thought the camel would have died of fright by the time he'd got it back to the little police station at Marlu Hill, but it didn't, so he phoned Dad to see if we'd have it.

All through lunch Emily wanted to know what I was going to call the camel. I said I hadn't thought of a name yet. She said I should call him Stuart or Christopher. I told her to rack off.

As soon as I'd finished off the beef sandwich Bobbie had made me, I said thanks to the cop for bringing the camel over and asked if I could get down from the table. Dad nodded and said I had to find a stick that was big enough for flogging a camel with before I went back in the calf pen. I was halfway down the steps into the yard, but I just caught the end of what he said before the fly screen on the back door slapped shut.

When I got to the calf pen, the poddies were ignoring the camel—like they knew he wasn't the same as them. The camel was all on his own except for a big mob of flies hovering around his head like a cloud. I decided then his name was Buzz.

I said it out loud to him that I was going to call him Buzz. He looked me in the eye and bleated before he stretched down to the ground and chewed at a little tuft of grass. I took that as a sign he liked it too and smiled to myself. As he lifted his head back up to look at me, I reached out and scratched his ears. The fur on top of his head was softer than it looked, but his skull felt all hard and bony underneath it. After a minute he got a bit excited and kind of reared up, but I had the stick next to me and all I had to do was show him it and he quietened down again. I was glad about that. I didn't want to hit him—not unless I had to, anyway.

FIVE

I'd had Buzz for a month or so when we had another phone call, which wasn't from Aunty Ve. Sissy picked up the phone. She'd stopped puking up by then and had started eating everything in sight. She was getting real fat—not as fat as Aunty Ve, but still pretty big. We'd eaten dinner and were clearing the table when Sissy handed the phone to Mum and said, "It's for you," before sulking back into her room. She still hardly spoke to anyone.

The phone call was from a Pommie wanting to find out about the house-girl job. I reckon Mum was as surprised as the rest of us because she seemed to fall over her words as she tried to answer the Pommie's questions. "We're in the desert, two hundred miles from Alice Springs," she said. "No, no . . . you'd have your own room in a building on the station. You'd be in the same building as our govvie, Bobbie—the girl who teaches the children . . . that's right, three children. Emily's seven, Danny's thirteen, and Sissy's fourteen." She didn't tell her Sissy was pregnant.

When Mum hung up the phone, she looked at Dad, who said, "So?" Mum reckoned the Pommie sounded OK and that she could start work at Timber Creek in a week, if someone could give her a lift to the station from Alice. I felt sick. I hoped every ute on the station would break down so no one could go and get her. Emily's eyes were wide and I could tell she was excited. "What's she called?" Emily shouted. Mum told her the Pommie was called Liz, and Dad laughed. He said we should call her Her Royal Highness—like the Queen.

A week later, the Pommie house girl arrived. Bobbie brought her back from Alice after she'd been to town to see a bunch of other govvies she was mates with. We all heard Bobbie's ute pull into the yard, so we went out to meet them. The door of the ute opened and the Pommie climbed out. I couldn't believe it when I saw her.

I knew straightaway she'd be useless. She was small and skinny, for a start. Her legs were thinner than the calves' and her arms were like Emily's. When we saw her we all knew she wouldn't be able to lift the salt meat out of the brine, or hook the side of a killer to the cool-room ceiling—so what was the point? I dunno why Mum and Dad didn't fire her there and then. Even Dad said he'd be surprised if the Pommie could carry a bucket of calves' milk. I don't think Mum had asked how big she was when she phoned up about the job. I guess she was just glad someone phoned.

The Pommie looked around her and smiled a little as she glanced at each of us and then at the buildings and the yard. She looked confused, I guess. A bit like she'd just been beamed onto the moon, or something.

Her hair was the same color as the spinifex, before it rained. And she smiled a lot; I dunno what at. She didn't wear normal clothes and her skin was whiter than ours. The fellas were sat outside the old demountable caravan where they lived, drinking beer. As they watched the Pommie, they pretended not to, like the dogs did when they waited under the table, hoping for a scrap of food.

Mum tried to shake the Pommie's hand—she was acting real weird. Emily jumped up and down and ran round and round the Pommie, getting in the way. She was behaving like it was Christmas. She kept trying to hold the Pommie's hand and to help her with her bags while Bobbie was showing her to the room she'd be sleeping in. If I was Bobbie, I'd have told Emily to rack off. The Pommie's room was in the same building as Bobbie's. Dad had spent most of the last week fixing it up. It had a bed and a rail for her clothes. He'd even found some carpet for the floor. When they got in there, though, I don't think the Pommie was too pleased with her new roommate. Emily had left her favorite poddy calf, Charlotte, in there. She reckoned the Pommie could have Charlotte if she wanted her. The Pommie smiled but I could tell she wasn't too keen. I reckon the amount of shit Charlotte had left all over the floor was what made her mind up. I was killing myself laughing. Emily was in big trouble, especially after Dad had worked so hard to fix the room up. Bobbie told Emily to take the bloody calf back to its bloody pen. It took Bobbie and Mum almost an hour to get the room sorted out. The dumb Pommie kept saying, "Please don't worry about it—really, it's fine." I dunno why she said that—we all knew it wasn't.

After Dad met the Pommie, he laughed and said she talked like the bloody Queen. She sounded slow—like she was thick, as well as posh. Each word took ages to come out, like when Aunty Veronica played records on the wrong speed to make us laugh. We hoped the Pommie worked faster than she talked.

The day the Pommie arrived was a Sunday and our neighbors, the Crofts, were coming over for a barbecue. Mum reckoned it would be nice to get everyone together to say g'day to the new Pommie house girl and make her feel welcome. Mum and Sissy had been busy in the kitchen all day, and Bobbie was helping the Pommie unpack her things. Emily wasn't allowed out of her room because of what she'd done with Charlotte. Me and the fellas were hanging around the cool room—that's where the home brew was kept. The grog always smelled bad, like something was off. I didn't like it, but Dad reckoned I would one day.

Dad and the fellas had talked about the clean skins that needed castrating. Lloyd said we should get the Pommie to help us. Dad laughed at that. He said, "Christ, Lloyd! I reckon you're the one who needs castrating; your brain's in your bollocks." We all laughed and Lloyd looked at the ground. I said the Pommie couldn't even castrate a kitten. Dad said I was right about that.

Mum came over with the Pommie. She said I had to show Liz how to feed the poddies, the pigs, and Buzz. I started to complain—I mean, why did I have to do it? Why couldn't fat Sissy show her round? Dad gave me a look though, so I knew I'd better just shut up and do it. Emily had been allowed out of her room by then, so she was there too—hanging off us like an itchy scab.

The Pommie didn't even know what a poddy was, so I had to explain it was a pet calf—one that had been orphaned, and then hand reared. She'd never even touched a calf before, so she reckoned I was an expert. I didn't get it—why would we want such a total drongo working for us? Everything took ages because there was a lot to explain. I had to start right at the beginning, with things like how to unhitch the gate and close it again so none of the poddies escaped; how to mix up their milk; how to distract them with the hose so you could get the calf feeder hooked onto the fence without spilling any milk; and how to make sure they all got a fair share.

When we got to Buzz, the Pommie's eyes nearly burst out of her head. She said he was handsome, but I could tell she was scared, and so could he. He nearly kicked her, but I pushed him away. I was showing her how to hold the teat onto the bottle while he suckled the milk, when he started to have a piss. It splashed up off the ground and sprayed the Pommie's bare feet. She only had thongs on and so she screeched like a bloody galah. All the poddies scattered like crows after a gun-shot, and Buzz ran off round the pen, bucking and kicking like a rodeo bull. I said to her, "What d'you expect? You can't get him to sit on a dunny each time."

She said, "His pee was really hot," like it was a secret. That made me laugh. What a drongo. She hadn't a clue.

I didn't bother telling her about how I wanted to break him in so I could ride him. I thought I might even race him. Dad said the Arabs did that in Africa. I wanted to take Buzz there and bring the cup back to Australia, but Dad said it would cost too much.

The Pommie liked Mo's piglets. I guess they were smaller, so she wasn't as scared of them—but they'd got fat enough for bacon. I told her how Mo had had three sisters: Eany, Meany, and Miny, but we'd eaten them. That's when the Pommie told me she was vegetarian. I was shocked. Dad always said it was unnatural. She asked me if there was anything I didn't like— pumpkin, eurgh. She said that was how she felt about meat. I reckoned that was why she was so thin.

Emily had got bored by then and had gone back to the house, but the Pommie wanted to go to see Buzz again. There was no way I was going to let her anywhere near him on her own—she'd probably leave a gate open or something. When we got there I showed her how to put a rope on him and walk him round the yards. He wasn't as feral as when I'd first got him, so Dad reckoned I was making progress. When Buzz and me walked together, it was like we were partners. Sometimes he'd test me, and I'd have to get a stick and flog him, but that didn't happen often.

The Pommie had a camera and she kept taking pictures of me and Buzz, like we were something special. She asked if she could hold the rope. I didn't want her to, but I wasn't sure what to say, so I let her. She put her hand on Buzz's cheek. She held it there and stroked him, real gently, just with her thumb. His eyes closed a bit and he made this low, growling sound, like he was purring. I told her to pack it in, I didn't want Buzz going soft on me.

Later, when the Crofts arrived, Mary and Ron went inside with old Dick, it was too hot outside for him. Penny wasn't with them, she'd gone into Alice to see her mum. While they all went inside, Greg came to sit with us fellas in the shady bit behind the cool room. When Greg sat down, he took off his hat, like he'd arrived at church. He said he was perishing after the drive over, so the fellas gave him a beer. After Greg tipped the bottle back and swallowed half of it in one go, he burped and the warm smell of rotten sugar wafted over. That was when Elliot asked Greg if he'd come to take a look at the Pommie house girl. They all laughed.

They carried on drinking the grog and telling stories about mustering. After a while we got interrupted when the Pommie showed up. Mum had asked her to get something from the cool room for the barbie. Everyone went quiet, like we'd been talking about her. Elliot's chair made a hard, scraping sound against the ground when he got up to let her past. None of the fellas looked at her when she smiled. Eventually Elliot said, "This is Greg Croft, he lives next door." The Pommie laughed and said she'd been speaking to Dick, who'd told her Gold River was fifty miles away. She said that in England, fifty miles wasn't next door—it was a holiday. Greg smiled and said if she wanted to take a holiday to Gold River, she'd be very welcome to stay with him. The others laughed, and the Pommie went red. Greg watched the Pommie walk back to the house, like the Blackfellas did when they were hunting kangaroo and they'd spotted a big red.

SIX

It was always a late one when the Crofts came over, so we were all tired the next day. While we waited for the Pommie to get us some tucker, no one said much. We all looked a bit like creased-up bits of paper, which someone had chucked away and then tried to straighten out again. The Pommie hadn't a clue where anything was, or what to make for us.

She'd asked what we all wanted for brekkie—that was her first mistake. Mum usually made something and we all just ate it. If you didn't like it, it was tough—you went hungry. But seeing as she'd asked, Dad laughed and said if the Timber Creek café was taking orders, he'd have a bacon sandwich. Mum asked for a poached egg on brown toast. I wanted rice bubbles and milk, followed by a bacon sandwich. The fellas said they wanted bacon and eggs with fried bread. Bobbie reckoned she'd just have toast with Vegemite, and that left Emily. Emily was in the kitchen helping. As we all waited longer and longer for some food to arrive on the table, we got quieter and quieter. Mum started checking her watch every other second—I guess she was worried about being late for work. Dad got real fidgety. He was like a bear with a sore head until he'd had a cup of coffee.

We knew something had gone wrong when the first lot of toast got burned and the smell wafted through from the kitchen. Dad raised his eyebrows and looked at Mum, who whispered, "Do you think I should go in and help?" Dad shook his head and said the Pommie would never learn if we did everything for her.

I could hear Emily telling the Pommie where things were kept in the kitchen. We don't use that pan for eggs, Liz. Mum always uses the other one. Why are you doing the toast in the grill? Mum always uses the toaster . . . It's over there, on the side. Why are you holding the tea towel against your face—don't you like the smell of bacon? Liz, can I have two slices of toast? When I stay at Aunty Ve's she cuts it into three pieces, with everybody jam on two of them and Vegemite on the middle one, so it's stripy . . . I wondered if the Pommie would know what everybody jam was—it's what the Blackfellas call apricot jam because everybody likes it. As I was thinking that, I reckoned I could smell burning again, so I got up and went to the kitchen door, just to see what was going on. Mum told me to sit back at the table, but I just wanted a quick look. And I'm glad I did.

I couldn't see the Pommie anywhere, but Emily was there. The bacon seemed to be smoking in the frying pan. Emily lifted it off the hob and put it down on Mum's plastic tea tray—the one Grandma bought her. She was too dumb to think that the hot pan would melt the plastic. So, then there was this sickly smell of burning plastic in the air, as well as a smoky smell. The toast under the grill was burning again, and before I could say anything about the tea tray, Emily put the tea towel down on the hob where the bacon had been, while she got the oven glove to pull out the grill and rescue the toast. When she turned away to put the toast onto the tray with the bacon, she saw it had melted. Just as I tried to warn her about the tea towel catching fire on the hob, the tea urn began to boil over. No one had thought to tell the Pommie not to fill it right to the top. Boiling water cascaded down the sides and across the floor, nearly scalding Emily's feet. I managed to push her out of the way and at the same time I shouted for Mum to come and help us. Mum just made it into the kitchen as flames from the tea towel suddenly licked at the ceiling and the water from the urn short-circuited the electric so the lights went off.

The dumb Pommie came back out of the pantry carrying a couple of jars of jam—she was saying something about not being able to find everybody jam, so would plum or apricot do? Her voice kind of trailed off to nothing as she noticed Mum's kitchen was about to start the biggest bushfire the Territory had ever seen. Luckily Dad was there. He reached over with his long arms and switched the hob off, then grabbed a pair of tongs and threw what was left of the tea towel into the metal sink where Bobbie was waiting to turn on the tap and put out the fire. Elliot had flicked the switch to turn off the urn. We all stood and stared through the smoke at what was left of Mum's kitchen. The Pommie's face had gone bright red and she was coughing because of the smoke. Eventually she said, "I was looking for everybody jam"—like that would explain everything.

I hoped the disaster at brekkie meant Mum would fire the Pommie. We didn't need a useless Pommie on the station, especially one who nearly burned the place down. I mean, no one else who'd worked for us had ever done anything as dumb as setting fire to the house before. But Mum decided to give her another chance. Seeing as the Pommie was new, and didn't know much about life on a cattle station,

Mum said Sissy would be in charge. She said Sissy could have the day off school to show Liz the ropes. That belly of hers was getting so big, she couldn't do any work anyway. I guess barking orders at the Pommie was as useful as she was going to get.

SEVEN

Everyone thought that when the Pommie arrived at Timber Creek, Mum'd be happier because she wouldn't have so much to do in the house, chasing around after us all the time. But it wasn't like that—not as far as I could tell, anyway. It was like having the Pommie there made it worse. After a few days I tried to tell Dad about it. He was in one of the sheds looking for a drill bit. I went in and said I was sick of the Pommie because she was useless and couldn't do anything right. But he just said that the house was Mum's responsibility and that she had a lot on and needed some help.

He nodded when I said the stuff again about the Pommie being useless, like he agreed with me, so I reckoned I was getting somewhere. I said how the Pommie wasn't much good at anything, which meant Mum spent most of her time checking up on her—like when she put Sissy's red socks in the washing machine with Mum's white work shirts by accident. The Pommie said she was real sorry. Mum said she had to pay more attention to what she was doing. Dad reckoned it wasn't the end of the world. He said we had to give her a chance to settle in. I said he should just fire her, but he held a hand up to me and said, "Leave it, Danny—I've got enough to think about without you bleating on about the bloody Pommie house girl."

That night Mum got home from work and found the casserole the Pommie had made for dinner in the oven. That would have been OK, except she'd forgotten to switch the oven on. It took ages for the casserole to cook—it wasn't ready until real late. That didn't just annoy Mum—everyone was mad. We were all perishing by the time it was ready. Mum reckoned we were all too tired to eat it. The Pommie was real flustered. She said she was sorry about a hundred times as we ate in silence. No one answered. We were too busy eating. Eventually Mum looked at Dad and said, "Well, it's not the end of the world, I suppose." Dad shook his head and said, "Not quite."

I realized living at Timber Creek wasn't like where the Pommie was from. When she came face-to-face with her first Blackfellas you'd think she'd spotted a spaceship. It was Davy Sugar, with Mick and Gil Smith. They'd called in to see Dad and to pick up a few things from the shop. Mum and Dad run a little shop at the station, just for the Blackfellas to use on their way to and from Marlu Hill and Warlawurru. They sell all kinds of stuff. Dad says it's just for essentials. They sell cans of Coke, bread, soap, tins of veggies, burgers, ketchup, lollies, cigarettes, bullets, biscuits, toothpaste, toilet paper— just the usual stuff. Anyway, Davy, Mick, and Gil were the Pommie's first customers, and I don't think they thought the service was that good.

When they all went to the shop, it was locked so they

came to the house to find someone to open it. When the Pommie saw them, she didn't know what to do. I was inside getting a drink of water so I said I'd show her. Mick, Gil, and Davy all followed us over to the shop. Gil was a bit like Mick's shadow. He walked just like his dad and he was about the same size and shape. I guess Mick was a pretty fit, strong fella in his day. Davy looked pretty short and kind of fat next to them.

Mick wore a hat—like a whitefella's hat, a bit like Dad's. He had a big, white beard and had a shirt and jeans on. Gil had a hat on too, but not like Mick's. He was wearing one of those beanies and he had on his usual T-shirt and jeans. It looked like the T-shirt was from an op shop, or something. It was real faded. On the front you could just make out the words Midnight Oil.

Davy was different. He was always scruffy and he smelled funny, kind of like smoke and sweat, or something.

Mick didn't say much. Dad reckoned Mick was an economical fella. He said Mick didn't move unless he needed to. I guess he didn't speak unless he needed to either. Davy was real friendly, but he kind of mumbled, so sometimes it was hard to hear what he said. He always did the talking when they were together. Mick just kept real quiet, except for saying g'day, of course.

Gil nodded at me and asked how it was going. I said I was OK and asked how he was. He walked over to the door and had a look around outside, like he was looking for something. As he walked back to the counter he noticed me watching him and he smiled a real big, toothy grin, so I smiled back. Jonny and Gil had been pretty good mates until Jonny went to boarding school. After that they didn't see so much of each other—just when it was the school holidays. They'd go off together—I dunno really what they did. Jonny didn't want me around if Gil was there. I hadn't seen him for a while. His hair had got long. I could see it poking out from the bottom of the hat, so he looked a bit like a surfer.

Gil nodded at Liz, as if to say who's the sheila? That reminded me that she was there. I told them Liz was our new Pommie house girl. She held out her hand for them to shake. Mick and Gil didn't say anything. Davy looked at the Pommie's hand and then back at her, before he shook it. She said, "Pleased to meet you." That made me laugh. I dunno why, just that no one else ever spoke like that, I guess. Davy asked if Liz was from London, so she explained she was from somewhere south of London. He didn't know where that was, so he just got on with asking for what he wanted to buy from the shop.

Davy asked for everybody jam, but he had to say it a couple of times because we couldn't hear him. The Pommie had found out what everybody jam was after she set fire to the kitchen, so that wasn't any trouble. Then he asked for four cigarettes. The Pommie gave him four packs because she didn't know we sold them separately. Davy got scared he was going to have to pay for four packs, but I sorted it out. Then he asked for a tin of mince, but the Pommie thought he said dinner mints—whatever they are. Then he wanted some bread and a kangaroo tail. The Pommie thought that was a joke until I showed her where we keep them in the freezer.

Davy said they'd stop off to see Dad and the fellas at West Rise. That was the water hole they were working at. Gil nodded at me as they left and said, "See ya around, Danny." They all got back in Mick's beaten-up, old red saloon, which was covered in dust from the desert. The exhaust threw loads of black smoke out as they drove away, making us cough a bit.

When we walked back to the house the Pommie made such a fuss about them, I asked her, don't you have Black-fellas in England? She said they did, but not like ours. She said the ones in England originally came from Africa or Jamaica—something to do with slavery. She said in England they had Indians, Pakistanis, Chinese, Africans, Arabs, Thais, Turks—everything, except Aborigines. I guessed that was what Bobbie meant when she said England was pretty crowded compared to Australia. That must have been why no Aborigines went there.

The Pommie asked me about Mick and Davy, so I told her about when Dad was a kid he used to go off with them, hunting kangaroo. I liked those stories. She was amazed by all that. I told her how Davy and Mick sometimes stayed at Cockatoo Creek Dam when life wasn't Aboriginal enough in Warlawurru and Marlu Hill. Dad said he didn't mind because they were decent fellas and the station's sixteen hundred square miles of desert, so there was enough room for us all. He put a water tank out there for them once, but one night they got real drunk and shot holes in it, so all the water ran out. The dumb Pommie smiled at that, but no one else thought wasting water was funny. I told her Dad was real angry about it, he didn't speak to Mick for a while after that. Then one day Mick showed up at the station. He'd been out in the desert, hunting or something, and he'd noticed we had a problem with one of the boreholes. I had to explain to the Pommie how we get water from under the ground by drilling boreholes—we pump it out for the cattle. Anyway, if there's a problem, it can be real serious. Dad didn't know anything had gone wrong, so he was glad Mick had called in. Mick reckoned he'd give Dad a hand to fix it and afterward they had a couple of bottles of the home brew in the garden together. I guess they were mates again after that. I liked Mick.

The Pommie and me were back inside the house then. As she got out the ironing board, she said, "So Mick's a neighbor too?" I told her the Crofts were our neighbors, not Mick. Mick just hung around in the desert when he got sick of things at home in Warlawurru. He didn't have a house in the desert, so he wasn't really a neighbor.

Sometimes Gil came with his dad. When Gil was little, Mick brought him to the station to play with Jonny. Mum reckoned Mick only did it because he wanted someone to babysit Gil. She said she felt sorry for Gil, being dragged about the desert with his dad and the other Blackfellas. Gil's mum wasn't around. She'd been killed in a car crash when Gil was little. Gil was in the car too—Mum reckoned it was a miracle he wasn't killed as well. The car hit a tree a few yards off the Tanami Road. No one knows how it happened. Maybe a big red ran out onto the road, or a wild horse, or something. Gil doesn't remember it—he was too little. Anyway, I reckon that's why Mum let him come to play.

I tried to remember when I'd last seen Gil. I reckoned it was probably during the Christmas holidays when he called in a few times. Last I heard, he'd got a job at the shop in Warlawurru.

That night, while Mum was in the dining room, looking at the books for the station, I asked her why we needed the Pommie when she didn't know anything about anything. Mum just said the Pommie would be fine once she'd got the hang of it. I asked how long that would take, but Mum didn't know. I said I reckoned it would take forever and that we should just fire her, like when Dad fired Olive Fish. She was the old govvie we'd had before Bobbie came. Miss Fish didn't last long. She didn't like us kids one bit—especially Jonny. She said he was a hooligan. We all reckoned she had a few kangaroos loose in the top paddock. I told Mum I reckoned the Pommie was the same. That was when Mum lost her rag and shouted, "For God's sake, Daniel. Enough. Can't you see I'm busy?" I went to my room and decided I'd have to teach the Pommie a lesson.

last long. She didn't like us kids one bit—especially Jonny. She said he was a hooligan. We all reckoned she had a few kangaroos loose in the top paddock. I told Mum I reckoned the Pommie was the same. That was when Mum lost her rag and shouted, "For God's sake, Daniel. Enough. Can't you see I'm busy?" I went to my room and decided I'd have to teach the Pommie a lesson.

EIGHT

Not long after that we found a mulga in the schoolroom—
that's a kind of poisonous snake, some people call it a king
brown. It was only a baby so Bobbie got a spade and hacked its
head off. Afterward, we all had a good look at it. It was only
small, but it could kill you. After it was dead I picked it up and
asked Bobbie if I could keep it. Bobbie asked what for, but I just
shrugged, I didn't want to give the game away. I guess Bobbie
didn't care what happened to the snake after it was dead, so she
told us all to sit back in our places and get on with our work.

I reckon the whole of the Territory heard the Pommie's
scream that night, when she pulled back her sheets and found
the headless mulga in her bed. We all ran out of the house to
see what had happened. The Pommie was pressed up against
the wall inside her room, scared to death, shouting, "There's
a snake in my bed!" Bobbie was there. She took one look and
knew straightaway what had happened. Dad, Elliot, and Lloyd
were all ready to kill whatever it was they thought was attack-
ing the girls. Dad had his pajamas on and was carrying a rifle.
Lloyd was only wearing his boxer shorts, but at least he had a
baseball bat. Elliot must have been asleep when the Pommie

screamed because he was holding a boot—I guess it was the first thing he'd found in the dark. When they realized what had happened Lloyd and Elliot shook their heads and wandered back to their demountable. I guess they didn't know whether to be annoyed about being woken up, or glad they hadn't come face-to-face with a mad axe murderer.

Dad looked at the Pommie and then at me and said, "Is this your handiwork?"

I nodded and laughed real loud and said, "Gotcha, Liz!"

The Pommie was still pretty freaked out I guess. She was holding her chest and shook her head. Dad picked up Emily and carried her back to the house. Mum reckoned we'd had enough excitement for one night and we all had to go back to bed. She said, "You OK, Liz?" as we all left. The Pommie nodded, but I could tell she was scared. I wondered how long she'd stick it at Timber Creek. The next day at brekkie we all laughed about it. I couldn't believe it when the Pommie smiled. She said she reckoned that while she was at Timber Creek, she'd have to learn to sleep with one eye open.

———————

A couple of days after that, the fellas were working near the station, castrating some bulls so I was real pleased. It meant I could have a ball fight. I went on my motorbike with a bucket to get some of the balls. They were pretty squishy, kind of horrible, like something out of a horror movie. I picked up almost a whole bucketful. Elliot helped me. He'd joined in with me and Jonny once when we had a ball fight at the yards. It was the best.

I drove back to the station with the bucket hanging from the handlebars. My hands were real sticky. When I got back to the house, Emily was in the garden, I could see her running around on the other side of the washing line where there were a couple of sheets hanging out to dry. It was perfect—the sheets meant she might not see me coming, so I could throw a couple of the balls at her without her even knowing I was there.

One hit her on the chest, leaving a real ugly, bloody mark, like she'd been shot, or something. She looked down and after the initial shock she laughed and pretended to collapse onto the ground in pain. We both laughed at that. She chased after me and tried to grab some of the balls. We chased each other round the garden, throwing the balls. We hid behind the washing on the line and jumped out at each other, I used one of the plastic chairs as a shield when I ran out of ammunition. I held it over my head as I searched the ground looking for balls we'd already used, so I had some to throw back at Emily.

Playing with Emily wasn't as good as it was with Sissy or Jonny. She didn't throw very well and she couldn't run very fast either, so it was easy to get her. I'd just made a perfect shot, which hit her right on the back, covering her in blood and slime, when the Pommie came round the corner from the side of the house. We hadn't heard her coming so when she shouted "What happened?" it took us a minute to understand what she was talking about. I guess seeing Emily and me covered in blood was bad enough, but then I noticed we'd accidentally got a bit on some of the washing too. "Look at what you've done!" she shouted. Emily and me were laughing at first, but then I guess we both knew we were in trouble.

The Pommie threw the laundry basket she was carrying on the ground. As she got closer to the white sheets and had a good look at the dirty marks she said, "Is this blood?" She noticed one of the balls on the ground then and bent down to look at it. That's when she said, "What is this?" Emily told her it was a ball. I reckoned the Pommie was probably thinking we meant a cricket ball, or something, so I said it was a bull's ball, just so she understood. She looked real shocked then and said, "A what?" Then her face changed again and she smiled and said, "Oh no. No way—nice try, but you're not going to get me this time. Very funny. Not falling for it, though." She reckoned it was another joke.

Emily looked at me and then back at the Pommie like she'd gone mad. I opened my sticky hand and showed the Pommie the ball I was holding. I pointed at a few of the others on the ground around us and said I'd been to get them because the fellas were castrating bulls. I guess the Pommie still wasn't sure but she came closer to where I was to get a better look at what was in my hand. I guess then she knew we were telling the truth. Her eyes filled up with water and she shook her head. She said something like "disgusting" . . . but I guess she didn't know what to say next because she just turned round and walked away. Emily ran after her and I heard her say, "Are you crying, Liz?"

The Pommie started to run then. I looked at the bed sheets and the bloody marks on them and I felt kind of funny. I didn't know what to do. I guess we'd made a load more work for her, but there was no need to cry about it. It was just ball blood.

The fun had kind of gone out of the ball fight then. I went into the kitchen—there was no one around, so I reckoned I'd make myself a beef sandwich. I carried the plate into my room so no one would see me eating it. Mum never liked us eating between meals. When I opened the door to my room I saw what the Pommie'd done to Jonny's stuff and that's when I really kicked off.

She'd been cleaning in our room.

NINE

Mum had told the Pommie to wash my bed sheets that morning at brekkie. Mine. Not Jonny's. But she was so stupid—she'd stripped and washed them both! Not only that, she'd pulled everything out from under Jonny's bed too. She'd taken all the books he'd slipped under there just before he switched the light off to go to sleep, and put them on the shelves with the others. She'd reorganized the plastic boxes of cars and games so the lids clicked shut. She'd even swept all his soldiers—the ones he'd painted—off the top of the nightstand where he'd left them to dry. I dropped the plate I was carrying and it broke. The beef sandwich landed upside down and left a greasy skid mark on the floor. I hadn't had a chance to touch Jonny's picture that morning. Things always went wrong if I didn't touch it.

I ran back into the empty dining room and looked out of the glass doors. That's when I realized the sheets outside covered in ball blood were ours. Both sets of sheets were fluttering on the line. They looked pale in the bright sunshine, the brown, bloody marks all over them from the ball fight made them look like injuries, or something. I pushed the doors open and felt the heat of the afternoon steal my breath. I ran straight out into the garden and grabbed at the sheets. I yanked them off the line, dragged them into the house. I could hear a tap running in the bathroom, so I went in there. That's where the Pommie was, leaning over the sink, splashing water on her face. My face was burning and my chest felt tight, even when I breathed out. When the Pommie realized I was stood behind her, I started to shake. I had all sorts to say, but everything I needed to tell her felt feathery, flying round in my head. She'd ruined everything. She had no business touching Jonny's things. No one was allowed to touch them. It all had to stay exactly where he'd left it. But when I opened my mouth, all I heard was, "You stupid cow, you washed Jonny's sheets!"

She looked at me, with the water dripping off her chin and a look on her face like I'd got a kangaroo loose in the top paddock. That's when I realized she didn't even know who Jonny was; no one had bothered to tell her. So then I hated Mum and Dad for forgetting about him, as well as her for ruining our bedroom. I started to blub a bit and as I ran to my room, I hoped Jonny couldn't see everything from heaven.

I dragged the sheets onto my bed and lay on top of them, face down. I breathed in the detergent smell and knew it had taken away the last trace of Jonny. I wanted to go to wherever he was.

When I heard a quiet knock at the door, I knew it would be the Pommie. No one else ever knocked. I ignored it at first. I didn't want to see her ever again. But then she knocked a bit louder and I heard the door handle scrape round, so I said, "Rack off!" but she came in anyway and sat down on Jonny's bed. I said, "Get off Jonny's bed, or I will get a stick and flog you." She stood up again and left.

I needed to get out of our room then. It didn't feel right any more. It was like Jonny was shouting at me from every shelf, every corner, even from the curtains. The Pommie had tied them back to the wall; pretty, like strangers. I couldn't work out if it was them or me that didn't belong.

I pushed open the fly screen and ran down the steps into the yard. It was real quiet. The generator had gone off, it must have overheated. When Buzz saw me coming he shouted out—gave a fanfare. From that far away, he looked a bit like a brown cloud on stilts. I wished he was bigger, and that we were further on in our training, so I could just swing my leg over his hump and let him take me for miles across the desert.

He rubbed his neck against me. He must have had an itch, but he nearly knocked me over, he was so strong. He knew we were going for our walk and got a bit excited. I guess that calf pen meant the same to him as the schoolroom for me. I threw the rope around him and unhitched the gate. He was impatient, so I had to have a word with him. I pulled his face round to look at me, his eyes were big and lazy, like he didn't want to hear it. I told him, "Buzz, I'm having a bad day, so don't you start with me." He made a little growling noise and blew a saggy raspberry with his lips, making them wobble like rubber. Then he sort of head-butted me—not hard, just like he was playing. I batted him away and kept walking, but he did it again. I didn't know whether to laugh at him or flog him. As we looked at each other, for no reason at all, I started to run with him by my side, all lanky and jerky, his hairy hump wobbled back and forth, while his neck stretched like Grand-dad's accordion.

We'd gone a fair way when I had to stop and have a puff on my inhaler. He was jumpy, all fired up, ready for more. Once I'd caught my breath we started to run again, but this time, I dunno why, I let go of the rope. I suppose I wanted to see if I really could trust him.

As we jogged through the dirt with the sun on us, the spiky grass whipped our knees. The rope dangled like a pendulum at his side, just within my reach. He didn't know I'd let go, so he kept to my rhythm and distance.

A few paces farther and the penny dropped. When I leaped over a big bush, the rope slid off Buzz's curly chest and for the first time it felt like he understood we were equals. He threw his head back into the sky. I felt sick and dry inside, knowing I had no control, but I kept on going. There was nothing between me, Buzz, and the desert—just the hope that he'd be loyal to me.

As we ran, I tried not to crowd him. I didn't want to push him away, but every now and then I'd look to see where he was. Once or twice I saw him doing the same. He was never more than a few yards away. I felt tired and sweaty from running around so I slowed down and started to walk. I didn't know if he'd stop, or just keep running. My chest heaved in and out. I put my hands on my hips to rest them while I watched Buzz. Fear slid down into my stomach. He stood still for a while, wondering if I would play some more. Then, bored of waiting, he decided to graze on the scratchy grass.

I almost ran over to grab him and snatch him back, but I wanted us to have more than that. I let him eat for a good while. I just kneeled down in the dirt and enjoyed the space we had. Every now and then he'd look over, chewing spiky sticks of grass, which stuck out of his lips. I guess he was just making sure he could still see my hat. That made me realize that I wouldn't need a rope; instead I'd just call him. Not like a dog, but more like a mate.

I got to my feet and turned my back to Buzz and whistled.

He looked up, like I'd disturbed him. "Come on, Buzz, let's go!" I called, swinging my arm over my shoulder. I shut my eyes and pleaded for him to follow. I didn't want to lose anything else today. I didn't look back again. I figured that if I was Buzz, and he checked up on me like that, it'd be like an insult, or something. I shut my eyes and prayed as hard as I could that Buzz would follow me and not the desert.

TEN

When I heard a thudding sound, I wasn't sure if it was my feet, my heart, or him. I breathed slowly to make myself as quiet as I could and then listened for a sign he was with me. I knew that if I lost Buzz I'd have nothing.

When I opened my eyes, it felt like someone did it for me because I couldn't believe what I saw. There, by my side, was Buzz, acting like everything was normal, so I swallowed my excitement and pretended it was a day like any other.

As we went back to the station yard, Dad stepped out of the open barn where he was working. He tipped his hat back to have a good look as Buzz and me walked past, shoulder to shoulder. The look on his face told me he was impressed. Noticing something different was happening, the fellas stopped what they were doing too. Elliot gave me a nod. I felt like I had something they all wanted.

When I got to the calves' pen, it was real quiet. The Pommie was round the other side feeding them, so I opened the gate for Buzz and wondered if he'd go in on his own. He hesitated. I opened the gate wider, so we could go through together. He liked that. I rubbed his neck and behind his ears until he purred.

The Pommie saw us and I could tell she didn't know what to do. We looked at each other for a bit, before she said, "I love Buzz's knees." I don't think anyone had ever admired his knees before. Mum always went on about his eyelashes and Dad laughed at how his fur was like Aunty Veronica's hair after the disastrous perm. When I looked down at his knees, they made me smile.

After that the Pommie said, "I'm sorry about Jonny . . . He sounds like he was a great brother." I guess Bobbie or someone had told her everything, so I said it was OK. I felt stupid, like when your flies are down. I looked at the ground for a bit and kicked at the dirt, as I tried to think what to say. Then the Pommie said she was going to go and feed the pigs. When she'd gone I gave Buzz his milk.

The Pommie didn't look at me at the dinner table that night and so I tried not to look at her either. But I wondered what she was thinking. When Dad was talking about Jaben Point, the Pommie asked where it was. Dad told her it was about ten miles south of the station—a rock that stuck up out of the desert. It was the highest point on our station and you could climb up it and get a view of the whole of the desert. That made me realize she didn't really know where anything was. She'd only seen the house and the yard, the poddies, Buzz, the chooks, and the pigs. The Pommie hadn't dobbed us in about the ball fight and the bed sheets, and I guess it wasn't her fault nobody had told her about Jonny. I reckoned I owed her one. I said I'd take her to Jaben Point the next day, if she wanted. She looked kind of surprised, like she didn't expect me to be nice to her. Dad said that was a real good idea. The Pommie shrugged and said she'd like to see it. I smiled at her and she smiled back.

So the next day, after I'd spent some time with Buzz and the Pommie had finished all her chores, I went to get the Old Rover.

The Old Rover was the station Land Rover. He was ancient, but real reliable, which was kind of how he got his name—he'd been roving around the station forever. He only had two seats and the one on the passenger side looked like the springy ghost of the seat that once sat there. The Pommie didn't complain about it, though. Emily would have. The only problem with the Old Rover was his steering wheel. The black stuff that covered the metal, Dad called it Bakelite, was all cracked, so when you gripped it, it pinched your skin. There was quite a knack to steering because of that.

The Pommie couldn't believe I could drive. I told her all of us could. Even Emily could ride a motorbike. The Pommie wasn't sure if that was a joke or not, but eventually, after I swore on Buzz's life that I was telling the truth, she said she believed me. She was amazed. She said it had taken her more than forty hours of lessons to learn to drive, and even then she failed her driving test twice. I could believe that.

As we headed out to Jaben Point, the Pommie kept taking pictures—just of the desert. When we saw a couple of big reds, she turned round so far in the passenger seat as she tried to take as many pictures as she could that I thought she was going to fall out. I dunno what else was so interesting, but she kept clicking away. She seemed to be taking pictures of the dirt track in front of us and the scrub at either side—the witchetty bushes, I guess. I asked her about it and she said it was because if she didn't take pictures of everything no one at home in England would believe where she was. I dunno why.

We turned off the dirt road and the Pommie saw Jaben Point rising out of the desert in front of us. She made me stop while she took some photos of me in the Old Rover with the point sticking into the sky behind me. She reckoned no one in England would believe a thirteen-year-old could drive, either.

When we got to where the fellas were working, Dad said I should let the Pommie drive back to the station. He reckoned it'd be good for her to get used to driving the Old Rover, so when the muster started she'd be able to take their lunch to the desert for them. I shrugged and jumped out so she could slide across from the passenger seat. She turned the key in the ignition and then stalled it twice in front of all the fellas. I looked up and saw Lloyd smile and shake his head. I've never heard a gearbox make the noises the Old Rover's did that day.

When the Pommie finally found first gear, I reckon she was so glad to have found it, she didn't want to change it again. The engine screamed and the wheels skidded on the dusty ground. Where it was sandy, it was real easy to skid. Eventually she worked out what the gear stick was for and slowly we started to move forward without the engine sounding like it was going to explode. I felt sorry for the Old Rover.

We got to the top of the rise, near the point, where there are fewer trees and the spinifex is real patchy. That's where the dirt track meets the dirt road. You can turn north to Timber Creek, or go south to Warlawurru. The view from there is pretty good. You can see for miles across the desert—the orange ground all patchy with pale-green and brown bushes and trees, and the odd lighter patch where there are rocks.

I was busy looking at the line where the sky meets the desert and wondering how far away it was, when I realized the

Pommie was driving the wrong way. I asked her where she was going. She shouted back, "The station!" And when she saw the look on my face, like she'd totally lost it, she added, "I don't know; everything looks the same to me." I couldn't believe that. We'd only just come from the station, but she couldn't find her way back there. How dumb's that?

I told Dad about it later on and he said, "Makes you wonder how they found Australia in the first place."

She was concentrating real hard on driving, so we didn't say much. When we got back to the station, the Pommie braked hard, but forgot to use the clutch, so the Old Rover stalled. The sharp movement made my neck hurt. I said to her I reckoned she could do with a few more driving lessons. She nodded and smiled. I dunno why, but as we walked across the yard to the house, I said I was sorry Emily and me had made a mess of the clean bed sheets with the bull balls. I said we didn't mean to. It was just a game. The Pommie shrugged. Then she said, "I guess you have to make your own fun out here—it's not like you can go to the park or the cinema or anything. I bet you and Jonny played some great games together."

I couldn't catch my breath. No one talked about Jonny like that, like he was ordinary. I had to use my inhaler. Then for some reason I opened my mouth to speak and I heard myself telling her about the time Dad found Jonny's cricket ball. It was about a month after the accident. Dad went up on the roof to fix the gutter. He wanted to make sure we were ready if the rains came. While he was up there he found the ball. It was stuck between the gutter and the house. Mum and I were at the bottom holding the ladder. Dad stood very still up there, clutching the ball against his chest. They told me to go and help Emily feed the chooks, but that's not a job for two people. I guess Mum and Dad just wanted to be alone with the ladder and Jonny's cricket ball.

The Pommie listened and then said, "Bobbie told me Jonny fell off the roof, right?" I didn't look at her. I just nodded. She held the fly screen open for me and we went into the dining room. The Pommie looked at me for a moment, like she was going to say something else, but changed her mind.

ELEVEN

When we all went over to the house for smoko the next day, the Pommie was in the garden hanging out some washing, so we went over there to eat the biscuits she'd left for us. Smoko was what we called the break we had in the morning. Bobbie reckoned it was because it was when people had a smoke. The Pommie said in England it was called elevenses because they had a break at eleven o'clock. Anyway, as she pegged the clothes onto the line she asked if I'd take her for another drive. She reckoned she needed to get used to the Old Rover. I looked at Bobbie to see what she thought. Bobbie shrugged and said it was a good idea. We all knew Liz needed the practice. I was just surprised she'd thought of it.

I asked the Pommie where she wanted to go, but she didn't know. She didn't know the station, so I said I'd take her to Simpson's Dam to see the memorial to old Arthur. That watering hole was the furthest one from the station, so I reckoned it'd give her plenty of time to get used to driving the Old Rover. It was right on the western side of our land. There was a pointy grey stone over there with his name on it. It said:

In memory of Arthur Simpson
A decent man who worked hard
Died June 12 1930

After we'd had lunch and the Pommie had washed up, we went to get the Old Rover. I told her she needed to be a bit gentler with him—he was an old fella and he didn't take kindly to being treated roughly. She smiled and nodded as she started his engine. She was concentrating real hard, finding the right gears and trying not to let the Old Rover skid on the sandy roads. When he did, she panicked a bit, like she thought she was going to crash. I told her not to brake—that just made it worse. After a while she started to relax a bit more.

The sun was real high in the sky and I was glad I had Greg's hat. The Pommie had on a pair of sunnies, like the tourists in Alice Springs. I said she should wear a hat too, but she said she didn't have one. I reckoned we'd have one she could use. I said I'd have a look when we got back to the station. The wind was cool as we drove along, but the Pommie didn't go very fast, so when I touched the top of my hat, it felt real hot.

We had to turn off the road to Warlawurru onto a dirt track, which was bumpier, to get to Simpson's Dam. There were bigger witchetty bushes and gum trees along the track, which gave a bit of shade. The Pommie didn't like it, though. She slowed down for each and every little bump and hole in the road. I told her the Old Rover's suspension was pretty tough, so she could speed up a bit, but she was scared she'd crash. We crawled along, zigzagging across the little dirt track as the Pommie did her best to drive round every little pebble and hole. Two wild horses came out of nowhere and crossed the road ahead of us. The Pommie stopped and said, "What was that?" Like she wasn't sure if what she'd seen was real or not. I explained how there were a few wild horses in the desert. They'd escaped from stations over the years and roamed free. I told her they were a pain in the neck and we hated them—we shot them whenever we could. She didn't get it, so I had to explain how they got in with the cattle sometimes during the muster and broke the fences and stuff. She was too busy looking at the road to really listen though.

Eventually, after almost an hour of crawling through the desert, we came out of the trees and bushes to a more open area. Below us was the dam—a kind of big hole in the desert, which was meant to be full of water. It wasn't full, though, because of the drought. You could see a mark stretching all around the dam showing how high the water used to be, but it was much lower than that now. I guess it was like if a pond dried up and became a puddle—only bigger.

Arthur's stone stuck up out of the ground next to the dam like a grey tooth. I pointed to it and told the Pommie to drive down there. She pulled up next to it and jumped out to have a proper look. She ran her hand over the top, like she was stroking Buzz. I told her how my great-granddad bought Timber Creek Station after Arthur died. Dad reckoned it had been a wild place back then. Not long before Arthur died, a bunch of whitefellas came out to the desert to kill all the Blackfellas. I think it was something to do with a Blackfella killing a gin-jockey.

The Pommie didn't know what a gin-jockey was. It was kind of embarrassing explaining it to her. A gin-jockey was what we called whitefellas who rooted with black women. The Pommie opened her eyes wide and said she didn't understand what the problem was. I guess she didn't understand anything. I told her how being a gin-jockey was bad—kind of gross. She shook her head and said she thought the word gin-jockey was bad and gross. I nodded. I reckoned she understood what I meant, but I was wrong. She said it didn't matter if you were black or white, people could be with whoever they wanted. I told her she didn't get it. She said, "If you like Mick and Gil Smith, why can't you like a black woman?" I shrugged. It's just that Mick was Dad's mate, so it was different with them.

Anyway, I carried on with my story and told her how when the whitefellas rode out into the desert to kill the Blackfellas, Arthur Simpson wouldn't join in with them, so he had a hard time because of it. The Pommie said he sounded like a nice man. She wanted to know more, but I didn't know anything else about it. She was real interested, so I told her she should ask Dad.

We had a little walk round the dam. The Pommie asked more questions about my family—stuff about how old Dad was when he took over the station from Granddad and if I was going to take it over one day. I said I reckoned I would. That's when she asked what would have happened if Jonny was still alive. I shrugged and said I didn't know. He'd probably have taken it over, but I reckon we'd have run it together. There was enough work for two fellas, easily.

When we came to a bloated carcass at the edge of the dam, covered in flies and stinking, the Pommie gasped, like she'd found a dead person. She wanted to know what had happened. I shrugged—cattle died, just like people. We hadn't had much rain, so maybe that cow had got dehydrated. She took a photo of the carcass and we kept walking. That was when she asked me about the muster. She didn't even know what a muster was, so I had to start right from the beginning. I said how it was the best thing about being a stockman, and how it only happened once a year. It was when we rounded all the cattle up at each of the dams and waterholes on the station, castrated some, branded them, and decided which ones to send to slaughter and which ones to keep. It was real important because it meant we made some money from the ones we sold.

On a station the size of Timber Creek, the muster took about a month. I told her how it was going to be my last one before I went to boarding school, and because I was thirteen, I'd get to camp out with the fellas, like Jonny did. I told her how I'd probably get to miss a bit of school because Dad would need me to help him and the fellas. It was real hard work—long hours and at the end everyone would be bushed. But it was exciting too—there was nothing better than chasing a big mob of cattle through the desert and taking them into the yards. She hadn't a clue what I was talking about, so I told her how we used the utes and motorbikes to chase the cattle out of the desert, round them up and herd them together. That's when she said, "And this will be the first muster without Jonny?" No one had ever come out and said it, even though we all must have thought it. I felt sick as I nodded, then she said, "So it's your chance?" I didn't know what to say. I nodded and looked at the sky. I said it was too hot. She agreed and we turned round and went back to the Old Rover.

The Pommie turned the key in the ignition and found first gear straightaway. She smiled at me and I could tell she was real pleased with herself. I smiled back and said she was getting better and that made her laugh. She said, "Driving lessons from a thirteen-year-old!"

I shrugged. It wasn't my fault she couldn't drive properly.

We were nearly back to the road that went from Timber Creek to Warlawurru when the radio buzzed and Dad's voice came through. He wanted us to go out to Jaben Point to collect a new poddy calf. While the Pommie drove I picked up the little black receiver and spoke into it. I told him we were on our way. Instead of turning toward the station, I told the Pommie to keep heading south. She smiled and said, "This is exciting."

When we got to where the fellas were working, they had the calf penned into one corner of the yard. Lloyd tipped his hat back when he saw me and the Pommie in the Old Rover. He said to Elliot, "Looks like the Pommie's got herself an admirer." Lloyd was OK normally, but sometimes I wished he'd rack off. I didn't know what to say, but Liz did. She smiled and said she couldn't find a better guide in the whole of the Northern Territory. I felt kind of tall then.

Anyway, we soon forgot about Lloyd when we saw the little calf. It was tottering around all lost and alone. Its mother was nearby but she was dead. We didn't know what had killed her. Maybe having the calf was too much for her. The calf was weak and wobbly, just a few steps away from death, so it was easy to catch. It fell down, like sticks—as though it wanted to be caught. I reckoned it would probably die. Liz helped me lift the calf into the back of the Old Rover. She couldn't believe how light he was. She said it was like lifting a polystyrene model, not a real calf. I knew what she meant. It was like he had nothing inside. I guess he didn't. He was hours, rather than days old and he'd already been attacked by dingoes. They'd got at him from behind. He had wounds all over his rump. I told the Pommie to drive us back to the station while I stayed in the back of the Old Rover with the calf.

When we got to the station, we laid the calf on the ground, inside the pen. He was all frothy around his mouth, and his eyes were really wide. His tongue lolled out in the dirt, like he didn't have the energy to be scared. Seeing him next to the others reminded me how little the newborns are—thin and weak like wet paper. The others towered over him like giants. They didn't come too close, though. I reckoned they could smell death on him. Emily, Bobbie, and Sissy had come out of the house to see the new poddy. I sent Emily to mix up a bottle of calf milk and then asked Liz if she wanted to name the new calf—just to piss Emily off. I knew she'd already have a name picked out, something stupid like Adrian, probably. I didn't expect the Pommie to come up with much better, but she said we should call him Dingo. I thought that was an OK name, for a Pommie.

Bobbie laughed when we told her he was called Dingo. She said the poor thing would never be able to forget his past. But I liked it because he'd survived the dingo attack—just. Emily got back with the milk, and Dingo just lay there in the dirt, his empty, brown body moving up and down as he breathed.

I showed Liz how you teach a calf to feed. I put a bit of milk on my fingers and then poked them into his mouth. I didn't think she'd want to try, but she had a go. Once her fingers were in his mouth I told her that when he started to suck them, she should swap them for the bottle. Nothing happened the first time. I thought he might be too far gone to care any more about milk. She tried again, her fingers sticky with calf spit and milk. He just lay there, his mouth slightly open. I told her to wiggle her fingers a bit, just to remind him they were there. She kept saying, "Come on, Dingo," like that'd make him live. She tried for a third time and I knew he'd worked it out when she yelped. They nip a bit when they latch on. She said it felt like he was biting her, so I quickly stuck the bottle into his mouth. And he drank.

I told Liz to build a shady area in one corner of the pen for him. We needed to leave him alone for a bit, to let him rest. I helped her find some bits of corrugated metal from one of the barns before taking Buzz for a run.

The Pommie and Emily wanted to stay with Dingo, so it was just me and Buzz—just how we liked it. No sheilas. It was a hot one, so we didn't run too far together. I didn't fancy having an asthma attack, so we slowed to a jog and then a walk. Buzz was real good, just going at my pace. When we came to a nice clear little spot by a dead, old tree I decided to sit down in the dirt. Buzz was just a couple of yards away from me, out of reach, chewing.

I picked at the dirt and felt the gritty ground crawl under my fingernails as I thought about the muster and how I was going to impress Dad and the other fellas. It reminded me of how it felt when we all had to pick up the dirt and throw it onto Jonny's coffin. I looked up at the sky then and wondered if he could see me. I told him not to worry about us. I was going to make sure the muster was the best one ever. That was when Buzz folded down into the dirt with me. He sat by my side. Chewing. I felt so happy I wished the Pommie had been there with her camera, just so someone else knew about Buzz and me. There was a crow sat high above us in one of the dead tree's empty branches. I looked up at it and hoped Jonny had seen us as I threw my arms round Buzz's neck and breathed in his smell. He headbutted me twice, and the second time it really hurt, but it didn't matter. I got up and shouted, "Come on, Buzz, this way!" as I ran out further into the desert with him by my side. I decided it was time we did some serious training.

I dunno what it's like to land an aeroplane, or how it feels when you dive with sharks, but I reckon it's probably a bit like the feeling you get when you teach a camel something new.

Being out in the open desert with Buzz felt good. As I ran with him, it was like my asthma had been a bad dream that I'd just woken up from—I could run forever. Buzz cantered along, like he always did, as though it was the easiest thing in the world. After a while I decided I'd better stop. As I walked around a bit, just thinking about what to do first with Buzz, he chewed some spinifex and sniffed around. I noticed him keeping an eye on me and so I wondered if he'd understand if I used my hands to tell him what to do. At first Buzz totally ignored me. I waved at him and tried beckoning him to come toward me with my arms, but he carried on chewing and when he'd finished, he dropped his neck so he could get another mouthful of grass.

When he looked up again at me I showed him the palm of my hand. Then I slowly bent down to the ground and placed my hand on the dirt. I dunno why I thought he'd understand that that meant he should kneel down, but I did. Buzz didn't get it. He kept eating grass. I stood up again and this time I said, "Buzz, kneel down." And repeated the movement. As soon as he heard his name, Buzz put his ears back. He knew I wanted him to do something, he just wasn't sure what. So, I waited a minute or two and then did the same thing again. "Buzz. Kneel down." I said the words in a way I hoped sounded serious. Buzz walked toward me then. I reckoned he thought that if he came a bit nearer, he might be able to work out what I wanted him to do.

I did it a few more times until he was standing right

in front of me. I touched his nose and repeated the words, "Kneel down," as I bent my knees. He flopped down into the dirt like a clumsy, broken old deckchair. He'd done it. Buzz had done it. I was so happy I threw my arms around his neck and shouted, "Yeah, Buzz! Yeah!" so loud in his ear he got spooked.

As he ran off I was a bit worried. I wasn't sure if he was playing because he thought it was a game, or if he was really scared of me. I ran after him, like we did when we sometimes played tag. I didn't want him to think kneeling down was a bad thing. The sun was in my eyes as I saw Buzz's dark shape ahead of me. He threw his head back and kicked his legs, like he was the happiest he'd ever been. I called his name again, just to get him to slow down, and I couldn't believe it when his legs eased off and he turned round to look at me. I knew he was saying something because then he blew a raspberry at me. I guess we both wanted to tell each other things. We just didn't know how.

I told Buzz to kneel down a few more times and I reckon three times out of four he did as he was told, which was good enough for me. After all, I didn't always do what I was told to. I lay down on the ground with Buzz next to me and stared at the sky.

———————————

That night, when Mum got back from work, she went out with Liz to see Dingo and give him a shot of antibiotics. Mum didn't like using the medicine; it was expensive. Liz must have persuaded her. Mum said the Pommie had really taken to the calf. After dinner Liz went back to check on

Dingo again and to give him some more milk, like she knew what she was doing. I never thought she'd be bothered—Emily never was. Mum said she hoped Liz wouldn't be too disappointed if Dingo was dead by the time she got up in the morning.

TWELVE

It wasn't long before the muster would start, so Dad said we needed to stock up. That meant we had to go and get a killer. It was great. I got to miss some school. During smoko, Dad came over to the house and said, "Danny, get your gun. I want you to come and help me get a killer." I looked at Bobbie, and she nodded her baseball cap at me, so I knew it was OK. As I ran inside to the gun cupboard I heard Bobbie explaining to the Pommie that a killer was when we shot a cow, brought it back to the station, and butchered it.

I took out Jonny's gun from the cupboard. When I was thirteen, Dad said I could start using it. He said it was inheritance. I rubbed the barrel with my shirt sleeve and took a box of bullets from the top shelf of the cupboard. I had a quick look down the barrel though I knew it was clean—I took good care of it. I stopped at the piano to touch Jonny's picture. I'd already done it once that morning, but it seemed wrong not to do it again, as I was about to use his gun. Outside Dad was waiting for me in the ute.

I'd been practising my shooting quite a lot and, as Dad had shot the last killer we'd got, I asked if I could have a go. He looked at me and narrowed his eyes a bit, like he was thinking about it. Then he nodded.

Out there on our own in the ute, listening to Willie Nelson, felt good. As we bounced down the track, dust smoking behind us, Dad said it was essential that I took my time and made a clean kill. "No suffering," he said. That was the most important rule. I reckoned Dad was a good stockman. Greg said so too. Dad believed in doing things right and got mad if anyone left a gate open or a tap switched on because it caused serious problems, which were entirely avoidable.

We drove out to Jaben Point so Dad could check the borehole. It had been pretty dry, so he wanted to make sure it looked OK before we started mustering. When the cattle were all herded together during the muster, it was important that there was enough water for them. He said the water situation looked about as good as he'd expected, so we turned back toward the station. As we drove, Dad seemed a bit fidgety, like he had ants in his pants. I was going to ask him about it, when he said to me, "Listen, Danny, I was wondering, has Sissy said anything to you about this baby?" I shrugged, and said no. She never spoke to me about anything any more. That's when Dad said, "You sure? She never mentioned anything to you about having a boyfriend at school—or anything? Anything at all?" I shook my head. We drove on in silence for a bit before I asked if him and Mum were speaking to Sissy. Dad asked me what made me think they weren't speaking to her.

I shrugged and said it was because Sissy only ever came out of her room for meals—and even then the only thing she ever said to anyone was when she wanted something passed, like the salt or ketchup, or whatever. Dad nodded and scratched his neck. That's when he said, "Listen, Danny, Sissy doesn't seem to want to tell us who the father is, and that's the only thing I'm interested in finding out right now." I asked him if he thought we'd ever find out who the father of Sissy's baby was. Dad shrugged and said, "You can't have a kid not knowing who its father is. It's just not right. No grandchild of mine is going to grow up like that—no way." We drove back to the station in silence. I racked my brain trying to think if Sissy had ever mentioned any boys, but the only person I could think of her talking about was her mate Natasha.

The cattle didn't know this, but the ones that wandered around near Timber Creek were the ones that became killers. Dad liked to pick a big, juicy one near the house, so it wasn't far to carry it back with the loader.

We stopped at this little rise and walked a few hundred yards through the scrub into the desert to this place called Sail Rock. It was a rock that sort of stuck out of the trees like a boat sail. It was a good spot for two reasons: you could climb the rock and get a better view to see where the cattle were, or you could hide behind it. That meant the cattle didn't know we were there, so they didn't get spooked. When you pick a killer, you want it to be nice and still, that way it's easier to get a clean kill.

Dad squatted down, so I followed. He jabbed his finger in the air toward my left. He'd spotted our killer—a big Hereford cow. We had two breeds of cattle, Hereford and Brahman. Hereford were good beef cattle and we had Brahman cattle because they could cope with living in the desert real well. Dad reckoned they were born survivors. As I looked at that Hereford cow, Dad gave me a nod. I carefully loaded the gun and turned round to face her. The sun was behind us—it felt hot on the back of my neck. I kneeled down in the dirt and tipped my hat up a bit, then raised the smooth butt to my shoulder. I could hear my heart pumping like mad as I stared for a good while down the barrel, making sure I had her head in the sight. I flicked the safety catch and held my breath. As I squeezed the trigger, the gun fired and then recoiled into my shoulder, like one of Jonny's punches. The desert screamed for a second, as birds and insects flew away from the smoky gunpowder smell. I lowered the gun and put the catch back on. Dad held his hand out to shake mine, then helped me to my feet.

We walked toward the cow. She was a big one. Dad said she'd provide plenty of good meat. One side of her face was wet with blood. I felt proud. Dad said, "It was a clean kill. Well done." I looked at Jonny's gun and wondered if he'd been watching me from heaven. That's when I asked Dad about Jonny's first killer. I wanted to know if he'd got it in one shot too. If he'd made a clean kill. I guess Dad didn't want to talk about it because he said he didn't know, reckoned he couldn't remember. I rubbed the barrel of the gun with my shirt sleeve and wished it could speak, like one of those genie-in-a-lamp things, so I could ask about Jonny's first killer. I guess that's just dumb though. Everyone knows that's just made up for little kids.

We went back for the ute and drove through the witchetty bushes and spinifex to where she lay. Dad took out his big knife and the saw to take off her head. When it came off it didn't seem real. It was more like one of Sissy's art projects. We let the carcass bleed into the desert, and that was when the fat black flies began to swarm. They were the same as the ones that hung around Buzz like a cloud.

Dad got a chain around the cow's front legs and with the ute dragged her out to the track. We drove home to get the loader and within half an hour we were carrying her into the yards, ready to butcher.

We left the hide, like a bloody rug, outside the cool room. Dad sawed the bottom of her legs off and even though there was a leg for each of our four farm dogs, they always seemed to find something to fight about.

Once that was done, Dad started butchering. There's a lot to learn. His dad taught him how to do it, and now he was teaching me. It was real interesting seeing the inside of a cow. Dad didn't waste any of it. That night we had the skirt and the other bits that didn't keep so well. The sides got hung up in the cool room. Dad chose some bigger cuts for salt meat; then there were ribs for the freezer, as well as the mince and sausages he made. Pure beef.

We were up to our elbows in blood when the Pommie wandered in. I reckoned she was on her way to see Dingo. She was always checking up on him. He'd got a bit bigger, mainly thanks to all the time she'd spent feeding him and filling him full of medicine. Even so, his back legs were still weak from where he'd been attacked. Anyway, I don't think she'd ever seen a killer before. She just stared at the hide and then the body Dad was sawing in half. I guess he looked a bit like a madman. I shouted for her to come and have a look at my killer, but she shook her head and went away again. Dad laughed, he said, "I don't think vegetarians make very good butchers, Danny." It wasn't like she had to eat any of it.

When Dad and me finished butchering the killer, he said he was going for a shower and that I had to do the same once I'd taken the hide to the farm tip. I said I wanted to do some training with Buzz first. Dad thought about it, and then said, "Fair enough—but afterward, you take the hide straight to the tip."

I washed the killer's blood off my hands using one of the hoses at the chook pens and then went to see Buzz. He head-butted me a couple of times, just to wind me up. I swatted him away and told him not to be a total drongo. We walked toward the gate, which took us out to the south of the station. Buzz got all excited when he saw the open desert and started skipping about. I teased him with the gate by opening it real slowly, which made him so impatient that when it was finally open wide enough for him to get through, he kicked his legs and almost flew into the desert. By the time I'd got the gate shut, Buzz was miles ahead of me, so I started to run after him. I shouted his name, so he'd know I was coming, but he didn't look back. It was like he'd been fired from a cannon. Nothing got in his way. The spinifex and little bushes seemed invisible for him, as I jumped and tripped over them.

I had to stop and have a breather. It was pretty hot and we'd run a long way from the station. Buzz didn't stop though and, as I kept an eye on his brown body on the horizon, I got worried. He'd never run that far away from me before. I needed my inhaler, so I told myself to trust Buzz as I sucked on it. I told myself he'd come back. As he got smaller and smaller in the distance, I knew there was no point in running after him—he was too far away to catch. So I stood still and shouted his name as loud as I could while I stared hard at the desert, trying not to lose sight of him. From where I was, I couldn't tell if he had stopped or not, and my eyes kept playing tricks on me. I'd see Buzz, then start focusing on a bush instead. I decided to walk toward where he was, hoping I hadn't mistaken a tree for him. It's harder than you think to keep your eye on a little camel in the desert. The heat haze confuses you and soon everything starts to look like a camel. Everywhere I looked, there was something on the horizon that could have been Buzz. I felt like crying. I shouted his name as I jogged toward what I hoped was him. I got so scared, I kept turning round to make sure the station was still behind me, so I'd know I was running in the right direction.

I was thinking about going back to the station to get the Old Rover, when one of the brown spots on the horizon started getting bigger, until it grew long legs and a neck. My chest loosened and the lump in my throat slipped away as I waved my arms and shouted, "Buzz! Here, Buzz!" As he ran toward me, relief flooded through my body. I guess that's how the desert felt when we had good rains and the creeks filled up. He skidded toward me so I could put my arms round his neck and tickle his ears. I didn't want to be angry with him— he'd come back to me. But as I threw my arms round him, I squeezed a bit harder than normal.

We walked back to the station together. I kept my arm on his neck the whole way. Just in case. I hadn't time to go chasing after him again. I had to take the hide to the tip or Dad would go ape.

After I'd put Buzz back in his pen, I jumped in the Old Rover. I reversed him up to the hide and went to get a hook. The hide was carpeted with flies. The Pommie came over to see what I was doing as I folded one side of the hide onto the other and then in half again. I explained I had to carefully hook the metal through the hide, without it ripping, so I could attach it to the Old Rover and drag it to the tip.

I was busy doing all of that when Dad came over. He'd been at the calf pen looking for me—and he wasn't happy. He asked me why I hadn't told him Dingo was crook. He reckoned the fact Dingo still wasn't well meant something serious was wrong with him. I shrugged and said it was the Pommie's calf, not mine. She smiled at Dad and said she reckoned he was stronger. Dad shook his head and shouted for Lloyd to bring his gun. Dad said, "You know the rules, Daniel. Why the hell we're throwing good money after bad on a sick calf like that, I don't know. Milk and antibiotics cost a lot." I knew he was right. I felt bad for going along with the Pommie for so long. Dad told the Pommie it was cruel to let Dingo carry on. "He's never going to get better," he said. The Pommie just stood there, silent, like she wanted to blub, but couldn't. I felt bad for her. Kind of guilty.

Lloyd brought the calf round into the yard and tied him to a post. Then he loaded his gun, held it to his shoulder and shot Dingo in the head.

The calf folded down into the dirt and a small pool of blood stained the bottom of the post.

THIRTEEN

Dad said Liz had to take Dingo to the carcass dump. I dunno why, but I said I'd do it. It meant unhooking the hide so I could lift the dead calf into the back of the Old Rover. Dad said I should take Dingo to the dump first because he didn't want a diseased carcass in the station yard any longer than was necessary.

That night, when I got back, it was too dark to go to the tip with the hide, so I went to check on Buzz. Liz was there with him in the calf pen. I wondered what she was doing. I could tell she'd been crying. She tried to hide her face from me. I didn't know what to do. I asked her if she was OK. She nodded the back of her head at me. Buzz was trying to butt us, like he wanted to play. He could be a real handful if he wasn't the center of attention.

I wanted to explain that sometimes it's kinder to kill an injured animal than to try to help it, but it came out as, "Dingo would have died anyway." It was like I'd hit her with the words. She turned on me with her wet cheeks and hissed, "How would you like it if they shot Buzz?"

I didn't see that coming and it made me stand back a

bit. Buzz's ears went flat, like he'd heard what she'd said. "I wouldn't let them," I said, half at her, and half to Buzz. She stared back at me and then looked down at the ground, like she knew what I'd said was right. Then she quietly said she wanted to go home. My stomach flipped then—I didn't want her to go. She said she wished she'd never come to Australia and that she hated it on the station with no one to talk to. I felt bad. I remembered how worried I was when Buzz ran off—I'd felt sick. I guess the Pommie must have felt something like that about Dingo too.

The Pommie looked up at the sky and said how fat our stars were. She thought they were like pebbles. She said the cities' skies have this skin of pollution over them, and because the desert doesn't have that, or any streetlights, the stars look brighter. I didn't know if that was true, but I've thought about it from time to time since then and I reckon it makes sense. The Pommie said we had different stars to England, on account of Australia being in the southern hemisphere. She said we look out on a different part of the galaxy, or something. I'd never heard that before. She also said our seasons were backward, so when we're having our summer, in England it's winter. That made me think about Jonny. I wondered if there was a northern and a southern hemisphere in heaven, and if he had to stay in ours, or if he could roam around like the seasons.

I asked Liz if she had any brothers or sisters. She didn't—not really. Just a stepsister who she said she hated. Her mum and dad were divorced. Had been for years. They sent her to boarding school, then university and after her exams she came out to Australia—just for something to do.

We fastened Buzz and the calves in for the night and then walked to the house together. She looked at the post in the yard, where Lloyd had tied Dingo, but she didn't stop. Then out of nowhere she said, "By the time this muster's over, you'll be an uncle." I dunno why she said that. Then she shrugged and said she'd never be an aunty. Uncle Danny—I hadn't thought of that before.

The next morning after smoko, Bobbie reckoned I should take the hide to the tip. She said it was starting to cause a stink. I said I'd have to miss a bit of school, but I guess right then, getting rid of the bad smell was more important to Bobbie than my education. I wasn't complaining.

The hide did stink a bit and it seemed to be twice as heavy as it had been the day before. Maybe because of all the flies on it. As I hooked it onto the Old Rover, the Pommie showed up. I said what I was doing and that Bobbie had asked me to do it—just in case she thought I was wagging. She didn't question it though. So I asked her if she wanted to come to the tip with me. She said she would because she'd never been before. I was surprised she wanted to come, especially with the hide. The Pommie stared at the blood that had gone brown and hard on my hands and under my fingernails. Then she looked at the hide folded like a hairy hanky behind us. She didn't say it was disgusting or anything, though. As we went along, the wind blew her hair back off her face and I noticed she'd closed her eyes. She looked different—kind of peaceful. I dunno how long I'd been watching her for, but I hit a rock at the side of the road, and that kind of reminded me to look where I was going. It kind of woke Liz up too. So we chatted about the muster and how it was only about ten days until things would get under way.

When we got to the tip, I think she liked it. While I unhooked the hide, she had a little wander along to look at all our old rubbish. It was just the normal stuff: old fridges; an armchair; a chest without any drawers; a pile of magazines and newspapers; broken pots and pans; Emily's old buggy; the Christmas wrapping paper, which was torn and faded; old tin cans; rags; cardboard boxes, which had gone mushy and deformed in the rains and then baked hard by the sun again. Nothing special.

When I started the Old Rover I shouted for her to get in. She looked like I'd interrupted her. She came over and smiled at me, then said the tip was like a museum to my family. I didn't get it. I thought museums were places where important things were kept. But then I realized what she meant. She handed me a card with a picture of a cricket bat on the front. I didn't recognise it, but when I looked inside, it felt like happiness and sadness were fighting over me. It said: To danny. happy 7th birthday. From jonny.

I didn't know what to do. I wasn't sure if it was mine, or if it belonged to the desert. The Pommie looked at me and said, "Should I have left it?" I shook my head and a tear fell off my face, onto my bloody hands, smudging the grubby card with blood. I was busy running my thumb over Jonny's words, trying to remember him giving me the card.

After a while the Pommie asked me about Jonny. I guess she saw the look on my face because then she said I didn't have to talk about it if I didn't want to, she was just curious. That made me shrug and ask her what she wanted to know. She shrugged back at me, and said, "Anything." I guess I could have told her about Jonny's cattle book and how he kept real good records in it about our herds. Or I could have told her about how Jonny was the best bowler his school had ever had—he won a cup for it. But I didn't tell her those things. As I looked away, everything I remembered about the day of the accident fell out of my mouth. I'd never told anyone about it before.

It was the October school holidays, so Jonny and Sissy were at home. It was real hot, so I wanted to go to Clear Water Dam for a swim. Jonny wasn't interested. He wanted to stay at home and work on his bowling. I didn't get it. He'd been practising his bowling for ages—it was all he did. It wasn't even as though I got to be in bat when he practiced, he just wanted to bowl the balls at the wickets he'd drawn on the side of the shop, over and over again. He reckoned he needed to perfect his technique. He wanted to bowl a ball of the century just like Shane Warne had in the Ashes series a few months before. It was boring. Anyway, I went to Clear Water Dam on the motorbike on my own. I was gone a while, I guess. Time stands still when I think back to that day now.

When I got back to the station, I parked the motorbike and walked past the chooks; they seemed all flighty and strung out, but I didn't think too much about it. I hopped up the steps to the back door and opened the fly screen as normal. I walked into the dining room. That's when normal stopped. I knew straightaway something bad had happened. It was weird. Everyone was in there—except Jonny, of course—but it wasn't dinnertime. No one was speaking. They were just kind of staring, but not at anything in particular. I didn't know if I was allowed to ask what was going on, so I just stood there hoping someone would tell me what to do. It was Mum who told me to sit down. I walked to the seat next to her and put my wet swimming things on the table in front of me. I saw Mum's hand on top of Dad's. Their hands were just resting in front of them on the tablecloth—like they weren't really theirs. Mum's voice was smaller than normal when she said, "There's been an accident." I listened and waited. It was like she didn't know what to say next. My mind felt woolly and empty all at once. Like sounds weren't real. Eventually Mum said, "It's Jonny." As I looked round the table I knew it had to be him. He was the only one missing.

I stopped talking to the Pommie then and put the card into my shirt pocket—it felt real stiff against my chest. Liz asked, "What happened then?" So I told her how I was too scared to ask Mum anything else. I stared at my swimming gear on the table in front of me for what felt like ages, wondering what to do. I didn't dare look up. I kept thinking if I could just get up and go outside, I could come back in again and things would go back to normal. I dunno why, but I couldn't move. I looked up and saw Jonny's picture smiling back at me from the top of the piano on the other side of the table and somehow I knew he'd gone. Dad pulled his hand out from under Mum's, his chair scraped back on the wooden floor, and he stood up and went outside. He didn't say anything. Not long after that Mum got up and went into their bedroom. I heard the door shut.

I looked across at Sissy and Emily on the other side of the table. Their faces were all weird, kind of blank or empty, or something, like they'd got stuck. I whispered to Sissy to ask what had happened to Jonny. I dunno why I whispered, but it seemed like the right thing to do. She started to cry—so Emily did too. In between all the tears, she got a few words out to explain everything. She said Dad had been in the yard, checking the generator. He thought he heard a scream, but he wasn't sure because of the noise from the generator. I guess he just thought it was us kids messing around. A few minutes later one of the dogs went over to him with blood on her nose. Dad knew something was wrong then, for sure. He followed her round to the side of the house and that's when he found Jonny and all the blood. He'd fallen off the house roof and landed on an old, metal fence post. Sissy said it went straight through him. By the time the flying doctor arrived, it was too late. Jonny had lost too much blood.

I needed to see where it had happened. I can't remember getting up from the table and walking outside. But I must have. I just remember being at the side of the house where our bedroom windows are. On the ground there were all these flies, with the fence post sticking out of the middle of them. Seeing all the flies swarming over the ground like they did when we left the hide of a killer outside the cool room, made me wave my arms and legs around to try and scare them away. I wanted to get them off what was left of Jonny, I guess. I touched the fence post too. Just with my fingers at first, but then I kind of held it. It felt hot from the sun, but there wasn't anything on it—it wasn't sticky like I thought it would be. I dunno if someone had wiped it, or something.

The Pommie kind of squirmed in her seat then. I looked up and noticed her face was all twisted and she looked like she was going to cry. She turned away. Then I heard her say in this real quiet voice, "I'm so sorry, Danny . . . I had no idea . . ." I felt like I didn't have anything else to say then, so I started the engine and drove back to the station. We didn't say anything on the way home. I tried not to think about Jonny, but my hands were trembling and they were real sweaty and kept slipping on the steering wheel. I dunno why, but that made me think about him even more.

When we got back, school had almost finished. The Pommie said that if I wanted, we could tell Bobbie we'd had engine problems with the Old Rover, and that's why we were so late back. She did all the talking, so I didn't have to say anything—I just nodded every now and then. Bobbie believed every word.

FOURTEEN

It was only about three days until Dad reckoned Reg and his mob would arrive at the station. Reg Evans had a team of fellas that traveled round the territory, mustering from station to station. Dad hired them to help us with our muster each year. I wanted to go to Jaben Point to see the fellas. I was pretty sick of being at the station with just a bunch of girls for company, but I knew the fellas would be busy building the yards over there and that was real hot, boring work—lifting fence panels and stuff. I was trying to decide, when the Pommie showed up at the calf pen. She needed help lifting some stuff into the Old Rover to take to the tip. I left Buzz and went to give her a hand.

She'd been clearing out the space under the house, so there was quite a lot of rubbish. Once we had it all loaded into the Old Rover, she asked if I'd got time to help her unload it at the tip. I told her she'd be able to manage on her own—the rubbish wasn't that heavy. She looked embarrassed then and said quietly, "Danny, I can't remember the way to the tip—so I need someone to come with me." I laughed at her and then she smiled at me and said, "I know—I'm useless."

At the tip, we soon got the bags of rubbish unloaded

and thrown into the pit with the other stuff we'd left there over the years. I hadn't been to the tip since we'd found the birthday card from Jonny, and it made me wonder what else was out there of his. I was having a quick look around and I guess Liz knew what I was up to because she said, "I think it was a bit further down." When I asked what she meant, she said, "Jonny's card." I felt a bit awkward then, like she'd caught me doing something I shouldn't have been.

Liz was real different to everyone else I knew. Not just because she was a Pommie, or that she was a girl, or because of her weird accent. It wasn't that she was nosy, or rude, or mean, or anything, but it was to do with how she'd talk about stuff, even if no one else would—like about Jonny.

As we both looked at the bits of rubbish around us, right out of the blue, she said, "Where's he buried?" Just like that. It sounded like she was asking where we'd left the keys to the ute, or something. I looked at her and said it wasn't far from the house.

The Pommie was lifting up an old magazine with the toe of her boot to see what was underneath it when she said, "Oh right, so it's not in a churchyard or a cemetery or anything then?" I shook my head. She thought about that for a minute and then looked up and said she reckoned that seeing as there wasn't a church anywhere nearby, Mum and Dad had probably decided to bury Jonny at the station, so he was nearer home. I felt sick.

As she stepped over a battered, empty oil drum to get a better look at something on the other side of it, she said, "So do you ever go to see Jonny's grave—you know, put flowers on it, or anything?" My belly felt like it was about to turn inside out, so I bent over and tried to breathe. The Pommie looked up when I didn't answer and said, "What's up? Don't you feel well?" I couldn't answer her. She came over to me and rested her hand on my back, like Mum did when we were crook. She asked if I was OK and said I should get in the shade behind the Old Rover. She helped me over to where it was and said I should sit down, so I did.

We were both sat in the dirt with our backs against the Old Rover's wheel. After a minute or two Liz said she was sorry she hadn't brought any water with her. I said it was OK— I'd feel better in a minute. That's when I told her about the funeral. I just came right out with it all, like whatever made her ask all those questions had somehow got into me too.

I explained about how they hired this big black car to carry Jonny's coffin from the house to the hole in the ground, which Dad had dug. I hated that black car. Jonny would've hated it too. I didn't know why we couldn't just put the coffin in the back of the ute and drive him there like that—like normal. That's how Jonny had always ridden round the station. He liked it.

Then there was everyone's clothes. Dad was wearing a black suit and Mum had on some black trousers. Aunty Ve had a black dress and Sissy was wearing a black skirt. Aunty Ve had brought me some black trousers to wear especially. I hated them. They were hot and itchy and I couldn't move in them. We looked like we were out of a bad dream or a real old movie, or something. The only thing that wasn't black was all the flowers. I dunno why, but people kept saying how beautiful they were. They weren't. They were the ugliest, stupidest flowers I ever saw. Jonny would've hated them.

The Pommie listened—so I kept talking. I told her about how at the funeral no one said anything. We all just sat around waiting and being quiet and polite to each other, like we didn't really know each other, like you do with strangers. I caught

Sissy's eye and we stared at each other for what seemed like ages. It felt like we could read each other's minds. Her eyes looked kind of empty, which was how I felt—empty and alone. I wanted to scream and shout, but I couldn't because I knew I had to be invisible.

Then, when it was time, we had to follow the stupid black car, which had Jonny's coffin inside it, surrounded by those ugly flowers. It made me mad thinking about it. When we got to where the hole in the ground was, we all got out of the cars and that's when the funeral happened. There was a priest and he said some stuff I didn't get. We sang some songs I'd never heard before and then they put the coffin into the hole. I hated that bit more than anything else. Mum cried. I'd never seen her cry before. Aunty Veronica cradled her in her arms, like she was a big baby. Dad was stood next to them. He didn't do anything—just stood and stared. It felt like I didn't know any of them any more.

After the funeral, when everyone had gone, Dad went out and ripped up the fence post Jonny had fallen on. He was still wearing his suit. I saw him through my bedroom window. He kicked the post with his boot; one way, then the other, then back again, but it wouldn't budge. The dry ground had swallowed it along with the blood. It was getting dark by the time he gave up and tied a chain around the post so he could yank it out with the ute. Sweat rolled off his face, like tears. Once he'd pulled out the post, he turned the engine off and rested his head on the steering wheel. He seemed to pant real hard. It had been so hot.

I looked at the Pommie then. She was crying. Why do girls always blub at everything? I didn't want her to cry. "Bloody pack it in, will you?" I shouted at her. She wiped her face with her hand and said, "I can't help it." I wasn't angry with her, just kind of sick of her, and everyone else. I wanted to be somewhere where none of that stuff had happened, where it didn't matter. I wanted to be with Jonny, I guess. We set off back to the station, but then the Pommie told me to stop. She said she wanted to see Jonny's grave. I didn't know what to do. I hated it there, so I dunno why I turned round and started to drive the Old Rover toward where Jonny was buried.

When we got there, the sky was pink and blue from the sun, which had turned bright red. It looked like it was somewhere near the end of the world. The grave was exactly where I knew it would be, but it looked a lot different to the last time I'd seen it. It looked older, like the desert had taken it over again. The stones round the outside were still there, as well as the bigger one, which had Jonny's name on it. Someone had put some flowers in a little bucket on the mound of dirt. I reckoned it would have been Mum. They'd gone brown.

I guess I'd wanted something to happen—for something to change. But it didn't. Jonny wasn't there. I knew he wouldn't be. He'd gone to heaven long before they'd put that wooden box in the ground—just as well really because if he'd seen the black car and those bloody stupid flowers, I reckon he'd have really kicked off. We didn't get out of the Old Rover. We just looked at the grave from where we sat. I guess there wasn't anything to say. After a few minutes I asked the Pommie if she'd seen enough and she nodded, so I started the engine and we drove home.

When we got home, I went to my bedroom and sat on Jonny's bed for a bit. It wasn't the same though since the Pommie had tidied everything up. I slipped down onto the floor and wriggled under the bed, where it was dark and smelled dusty. I wondered if that was how it felt to be in a box under the ground.

FIFTEEN

The radio in the kitchen fizzed and Reg Evans's voice filled the room. Dad knew Reg was meant to be arriving at the station that day, so we were all waiting to hear the rumble of their truck and the utes and bull catchers. When Reg radioed and we heard him say, "Reg Evans to Timber Creek—you read me, Timber Creek? Over," we all cheered. That made him laugh. He said he reckoned there weren't many places in the Territory where you got a welcome like that. Dad said they'd sink a few cold ones when Reg and the fellas arrived. Reg laughed and said he reckoned he'd be ready to blow the froth off a couple.

When we heard the truck horn honk twice and then give a much longer belch, we knew Reg and the fellas had arrived. We all ran outside to see them. A cloud of dust surrounded them as they pulled into the station. The farm dogs chased after the wheels on the bull catchers as they drove into the yard and skidded to a stop, like they were giving a show, or something. Dad went over and shook Reg's hand. Reg gave Mum a kiss on the cheek and said it was good to see her. I guess he knew Jonny wouldn't be there—I dunno if Mum and Dad told him, or if he'd just heard on the bush telegraph. Either way, no one said anything about Jonny. I guess it was just easier that way. He pretended to give me a dead arm and then picked Emily up, turned her upside down and pretended to drop her. She giggled like crazy. He nodded at Sissy. There was no way he could lift her up, her belly was way too big by then. I dunno if anyone had told Reg about Sissy and the baby before he arrived at the station. Sissy looked embarrassed and stared at the ground the whole time. Reg tipped his baseball cap at Bobbie next—he remembered her from the year before, but he'd never met the Pommie. Dad explained who she was and Reg said, "You're a long way from home out here then? You finding it OK?" The Pommie said she reckoned she could handle life on the station—like it was the easiest thing she'd ever done.

Reg nodded, smiled, and then pointed at his mob of fellas. He said, "Well, this is Rick Smith." Rick said g'day. He was about Dad's height, but had fair hair and real brown skin. He tipped his hat at us all and I saw the scar he had on his cheek. I dunno how he got it. Then Reg pointed at Ed and Spike Barron—they were brothers. They both said g'day. They were about the same age as Lloyd and Elliot, and while Spike had a happy expression all the time, Ed looked like he was thinking too hard. They were both taller than anyone else I'd ever met. The Pommie and Bobbie grinned like idiots. Lloyd and Elliot shook hands with the fellas too. Reg lifted a box of VB beer out of the back of his bull catcher and handed it to Dad. Dad smiled and said it was just what the doctor ordered.

It was real noisy at the station that night. There were so many people, all talking and laughing. It felt a bit like a party. We had dinner in the garden. We'd taken the tables out to make room for everyone. It was nice, even the mosquitoes didn't spoil it. Everyone was thinking and talking about the muster. Dad said he wanted to make sure it went smoothly. He said, "I don't want to have to shoot any cattle because they've got stressed in the races." That's when the Pommie said the stupidest thing. She said, "I thought the idea of mustering was to catch the cattle, not race them." There was a moment when no one said anything at all, like we were all trying to work out what the hell she was talking about. It was Reg who started howling first. He laughed so hard he began to choke. Mum was so concerned about him she got up, ready to whack him on the back. The Pommie just sat there, looking embarrassed, but not knowing what she'd said that was so funny.

Once he'd calmed down a bit Reg took out his tobacco tin from under his tattered cap. Seeing those leathery hands delicately make a durry made me think of Dad, before Jonny died, when he sometimes played the piano. Reg lit the durry, took a drag, and picked a stray bit of tobacco off his lip.

Liz's face was blank. I ignored her at first. She was being such a dumb Pommie, I couldn't be bothered with her, but then she looked at me like I should help her so I explained that the races are the narrow walkways we use to guide the cattle from the yards onto the road train, when they're being trucked. I don't think she understood, so I said it wasn't an actual race— we didn't care which cow was fastest. The Pommie pretended to understand.

If I was the Pommie, I'd have kept quiet after that. I'd have just got on with clearing the plates, or something, but she didn't. She started asking all kinds of questions about how we decided which cows to truck and which ones to set free. She wanted to know how we could tell if we'd mustered them all, what happened if we went out to muster and there weren't any cattle there. She was pretty clueless when it came to how a cattle station worked. I don't think Reg minded; he and the fellas were real patient, answering all her questions. Mum wasn't happy. After a bit she said the Pommie could go out with the fellas one day to see what the muster was like for herself, but then she added, "Right now, we need to get these plates cleared." Even the Pommie wasn't too dumb to take that hint.

I guess Reg had had enough muster talk because he tapped me on the shoulder and said, "So what's this about you having a camel to break in, Danny?" I felt a bit shy then, like when you want to say something, but don't because you're scared someone will take the piss out of you. I just said, "We've got a way to go before I'll be able to ride him," like Buzz was more trouble than he was worth. Reg knew more about me and Buzz than I expected. He said, "Sounds like you're making good progress though. Elliot reckons you've got the camel eating out of your hand."

I looked round and everyone was listening to me and Reg—wanting to hear what I thought. I felt this big smile fill my cheeks, like when I shoved too much food into my mouth. I said he could come and see Buzz if he wanted. That's when Reg told me about this place down near Uluru. He called Ayers Rock that, just like the Blackfellas. He said he'd been mustering at a station down there, when he met a fella who kept camels and made good money at it. Reg said this fella had a whole bunch of them, all broken in and easy to ride, and that he used them to take tourists on desert safaris. They didn't go anywhere special, just to see what the desert was like—for fun. Reg said I should ask Dad to take me down to meet that fella, to find out how it was done. He said it could be a money spinner. He reckoned I could be the first Dawson millionaire.

I looked at Dad to ask if we could go, but his eyes didn't meet mine. He looked down at the ground, kicked at the dirt, then looked up at my chest and smiled. "We'll see, Danny," he said. I reckoned it would cost a lot of money to go all the way to Uluru—and who'd look after the station?

The fellas watched the Pommie clearing the table, like they were waiting for her to drop a plate, or something. Then Mum told Emily and me it was time for bed—in front of all the fellas, and Liz, like I was a little kid. It was embarrassing, and I was going to say something, but Dad knew I'd kick off, so he stared at me, with his don't you dare—not if you want to stay out at stock camp look. So I just said good night and went quietly.

SIXTEEN

When I woke up, it was still more or less dark. The muster was whirling round in my head. I knew I wouldn't go back to sleep, so I got up. With everyone else still in bed, the house felt funny, like a stranger. I took a piece of bread from the kitchen to eat on my way to see Buzz. When I got there, Liz was already feeding the poddies. She smiled when she saw me coming and said, "Excited about the muster?" I nodded and she said she was too.

The Pommie didn't know anything about mustering, so I started right at the beginning, by telling her about Reg. He'd mustered cattle from station to station in the Territory all his life. He was the best in the business. Liz said Reg reminded her of a desert version of a snow leopard. I didn't know what she meant. She reckoned animals in snowy places are nearly always white, so they're camouflaged. She said it was to do with survival of the fittest and that Reg was the same, except he'd gone orangey-brown to match the desert. I kind of knew what she meant. He did look a bit like his skin was made from dust and dirt, all craggy and hard, like a boulder.

His team changed from year to year, except for one Black-fella, called Jack Black. Dad reckoned Jack was named after a card game he won when he was a kid. Jack and Reg had worked together forever.

The Pommie was real interested—wanted to know every-thing about them. So while I fed Buzz, I explained how Reg lived a different kind of a life to most whitefellas. He was about Dad's age, maybe older, but he didn't have a wife or kids or anything, and he didn't like being in the house much. He looked itchy whenever Mum invited him inside—that's why we always ate outside when he came over, even if we weren't having a barbie. He preferred to be out at stock camp with the fellas. Some people said he was more like a gin than a white-fella. Dad reckoned it didn't matter when you were as good at your job as Reg was.

Jack Black was a bit of a legend. Everyone in the Territory had heard of him. He wore this great big black hat and had these teeth, which were whiter than any whitefella's, but real crooked, like someone had broken a fence up in his mouth.

The Pommie brought the empty calf feeder over to be rinsed and said she wondered why Jack hadn't come to the house for dinner, so I told her it was because he's a Blackfella. She didn't get it, so I told her how Blackfellas didn't come to a whitefellas' party. Even when they were mustering, Jack didn't camp with Reg and the others. She wanted to know why Jack didn't sleep or eat with the others if he and Reg had worked together for so long. I shrugged and said it was just how it was. I tried to explain that it was like that with Mick and Davy— they never came into the house. They only ever sat outside with Dad. Liz asked if anyone had ever invited them inside. I shrugged. I didn't know the answer to that. Then she asked about Gil. She wanted to know if he came into the house when he used to come over and play with Jonny. I nodded—they often played together in our room when they were little. I guess maybe because Gil was a kid, and because he was Jonny's mate, it was different. The Pommie agreed.

She didn't ask me anything else about Jack, so I told her about how Reg chose his team real carefully. He made sure his men were all decent, trustworthy fellas because of a nasty incident that happened a few years before. Reg had had a fella called Gibson working for him. Gibson was a drinker. Reg didn't know that, though. Gibson had been drinking whisky this one day and because they were at opposite ends of the yards, Reg hadn't noticed. They were trucking the animals up the race onto the road train, but Gibson couldn't count how many animals he'd let through onto the trailer because he was so drunk.

Liz didn't know what a road train was. I told her it was a big truck with three double-deck trailers behind it. She said they didn't have them in England.

Getting the cattle onto the trailer could be tricky. They could get scared, so you needed to lead them on slowly, one at a time, to let the drivers load them safely. The cattle stayed in the trailers for days while they were driven across the country to a slaughterhouse, so they needed to be loaded properly. It was a dangerous job being a road-train driver. If you were inside a trailer and a bull kicked off, it was bad news. But that wasn't the problem on this occasion. It was Gibson's job to count how many had gone through his section of the race onto the trailer, only he wasn't really awake. One after another they went into the trailer, faster than the driver could manage them. It was pretty noisy, with all the hooves stamping around and the cattle braying at each other, so no one heard the driver. By the time Reg and the others realized what had happened, the road-train driver was nowhere to be seen, but they could hear him crying out. It took them so long to get the cattle, crammed like sardines, back out of the trailer, that by the time they found him, he'd been trampled to death. The Pommie's eyes grew wider when she heard that.

I don't think anyone I know ever asked Reg about it, but the story went that he drove Gibson and the driver's body back to Alice. The corpse in the front, wrapped in Reg's blanket, while Gibson was tied up in the back of the ute. Reg dropped the road-train driver off at the funeral home and then took Gibson to the police station. Greg told me Reg dragged Gibson out of his ute and then quietly beat the crap out of him in the street. Greg reckoned the cops turned a blind eye.

I don't think Liz knew what to say then. Her face turned, like she'd tasted meat. I thought I'd better change the subject, so I told her what I knew about the rest of Reg's mob. The Barron brothers, Ed and Spike, had come from South Australia to find work after their father's cattle station went bust. They were new, but Reg told Dad he was impressed with them. Then there was Rick Smith. He was a very quiet man. He'd been in prison, I dunno what for, but he was Reg's mate's mate, so he was OK. I guess Rick must have been useful or Reg wouldn't have kept him.

As well as Reg's mob we usually hired in one or two Blackfellas to help too. On a cattle station as big as ours, it was always good to have a few extra people on the ground, just to help with anything that came up. But Dad said we couldn't afford it this year. I guess it was because we had to pay the Pommie and with the baby coming too. I'd heard Mum say babies cost an arm and a leg. I didn't say that to the Pommie though. I just told her Dad reckoned we'd be able to manage this time just with our fellas and Reg's.

We'd finished feeding the animals and were on our way back to the house so the Pommie could make our breakfasts. As we walked along I told her how at each water hole on the station, the fellas would set up the yards, using these real big fence panels. That's heavy work, hot and a bit boring. But then you get to do the actual muster—that's when you go out in the utes and bull catchers and round up the cattle. That's when the fun starts. Driving across the desert, taking a big mob back to the yards. It's the best.

When we got back to the house, Dad was there and he reckoned we could all skip school and go mustering—everyone except Sissy. She was too pregnant to muster. Man, I was so stoked I threw my hat in the air and whooped like a madman.

Dad tipped his hat back a bit, looked at me and smiled. I said I didn't want to muster with the girls. I was sick of being with the girls all the time. He laughed and said he reckoned there'd come a time when I'd feel differently about that. I got worried then. I thought he was going to make me go with them, but he said the girls could all ride with him in his ute. Elliot said I could be his co-driver if I wanted. I nodded and we all ran out to get in the utes to head to Jaben Point. We always started the muster at Jaben Point, then we moved to Wild Ridge, then Simpson's Dam, before heading over to Cockatoo Creek, Gum Tree Creek, and last of all Timber Creek.

When we got to Jaben Point, Reg was waiting for us. He rubbed his hand in my hair and called me the camel man. I liked the sound of that. He said I could ride with him in his bull catcher! I couldn't believe it. I didn't know what to say. I just nodded. I was totally stoked. I looked at Elliot, to see if he'd mind if I went with Reg instead and I could tell he understood. I couldn't stop smiling. Reg's bull catcher was a lot better than Elliot's old ute.

Lloyd was going to be on one of our motorbikes, and so was Ed Barron. Jack and Rick were in another bull catcher and Spike Barron was in a ute. We got in the vehicles and left the yards like Wacky Racers in convoy. Reg gave the signal and he and Dad led us into the desert. There were some deep ravines in the earth around the Soak, that's what we call the water hole out there, so we had to be careful. We couldn't just look at the cattle we were chasing, we had to keep a real close eye on what was around us. Reg revved the bull catcher and we shot forward into the desert.

The team fanned out from the yards all heading south, to see what that part of the desert was hiding from us. Reg grinned at me as we bounced through the grass and dirt. "Here we go, Danny!" he shouted. I was so happy. I couldn't wait to find some cattle. We ran into a handful nearly straight-away. They were scared of the sound of the engine and started running. Reg swung the bull catcher round the side of them to herd them back toward the yards. As we came in a loop we met Ed Barron on his motorbike, so he spun round and took our cattle with him. That left us free to go into the desert again and find more.

When we set off this time, we went in a different direction. Reg's hands frantically turned the wheel and we doubled back. We'd only been going for a second or two when Reg had to slam his brakes on. Four wild horses came from nowhere, their hooves like engine pistons against the track in front of us. "Jesus!" Reg shouted and hit the steering wheel. We all hated the wild horses. They were a damned nuisance when we were mustering. If they got caught up in the muster and ended up in the yards with the cattle, they could start kicking and break the fences. That was the worst. It was like getting a crack in a hose—the cattle would run out back into the desert and we'd have lost them and a day's work.

The horses ran by so fast, their scraggy manes and tails reminded me of tattered sails. They'd gone as soon as they arrived, so I wasn't sure if I'd really seen them.

We set off again and this time we mustered a good few cattle. We uprooted one cow and then we found another, which ran with it to try to get away from us. Round another bush there were three more, until we had a small herd. As we brought them back toward the yards we saw Dad and Jack bringing a real big mob in, so we joined them in what Reg called a nice little pincer movement.

That big mob of cattle ran along like a dark cloud. It moved like weather, rolling along the earth with its own energy. We followed it. We were traveling slower than before. It was hot and once we had a mob together like that, we didn't want to stress them any more than we already had by making them run even faster.

Once we got them to the yard, Spike Barron was waiting to open the gate. The cattle were too scared of us to realize it was a trap. As soon as the last one went through, Spike swung one gate shut and then Rick jumped out to close the other one.

"Nice work, fellas. Over." Dad's voice echoed from the radio in Reg's bull catcher. Reg picked it up and replied, "A good mob there, Derek. Over and out."

We all knew there were more to muster, so we didn't stop. We headed north of the yards and found Elliot with a small mob of cows and calves jogging along, tired and afraid. Reg said they looked like a sorry bunch of refugees. I didn't know what that meant, but those cattle looked perished.

We carried on like that all day, going out into the desert and bringing more and more cattle back to the yards, until it was nearly dark and it was too dangerous to muster any more. The fellas agreed to leave the cattle in the yards overnight so they could cool off a bit. There were one or two crazed cattle. They'd gone mad because they hadn't had enough water. When they got like that they could be real angry, but Dad said it was because they weren't in their right minds. Dad hoped that if we left them in the yard with the troughs of water they might have a drink and calm down overnight, so they'd be easier to draft and truck the next day. Reg agreed.

At breakfast the next day, Dad was at home and said he wanted me to go with the Pommie to Jaben Point to help draft the cattle. He reckoned there was a good mob over there, pretty healthy too. He said I had to go to school that morning, but afterward he wanted Liz to take them some lunch. He said the two of us could stay and help take down the cattle numbers as they were trucked. That's a real boring job, but I was still stoked. I was going to be out with the fellas again—I felt like jumping up and down. Emily said she wanted to go to Jaben Point too. Dad smiled and said she could go as long as she promised to stay out of the way and not cause any trouble. Emily swore on Charlotte's life—that was her favorite poddie calf—that she'd behave herself.

When our lessons were finished, I ran out of the schoolroom into the hot yard. It felt good, like nothing mattered except cattle and water. Liz had lunch ready and we all bundled into Bobbie's ute.

When we reached the top of the rise at Jaben Point looking down on the yards, we all breathed in, like we were about to dive into deep water. The yards were bursting with hundreds of cattle. The Pommie couldn't believe it. As we drew closer her mouth fell open at the sight of all the cattle, the size of the spread, and the amount of dust that had climbed into the air. When we stopped, Dad waved over at us. He was sweating and dirty. The Pommie was so busy staring at the cattle that it was left to Bobbie to set out lunch for the fellas under the shade of a gum tree. The food drew everyone in like a magnet but Liz was in some kind of daze.

While Dad and our fellas got stuck into the food, Reg and his mob brought their tucker over to the tree too. We all sat round, quietly eating and trying to hide from the sun and the flies. I heard Dad say the cattle at Jaben Point were good, pretty healthy and lots of them. He was pleased with how it was going. I could tell.

While Dad ate and chatted with Reg, the Pommie came over to get herself some lunch. With so many people and cattle in one place, the flies were having their own muster. We all smiled when we saw Liz fighting a losing battle to keep them off herself and the food. She twitched and slapped the air like someone had connected her up to a faulty circuit. Bobbie felt sorry for her, so she got up and went to help. Between them, they managed to cover the food and put it back in the ute. When they came back Bobbie said, "If anyone wants a sausage-surprise sandwich, just help yourselves." Reg liked that, he said, "What's the surprise? It wouldn't be the outback raisin, would it?" Bobbie laughed. Lloyd got up and helped himself to more food. The Pommie's face crinkled like paper when he bit into a sandwich before he'd even checked to see if anything had crawled inside it.

It was then that the rumbling started and we all looked up to the top of the Point where we saw a truck dragging wagons and a cloud of dust behind it. Its horn belched a greeting at us, and for no reason at all I jumped up and down and waved my hat around like we'd won a competition on TV. Dad was on his feet then and looked at me funny, like he couldn't decide whether to laugh at me or flog me. So I stopped, put my hat back on and smiled at him. I reckon he was just as excited. He pretended to give me a dead arm and said, "Here we go, Danny."

SEVENTEEN

I looked round and Liz was there, smiling too. Even though she didn't know what it all meant, I thought it was kind of nice of her to try and join in.

We watched the road-train driver, this real nice guy called Bob, maneuver the wagons into position at the far end of the yards. He looked like a multicolored bear. His beard was really big and it was dyed blue. Then he'd got this long, curly hair on his head, which was so thick, it was a bit like black fleece. His arms were covered in tattoos of everything from spiders' webs and goblins to naked women and pictures of VB beer.

As Bob slotted the trailers into the right place, Jack Black wandered out of the heat like a scorpion. Seeing the Pommie, Bobbie, and Emily there, Jack pointed at them with his chin and said, "What's this? Reinforcements?"

Reg laughed and explained who everyone was. Jack remembered Bobbie from the last muster, but he'd never met the Pommie before, so he tipped his hat at her—polite. She smiled back. Jack looked at the sky and said, "Too hot." Reg nodded and everyone knew it was time to get down to business.

The Pommie didn't know how the drafting worked. I explained that after we'd mustered the cattle into the yards, drafting was what we called it when we decided which ones we wanted to truck—in other words send to the slaughter-house—and the ones we wanted to keep, which meant they went back out into the desert.

It was a pretty dangerous job, in some ways. If you didn't pay attention you could get into all sorts of trouble, but we worked as a team and that meant we did our own jobs and kept an eye out for everyone else, to make sure it went smoothly.

It was simple really. It started with a sliding gate, which moved up and down like a guillotine, at the far end of the yard. That was where Ed Barron was working. He sat on top of the fence like a great big jabiru waiting for Reg to give him the signal to lift the gate up and let a handful of cattle out of the main yard into the smaller one. That was where Reg was waiting for them.

The cattle were happy to get out of the main yard, so they rushed through that gate as soon as it was open, thinking they were going back to the desert. Each time Ed opened the gate, he had to be careful not to let too many cattle through at a time—that would be dangerous for Reg on the other side.

Once they were in the next, smaller yard, Reg would walk round them like a ringmaster. He did that to get a good look, so he could decide which ones to turn loose, and which ones to truck. The Pommie reckoned Reg was like a cattle god. I dunno about that, but it was pretty amazing to see him work. The cattle could charge you, try to stab you with their horns, or just crush you against the fence panels. They were pissed off and scared—you couldn't blame them really. Because of that, Reg needed eyes in the back of his head. He was clever with cattle. It was like he could read their minds.

I was watching Reg work that yard. One minute he was busy walking round and round, deciding which cow to pick out for trucking, and the next he leaped up at the fence, with more bounce than a big red. When I looked I saw he'd just missed having his leg stabbed by a Hereford's horns. No one else had seen it coming, not even Dad. Reg was real fit and strong. He held his cattle prod like a musketeer's sword and when he made a run and jump for the fence, he held it high in the air.

The first one Reg picked out for trucking was a young Hereford bull. He separated it from the others with his cattle prod and herded it toward another gate where Dad was waiting. Once the bull was near the gate, Dad slid the metal panel up to let it through. The sound of metal scraping on metal didn't stop that bull. It ran straight past those weird sounds into the narrow race, toward the road train. The bull's horns were too wide for the race though, so they hammered against the metal fence panels as he ran through. It was a horrid sound. It made the Pommie wince, but it was nothing compared to the face she pulled later when a cow got scared and ran so fast down the race that it knocked a horn clean off. When the Pommie looked down and saw that old bit of horn, like a bloody ice-cream cone, I thought she was going to puke. I kicked it away and she pretended not to notice, like she was thinking about something far away, out into the desert.

A bit farther down the race from Dad, Jack was waiting at the next gate. That one was usually kept open, but it was there for safety, so if there was a problem, Jack could shut it, and stop too many cattle going through to the road train.

I was working in the section of the race after Jack's gate, with Elliot. We had to tag each of the cattle before they were trucked. Elliot straddled the top of the race and leaned down to tag the cows with sticky labels as they came through. He shouted out each number and I wrote it down. Those bits of paper went with the cattle to the slaughterhouse. Next to each number I wrote a description, like Hereford bull. That way, everything was in order. Once we'd tagged each one, Elliot opened our gate and let them through to the next section, where Rick was waiting for them. His job was to make sure they went up the metal gangway onto the road train without any problems. Bob, the driver, was waiting on the trailer to load the cattle. He was a real nice guy, but I thought the cattle might look at him with all his tattoos and be even more scared.

After Reg had picked out the cattle to be trucked, he herded the ones that were left into another yard where Lloyd and Spike were working. It had troughs of water in it, so the cattle could have a drink and calm down, before we let them back into the desert. If Dad thought any of the cattle in there needed castrating or branding, he let Lloyd and Spike know and they'd sort it out—that was their job.

The noise from the cattle braying, the sound of their hooves on the metal gangway up to the trailer, and the hammering of their horns on the fence panels, was deafening. At times it felt so loud that it made the ground shake. I could feel it in my chest. Above all that noise we had to make ourselves heard: Elliot had to make sure I could hear each cow's tag number; Reg had to tell Ed when to let the next lot of cattle into the yard; Bob had to let Rick know when to let the next one onto the trailer. It was like we were all working inside a machine—an engine, ticking over nicely, so it wouldn't overheat.

We'd settled into our rhythm pretty well. Everything was going OK until I heard hooves kicking against the inside of the trailer like a jungle drum. Then there was shouting and we all stopped what we were doing and looked. Rick and Bob were struggling with a stubborn bull inside. It was so hot, I could feel the sweat trickling down my neck into the small of my back.

Jack shouted, "Wo! Wo! Wo!" So we all knew not to let any more through to the road train. But then a heifer ran so fast down the race to get away from Reg in the yard, it had run into an older cow in front. The younger one piggybacked the cow until it collapsed.

There was nothing Jack could do. He couldn't let his cattle through into our section because we already had two cows waiting to go through onto the trailer. We couldn't let them go because that would be real dangerous for the fellas inside the trailer. I felt sick. Jack looked back and forth at the squashed cow and the stupid heifer on top. Seeing the stress on the cow's face, as it heaved under the weight of the other one, he used his prod to try to get the heifer off her. The cattle couldn't turn round in the race, it was too narrow. You could sometimes get them to back up, but it wasn't easy. I could hear Jack muttering under his breath. He looked worried.

Reg had the measure of things and had jumped out of the yard and was running past the race toward the truck. He jumped over the fence and ran into the trailer as the drumming inside got louder.

No one spoke. We waited and listened to the bucking bronco inside the trailer and the odd call from Rick to Bob and back again. The cattle held in the race were all quiet except for the two in Jack's section. The bottom one was making a kind of rasping sound as it gasped for air under the weight of the heifer. The heifer seemed to be screaming. Dumb animal— it didn't have anything to scream about. It was the other one that was being crushed. I looked back at the trailer and said,

"Come on, fellas," under my breath, hoping they'd sort it out so we could let the others go and free the crushed one in Jack's section. I looked over at the Pommie and Emily. Emily was standing, staring at the road train and the Pommie was staring at the cattle in Jack's section. She was kind of biting her lip, like she wasn't sure about something.

We all stood still, adjusting our hats and wiping away the sweat from our foreheads. Then the drumming inside the trailer stopped and Reg appeared with Rick. Reg gave Elliot a thumbs up to let the next one through. He looked a little redder than he had when he went into the trailer—but that was all.

The two cows in Jack's section of the race were a bit like tired old boxers by then. Too exhausted to spar with each other. We let the ones we'd tagged go through to Rick and Bob to be loaded onto the trailer. Once they'd gone we shut the gate and Jack opened his. The heifer scrambled forward, digging her hooves into the other one's back. Once she'd come through to our section, Jack shut the gate again. Reg bent down next to him like you do when you're looking under a ute. He wanted to find out why the older cow was refusing to budge.

Once we'd tagged the flighty heifer and let her go through to the truck, Jack opened his gate again, to try to persuade the cow to get up. Both he and Reg used their prods to try and startle her into action. They gave her a quick poke in the rump, but she looked lifeless, except for this slow panting noise she'd started to make. Reg looked at Dad. He grimaced and said, "I don't like the look of this one, Derek." Dad jumped down off the fence and came round the side to take a closer look. He shook his head and Jack closed his gate again.

They unhitched the part of the fencing that the cow was leaning against, while Elliot went to get a bull catcher. Dad walked to his ute. He moved like he meant it. When Jack tried to lift the fence panel away, scraping it through the dirt, the cow's body followed until she'd slumped onto her side. One of her hind legs, wonky and broken, flopped out from under her. We all winced at that. "Jesus," Reg said, under his breath.

Dad came back with his gun. He loaded the rifle and in one movement he raised it to his shoulder, took aim and fired at the cow's head. There was a moment's silence after the gunshot, like we'd got the whole desert's attention. The cow's body finally relaxed and became still. Jack bent down to examine her broken hind leg. He held it in his big hands. His fingers were so thick with calluses, it looked like he was wearing gloves. He rubbed his hands up and down the thin skin that covered the broken bones; touching it real carefully, like a doctor who didn't want to hurt a patient. He was looking down at the cow, so all I could see was the top of his wide hat, which shook from side to side like a wagging tail. "That's bad," he said quietly.

Elliot put a chain round the cow and Emily jumped down from the back of the ute where she'd been sitting with Bobbie. Seeing her suddenly at his side, it was like Dad's anger at losing a cow had dried up. "You surfing, Em?" he asked, and she smiled that big, stupid grin she uses when she wants something. As Elliot waited with the bull-catcher's engine running, Emily climbed onto the dead cow's body, leaving dusty orange boot prints on its fur. She found her balance on the cow's round belly and waved at Elliot to let him know she was ready. As he set off, she stretched her arms out and pretended to surf. Her face looked real serious, a bit like the look she had when I tried to teach her how to tie her shoelaces. As Elliot dragged the cow slowly away it swept a sad-looking mark into the desert.

Emily hadn't done much cow surfing before—she was just learning. She hadn't got the hang of it properly, so when she didn't bend her knees enough, her arms swung upwards. She did her best to stay balanced, but then her boots began to slide on the cow's short fur. As she fell, her head went backward into the cow's mound of a belly and it knocked her hat forward so she couldn't see. Then she slipped into the dirt with a jolt as the cow continued on the dust wave without her. I shut my eyes and waited for her to start to blub like the other times, but she didn't cry. She lay on the ground laughing. Dad went to pick her up and hoisted her onto his shoulders, like a champion, even though she'd fallen off.

Everyone forgot about the dead cow then, except for the Pommie. She was just stood there, staring, as it disappeared into the spinifex. Her mouth was turned down, like she'd smelled something rotten.

EIGHTEEN

The next morning I got up early again. I couldn't stop think-ing about the muster. I was real excited. I felt good—I had no idea it was going to be the second worst day of my life. I went straight out to see Buzz—to take him for his walk just in case I didn't get a chance after school. I was hoping I'd be able to go out with the fellas. On my way back to the house, I saw the Pommie. She smiled at me, waved and asked if I was going mustering again with the fellas. I shrugged and said I reckoned I would after school. We walked back to the house together.

I was busy telling her how it was easiest to use a winch on one of the bull catchers to drag a dead cow out of the races, when she stopped and squinted like she was trying to read a real long word, far away. I looked toward the house, following her gaze. There was a fella climbing out of Sissy's bedroom window. The sun poked its head up, like it had just spotted him too. Its rays caught against the fella's golden hair as he landed on the ground and started to walk away.

The Pommie nudged me, to see if I'd seen him, so I just said, "Gil Smith."

She looked at me like I was crazy. "But he's blond," she eventually said. My mind flicked back to the day in the shop when he'd come to the station with Mick and Davy and I remembered the hat he'd been wearing. I guess the Pommie hadn't noticed his hair because of it. I couldn't be bothered to explain to her that Blackfellas sometimes had fair-haired kids—my mind was too busy remembering that day in the shop and how Gil kept looking outside, like he was hoping to see something—or someone. It must have been Sissy he was looking for—that's why he'd come to the shop with Mick and Davy. I swallowed hard as I realized Sissy had been rooting with Gil Smith—a gin! It felt like someone had punched me in the belly. I didn't know if it meant Sissy was a gin-jockey or not—we usually just called fellas that. My mouth fell open. It was dry. The Pommie looked at me and tugged on my arm, she said, "It might not be what you think." But I knew. I felt like kicking Sissy's big belly.

Gil was a couple of years older than her. He was Jonny's mate, or used to be. Jonny wouldn't have been mates with him any more, not if he knew he was rooting with Sissy. No way. My mind raced and I remembered Gil being at the station a few times at Christmas when Sissy was home for the holidays.

The Pommie put her hand on my shoulder, but I didn't want her or anyone near me. I sat down in the grass for a moment, like I needed to catch my breath. She stood quietly next to me for a bit, and then said, "What difference does it make? Really?"

I dunno if I was annoyed with her for asking such a stupid question, angry with myself for not realising it was Gil's baby sooner, or just mad with Sissy. Anyway, I didn't let the Pommie finish. I got up and walked toward the house. I didn't know what I was going to do. I felt like I wanted to puke. I reckoned that when Dad found out he'd kill her—and Gil.

The house had started to stretch and yawn, the dunny flushed and the early sun streamed through the glass doors in the dining room as I touched the sides of Jonny's picture. His smile made me want to scream. The Pommie followed me inside the house. I wanted to shout and trash things. Sissy had ruined everything. She'd wrecked the muster—my last muster—before it had even started and she'd wrecked everything else too. I felt like we were all going to be in trouble because of her belly. The Pommie took me by the arm and pulled me into the kitchen. Her voice was like a loud whisper, "Danny, you can't say anything—it's not your secret. If Sissy wants to see Gil, it's nothing to do with you."

Elliot came in then and said, "G'day, musterers," as he tipped his hat. The Pommie stopped talking. She looked like she was the one who'd been caught rooting with a gin. My smile was so stuck on, I thought it was going to slip off my face. Luckily Elliot was too busy jabbering on about the muster to notice.

All morning all I could think about was Gil Smith. I couldn't get it out of my head. I guess it was the same for the Pommie because at smoko I caught her looking at me with this real serious face. I wished she'd rack off.

The fellas were out with Reg's mob all day, taking down the yards at Jaben Point. After school I knew I'd explode if I had to stay in the house with my gin-jockey sister, so I took the Old Rover and went straight down to the yards to help the fellas—I didn't even ask if I could leave the dinner table. Bobbie yelled something after me, and I yelled back that I was going to Jaben Point, just so they knew where I was.

It was no fun at the yards though. I couldn't stop thinking about Sissy and Gil. Lifting fence panels isn't exactly exciting work. My brain felt dead by the end of it. I was glad when

Dad said the light was fading so we'd call it a day. He and the fellas were going to stay out at Jaben Point with Reg and his mob, so they could get a good start in the morning. I said I wanted to stay too, but he shook his head. Reckoned I had to go to school in the morning because he didn't want me being the class dunce when I started boarding school. I guess he knew I'd be disappointed, so he said I could go and help them after school. I asked if I could camp with them then—he said he'd think about it. I didn't want to rock the boat and ruin my chances of staying at stock camp, so I did as I was told. He said I had to radio when I got back to the house, so he knew I'd got home OK. Like I was a little kid.

On the way back to the station, I thought about Buzz and what I wanted him to be able to do. As I pulled into the yard at the house, it was in-between day and night. Not dark enough to make your hands disappear in front of your face, but not light enough to stop me tripping over the calf feeder. I ran to the calf pen to see Buzz, but it wasn't until I got there that I saw the gate was open. Man, I had a panic. There was only Charlotte there.

The rest had gone.

I kicked the empty calf feeder as I ran back and shouted for the others to help me find Buzz. Mum was home. When she heard me shouting she came out and saw Tough, Pod, Elaine, and Archie in her garden, chewing the plants up. She got real mad—I could hear her shouting. Buzz wasn't with them though. That's when my chest really did feel tight. Like finding out about Sissy and Gil wasn't bad enough, I'd gone and lost Buzz too.

I tried to stay calm, to think about where Buzz might have gone. I had a couple of puffs on my inhaler and then ran into the house. It was getting darker, so I got a flashlight and went out to the back yard where I usually took Buzz for training. I kept calling out his name, over and over again, hoping I'd catch the glint of his eyes in the beam of light I was casting back and forth across the desert in front of me.

I dunno how long I was out there for, scouring the desert, round and round the house in circles. It had gone quiet in the yard. I guess they'd caught all the poddies and put them back in their pen. After a while I could hear Bobbie and Liz shouting Buzz's name too. Mum must have taken Emily inside for her bath.

The spinifex felt sharp against my bare legs. I fell over a couple of times, and I could see in the torch light that I'd grazed both knees and had a nasty scratch down the back of my leg. I had to find Buzz.

I heard a ute start. The engine got louder and then I saw its headlights on full, swinging into the desert in front of me. Bobbie shouted for me to get in.

I ran through the darkness toward the ute. My torch light jumped over dust to bushes, to dust to spinifex, to dust again. I fell over. I wanted to cry. Not because I was hurt—I couldn't feel anything anyway—just because I was scared. I wanted to find Buzz, to know he was OK. He'd never been out of the calf pen on his own before. I didn't want the dingoes to get him and I didn't know if he'd be able to find water on his own. I swore on Jonny's grave that I'd spend time with Buzz every afternoon, if God would show me where he'd gone. I hadn't thought about God for a while, not really. I didn't think there was much point, after what happened to Jonny, but I guess I was desperate.

I wiped my face as I got into the ute, I didn't want Bobbie or the Pommie to see my wet eyes. We drove round and round and round that desert, going farther and farther away from the house. My stomach was churning, somewhere far down inside. Mum radioed to see if we'd found him. Dumb question. We'd have radioed if we had. She said dinner was ruined and we had to go back to the house. She said we were looking for a needle in a haystack, blindfolded.

I told Bobbie that her and the Pommie could go back, but I wasn't giving up. I had to find him. Bobbie didn't argue with me. She drove in these real big loops back to the house, just in case we'd missed him. But then we were back in the yard and there was no sign of Buzz. I wondered out loud how Buzz and the poddies had got out of the calf pen. That's when Bobbie said, "Sissy says she might have left the gate open by accident after she fed the poddies this afternoon."

Sissy—the stupid gin-jockey bitch! I ran to the house ready to belt her. I didn't care about her big belly. I reckoned she'd have been too busy rooting with Gil to think about shutting the gate properly. I flew up the steps and flung the fly screen open so hard it smacked against the wall. I gave the door a shove and burst into the dining room. Everything was spinning. She was sat at the table with Mum and Dad, like a fat frog.

"No sign?" Dad asked. Mum had radioed him to come home too. I didn't want to talk to him. I just went straight into it, shouting and screaming at Sissy. I threatened her with every bad word I could think of. Mum was there, but that didn't stop me from swearing. I told Sissy she'd better find Buzz, or I would beat the crap out of her, smack her stupid face in, belt her good and proper—said I'd get a stick and flog her. Everyone was shouting. Dad was trying to get hold of me, then he'd forget about me and start to argue with Mum instead. Sissy just sat there, saying nothing. Not even sorry. That's when I said, "I'm gonna kick your fucking gin-jockey belly."

It was like I'd fired a gun in the house.

Everyone shut up while they had a think about what I'd said—including me. I guess Sissy realized then that I knew about her and Gil. Her eyes opened wide. I don't think I've ever seen anyone look as scared as she did. Mum just stood there with her mouth open. Dad tried to grab my arm, but missed. "You don't EVER swear like that in front of your mother, Daniel!"

I was confused then. I didn't get it—why wasn't he mad at Sissy for rooting with Gil? I looked at him and asked, "What?"—like he'd gone mad. I guess he didn't like the tone of my voice, or the look on my face, or something, because he shouted, "Who do you think you're talking to, you little mongrel!"

I think I was walking backward because he seemed to be moving, but he wasn't getting any nearer. I saw his face twist and suddenly he started to move like he meant it. So I turned and ran. My boots skidded like glass on the floorboards as I dashed into Emily's pink room and on to where the walls turned blue and it became Sissy's bedroom. As I struggled to open the window wide enough for me to get through, I heard Dad's boots heavy behind me. I jumped up and wriggled through the gap in the window. His big hands caught my right foot. I was dangling there, outside the window, upside-down, like a doll. It all happened so quickly. I'm not sure if I wiggled my toes to make my foot slide out of my boot, or if gravity sucked me onto the ground. All I know is that I landed heavily on my shoulder. As I scrambled to look up behind me, I saw Dad's furious face at the window. He was looking at my boot in his hand. Then he was gone and I knew he would come after me, so I ran—one boot on, one boot off.

I just ran and ran and ran. It felt like one leg was longer than the other without my right boot on, but I kept going as fast as I could. Every right footstep landed on spiky stones and sharp grass. I hopped past the ammonia smell of the chooks. I heard feathers ruffling inside their house. I kept going. I jumped over fences, leaped over spinifex. I fell. I got up. The witchetty bushes scratched me and the grass whipped me. I felt the darkness against my face as I ran, and the dust against the white skin on my right ankle. I didn't stop until I thought my chest was going to burst. I knew I was going to be in trouble if I didn't slow down. I couldn't feel my inhaler bouncing against my thigh. I touched my pocket where its blue-plastic hump should have been, but it wasn't there, it must have fallen out when I jumped out of Sissy's window. I didn't feel angry any more. Just scared. I could hear the ute revving, wheels spinning and screeching. I knew then that I couldn't go back. I was on my own. I slowed to a jog and made for the open desert.

NINETEEN

The ute's engine growled louder, so I lay with my belly on the ground, hoping I'd ducked down below its headlights. It was then I remembered what the Pommie had said about Reg, so I started rolling over and over in the dust, covering myself with the dirt. I wanted to be a desert snow leopard too, so Dad wouldn't be able to see me.

As the ute got closer and closer, I started to think he might run me over. I shut my eyes tight and braced myself. It came nearer and nearer. I held my breath. Dad drove past me. He must have only been a few yards away, but he couldn't see me in that dusty disguise. The ute hummed toward Warlawurru like a mosquito. I stayed down on the ground, which was getting wet from my tears. I had no Jonny, no Buzz, and my sister was a gin-jockey. I guess I had no family really. It was cold on the ground.

When I saw Mick Smith's white beard, I thought I was with Father Christmas. There was still a star or two in the sky behind him, so it looked a bit like heaven. I'd forgotten where I was, until he said, "G'day, Danny." It was like he slapped me awake when I didn't even know I'd been to sleep.

I think I said Buzz's name out loud. It was like my mind's starter motor was just cranking up. Gradually I remembered he was lost, and so was I. Mick sat down. I didn't ask him if he wanted to. He just squatted on the next patch of dust, like I'd invited him.

He was looking out at where the sun was getting ready to yawn, when he said, "No swag?" I guess it was pretty stupid to sleep out in the desert without a swag, or even a blanket. That reminded my body to feel hungry and cold. I felt like I was going to perish. I guess I had the look of a crazed, dehydrated cow because he held his water bottle out to me and pointed at it with his chin, telling me to have a drink. He gave me his jacket too. It smelled like the inside of the chook house when you go early to collect the eggs. Clean, dry, lived in. Its warmth ached against my sharp shoulders. My dirty, bare legs stuck out underneath and in the grey light, the dried blood on my knees and shins looked like cement.

We didn't say anything else for a while. Mick just let me think. That's when I realized that when Sissy's baby was born we'd kind of be related. After a bit he looked right at me, and said, "Buzz? That the camel?" I nodded and so did he, like it all made sense. Mick leaned back until his hat rested on some spinifex. He looked real comfortable. More comfortable than any whitefella's ever looked, even in a bed. I guess I was the one who hadn't been invited. I turned round and started to think of tracking Buzz and how I could find him out in the desert. I swatted at the thought that he might not have survived the night and rested my head on my knees.

"You want to see Buzz?" Mick asked. I turned to look at him, wondering what he meant. I thought he was offering to help me track him. Dad reckoned Mick was a great tracker. But then he said, "Ya dad's got him back at Timber Creek—found him while we were looking for you."

My chin shook against my bottom lip, so I covered my mouth with my hand. When my eyes started to get wet again, I covered them too. I know Mick saw. I just didn't want to see him, seeing me blub. I could feel the salty streaks dry and go tight against the dirt on my face. After a minute or two, I got up and said, "I'm perishing." I gave Mick his coat back and said, "Thanks." The blue desert was streaked with orange when I set off toward Timber Creek. Mick didn't try to take me back there, like you would a little kid. He let me go on my own.

———————

Where I'd slept wasn't that far from the house, which was lucky because my right foot was cut to bits. I limped home, afraid of what might happen when I got there, but I had to go—I needed to see Buzz. I decided that if Mum and Dad didn't want me any more, I'd get a few of my things, Jonny's cattle book, the card the Pommie had found at the tip, and with Buzz, I'd head toward Marlu Hill. I reckoned someone would give us a lift from there to the Tanami Road and then there might have been a road-train or a ute driver who would drive us to Alice Springs. Aunty Veronica lived in Alice, so I thought I could go to hers.

When I got to the farm gate, I tried to sneak in quietly, so I could see Buzz before I had to speak to anyone else. I wanted to make sure he was OK. Seeing the house and Sissy's window made me think of her. I wondered if she was OK. Even though it was her fault that Buzz escaped, knowing he was all right made what she'd done seem less important. It was like the morning had taken the sting out of me. All my anger had gone cold during the night. I felt a bit sick about what I'd done, telling Mum and Dad her secret like that. I hated her for rooting with Gil, but I guessed the Pommie was right, I should have kept my big mouth shut. I called myself a stupid bastard then.

As I closed the gate quietly and limped across the yard to the calf pen, I looked over my shoulder. Elliot and Lloyd were outside the house having a smoke. I wondered what had happened. They were meant to be staying at stock camp with Reg's mob. When they saw me, they both looked like they'd spotted a wanted man. I didn't stop.

Buzz was waiting for me, like a lanky old carpet. When I saw him, a smile filled my cheeks and it felt strange. I guess it felt like I'd been miserable for so long, my face had forgotten how to do it. I rubbed Buzz's neck and ears. He seemed different, though, like he didn't know me. My heart thudded against my chest. I thought I'd win him back with some milk, but he got spooked. His ears went flat and his eyes looked wide and empty and then he reared up. At first I thought he must really hate me, but then I turned round and saw what it was that had got him going. Mum was running toward us. She looked weird in her nightie, outside, in the daylight. Her face was pale. I thought she was about to rugby tackle me, but her arms came out like these big mechanical-digger buckets and hugged me, hard. There was just her thin nightie between her big warmth and my dirty, scratched skin. Her hug wasn't just nice, though, she wanted to hurt me too. We stayed like that for ages, with her pressing her hard chin and then her cheeks into the top of my hat as I looked down at the ground, squashed into her belly. I started to want her to let go of me.

Clutching my shoulders Mum pushed me away from her body, but held me there, at arm's length. She looked me in the eye, then looked me up and down, like she was checking for something. Once she was sure it wasn't there, her wet eyes became hard as she said, "Don't ever, EVER, run off again." She shook me. I nodded as tears came into my eyes from nowhere. She told me to go to the house and get some food and a bath. I said I had to feed Buzz first. She stared at me again. I stared back. I think she knew I meant it because she said OK. She didn't go back to the house, though, she waited for me to give him his milk. She wrapped her arms around her nightie as it quivered in the cool air. I think she thought I might run away again.

I didn't say anything else. I just took my time and made sure Buzz had his brekkie. He looked OK. I checked his legs and underneath, but I couldn't see anything wrong with him. I ran my hands up and down his back and sides as he head-butted me, but I couldn't feel any bumps or scrapes. Mum said Dad found Buzz during the night when they were all out looking for me. He told her I'd done a good job with Buzz. She reckoned Dad only had to call Buzz's name once, before he followed him back to Timber Creek.

I should have felt tall when I heard that. Proud. But I didn't. I realized that the reason Elliot and Lloyd were at the house was because Mum and Dad asked them to come back from stock camp to help find me. I didn't know they'd all come looking for me. I was glad Dad found Buzz, but it made me feel bad about Sissy.

I asked where Sissy was. Mum said she was in her room, as usual. I asked about Dad and she said he was in the dining room—waiting to see me. I'd had to go and see Dad in the dining room before, for all kinds of different things. Once it was because I'd got distracted and forgot about a hosepipe I'd switched on to fill a trough. I left it running for half a day, and when Dad saw the great big wet mark on the dirt, he went mad. I wondered if Sissy had been called into the dining room too. I reckoned she'd have to explain why she'd been rooting with Gil.

I was a bit scared about having to face Dad. I'd never run off like that before and I'd never seen him look as angry as he had that night, either. Mum let me go into the dining room on my own. I wanted to touch Jonny's picture first, but Dad was waiting for me, with his back to the door. Everything went quiet when I walked in. Emily stopped eating her brekkie, so did Liz and Bobbie. Liz gave me a real nice smile, before they all left the room. I reckoned Emily wanted a ringside seat, but she knew she wasn't welcome. Once they'd gone and we heard the door click shut, Dad scraped his chair back against the floorboards. It made the hollow space under the house sound bigger than usual.

Dad nodded at another chair and told me to sit down. His hands were clasped together, resting on the table. It looked like he was keeping them like that, so one of them couldn't get loose and whack me. I guess he was pretty mad. He spoke in this real quiet voice, like he was trying hard not to shout. He said I looked a dirty mess and that after he'd finished with me I had to have a shower. He said that from then on, if I put a foot wrong at school, Bobbie would give me a thousand lines. I knew that wouldn't be all—he was just working up to what he really wanted to say.

Dad looked at me real hard and said Mum had been awake all night worrying about me. I saw the anger in his eyes. He looked back at the table, like that was where he'd left a list of all the things he needed to say. After a second or two he said I had cost the station money. He'd called Elliot and Lloyd back from stock camp to help look for me and because they'd been up all night, he said he had to give them the day off, so they could get some rest. He reckoned that meant Reg and his mob had more work to do, which would cost more money. "You are very lucky no cattle suffered because of all this," he said.

Dad said I wouldn't be allowed to go mustering until I'd done enough chores to work off each of the hours of worry I'd caused Mum. "By my reckoning that's about twelve hours, Daniel," he said. I took a deep breath and said, "OK." I was waiting for him to say something about Sissy and Gil, but he didn't. He said I was lucky he didn't take me outside and flog me. That was it. He stood up, put his hat on, and went out. I guess I was glad he didn't hit me, but I think I might have felt better if he had.

I tried to be quiet for the rest of the day—to blend in with everything, so no one would really know I was there. I had a shower and I was so tired my eyes kept closing. It was quiet everywhere. The fellas were asleep in the demountable outside and Mum was resting inside. Bobbie said there wouldn't be any school that day because everyone had been up all night. She looked tired. She was swinging like a lazy goanna in her hammock with this look that said, Don't speak to me. The Pommie was just getting on with her cleaning and things as usual. Emily was real annoying—she wasn't tired. She'd slept all night and didn't really know what was going on, so she kept asking all these questions, which bounced against my head like the tapping sound beetles make when they fly into a closed window. I wanted to know what had happened to Sissy. I didn't see her all morning, but there was no one to ask.

At lunch time Mum had changed out of her nightie into a shirt and trousers, so everything felt normal again—except for Sissy. She waddled out of her room and sat down carefully, like someone had flogged her. Her belly button poked through her T-shirt like a weird thumb. When I looked at her, she gave me this look like she hated me. I guess I had dobbed her in about Gil. I reckon if it wasn't for that big belly, she'd have come round the table and strangled me, or something. I couldn't look at her. Elliot and Lloyd said they were going to go back to work, and even though Mum said they didn't have to, they said they would anyway.

Everyone got down from the table, except me and Mum. Bobbie and Emily went with the fellas to Jaben Point and Sissy disappeared back to her room. I reckoned she'd never speak to me ever again. I was waiting to hear what my chores would be when I began to wonder what Sissy's punishment was. She hadn't stayed at the table to hear what her chores were. Mum seemed happy again, so I asked her what Dad had said about Sissy and Gil. She looked at me and asked what I meant. So I said because of the baby. Her eyes narrowed and her mouth fell open.

Mum leaned forward and touched my arm—kind of pinning it down.

Then she said, quietly: "What do you mean, Sissy and Gil and the baby?"

TWENTY

"Sissy! SISSY! Get in here now!" Mum was shouting at the top of her voice but there was no sound from Sissy's room. Mum shouted for her again and when there was no answer she went to Sissy's bedroom and opened the door. Sissy wasn't there. I could tell by the way Mum shut the door again. She came back into the dining room where I was. I guess Mum and Dad hadn't understood what I meant when I'd called Sissy a gin-jockey the night before. Maybe they just thought it was another nasty name I was calling her—like when Sissy called me gay.

Mum looked at me and said, "I want to know everything. NOW!" Like I was the one who'd been rooting with a gin. While I tried to think what to say I looked at the floor. Mum was looking at me. Waiting. When I looked up she didn't seem angry, more afraid. She moved her chair round nearer mine and put her other hand on my back—to see if being nice to me would help me spit it all out. She said, "It's OK, Danny, just tell me."

I wasn't sure that she meant it. She nodded at me and said, "It's OK," more quietly than before. I looked at my hands, then said how I'd already told them: Sissy was a gin-jockey—she was rooting with Gil Smith.

Mum breathed in suddenly and stood up real fast. After a second she said, "What makes you think that?" Like I'd made it up.

My stomach went tight. Mum said again, "Why do you think that, Danny?" I looked at the floor and said I'd seen Gil climbing out of Sissy's bedroom window and that if Mum didn't believe me, she should ask the Pommie about it.

Mum shouted through to the kitchen, "Liz! Get in here, will you?" The Pommie came through. She was drying her wet, soapy hands on a towel. Before Liz could speak Mum turned to me and said, "Danny, go to your room. Now." I got down from the table and walked quickly to my room, which was just off the dining room. My bedroom door was opposite the piano, where the picture of Jonny was. I didn't know if I was in trouble or not. It felt like I was. I wanted to touch the picture of Jonny on top of the piano, but I couldn't with Mum and the Pommie there, so I just looked at it real hard instead as I shut my bedroom door.

Mum shouted at the Pommie. I heard her muffled voice through the thin bedroom wall. "Danny reckons you saw Gil Smith climbing out of Sissy's bedroom window—is it true?" The Pommie must have nodded because then Mum said, "Why the hell didn't you tell me?" The Pommie said she didn't want to cause any trouble. It wasn't really anything to do with her. She said Sissy was already pregnant when she arrived at Timber Creek. Mum couldn't argue about that. The baby wasn't Liz's fault. Liz said she thought we all knew the father was someone at the station because Sissy must have got pregnant at Christmastime when she was at home for the school holidays. Hearing the Pommie say that made Mum real angry. She hit the roof. She shouted, "Get out! Just go, will you?" I heard the Pommie say, "I didn't know what to do—I'm sorry." I guess Mum didn't want to hear it though. She shouted, "I said GO!"

It went quiet then in the dining room, so I opened my bedroom door a crack. There was no one there. I could hear Mum on the radio in the kitchen. She was telling Dad he had to come home straightaway. I felt sick. I wanted to go and tell Sissy—to warn her. But I was scared. I knew Dad would blow his stack when he heard what she'd been doing. I ran to my bedroom window to see if I could see Sissy somewhere on the station. I wanted to shout for her to run, to just get in a ute and run away. I couldn't think what else to tell her to do. I couldn't see her anywhere. I was wondering how much trouble I'd be in if Mum caught me looking for Sissy outside, when I heard the door to the dining room open.

Mum said, "Ah. Just the person I was looking for. You'd better sit down, young lady." I heard Sissy try to ask what was going on, but Mum just said, "Gil Smith." I guess Sissy knew then that the game was up and tried to run because Mum shouted, "STAY WHERE YOU ARE! YOU ARE GOING NOWHERE. NOWHERE. YOU HEAR ME? Your father's on his way home right now." Man. I had never, ever heard Mum shout like that before. It made all the hairs on my arms stand on end, my belly flipped too. I felt scared. I guess Sissy did too because that's when I heard her start to blub. Quietly, though. Not like normal. I wondered what to do. Things were going to get a lot worse once Dad got home, that was for sure. I sat on the end of my bed, near the door, which was still open a crack, and waited.

I dunno how long it was that I sat there and listened to Sissy whimpering, but it felt like about a year. When Dad eventually arrived he slammed the door to the dining room shut, so I knew straightaway he was annoyed about being dragged back to the station when he was busy with the fellas. I swallowed hard when he said, "Well? What is it? This had better be good, I've got better things to do—" But he never finished because Mum told him to sit down and listen.

I heard Dad scrape the chair back on the wooden floor. I couldn't see him properly through the small gap in the door, just his left forearm. But I was too scared to open it any wider. I could tell he was resting his elbows on the table, like always. He said again, "Well? What is it?" Sissy had stopped whimpering by then and there was this silence, while I guess Mum worked out the best way to tell Dad Sissy was a gin-jockey. Eventually she said, "Danny reckons Sissy has been sleeping with Gil Smith." Then there was silence.

Dad took his elbow off the table and put his hand down. "Sissy?" Silence. "Sissy? Is this true?" he asked, real quietly. Sissy must have nodded her head because she didn't say anything. But that's when Dad slammed his hand down on the table and said, "NO. NO WAY. A GIN?" Silence. "Jesus Christ." Silence. "The little mongrel!" Silence. "I am going to break every bone in that little bastard's body. You hear me?" Sissy was crying again then. Dad stood up and started pacing around, slamming his hand down on the table and shouting, "No! The mongrel!"

Mum followed him about trying to calm him down a bit. Then all of a sudden he sat back on his chair and I reckon he was rubbing his face with his hands, but I couldn't really see. Then he jumped back up again and said, "Where?" No one answered him, so he slammed his hand down on the table in front of Sissy and said, "WHERE? WHERE? DAMN IT!" Sissy didn't answer, so then he said, "Was it here? Here on the station?" She must have nodded because then he asked if it was in the house. Mum answered that. She said I'd told her how Liz and me had seen Gil climbing out of Sissy's bedroom window.

Dad went ape then. He went into the other room and came back carrying a rifle and a box of bullets. It was weird, though. It was like he didn't need to shout any more—he'd decided what to do, I guess. He'd got it all figured out. "I'm going to Warlawurru," he said. We all knew what he was going to do. But he said it calmly, like it was the most normal thing in the world, like he was going to the Crofts to borrow a trailer, or something.

Mum was scared then. I could tell. "Just sit down, Derek. Sit down—please. Please."

Dad wasn't listening, though. He picked up his hat and turned to go out the door. That's when Mum jumped up and grabbed his arm. She screamed at him to stop and just think—please, think about what you're doing. He pushed her off, so she kind of stumbled backward a bit, but she was fast. She got her balance and kind of threw herself between Dad and the door, so he couldn't get out. Dad said, "Get out of my way, Sue. Now." But Mum wasn't budging. She told him there was no way she was going to let him out of the house until he had calmed down. "You kill him, you'll get life. D'you hear me? Life. What bloody use will you be to us then? You know what it's like. The law's different nowadays—they listen to the Blackfellas. You so much as lay a finger on him and they'll lock you up and throw away the key."

I don't remember doing it, but when Dad shoved Mum I must have opened the bedroom door because when Dad threw his gun on the floor, I was standing in the dining room. He kind of shouted—not words that I could recognise, more of a real loud moan. Then he pushed past Mum, so he could get out of the house. Mum ran out after him. I could hear her shouting, "Derek! Derek! Come back. Just come back. Please. We need to talk—" The ute's engine started and I heard the wheels screech as he raced out of the yard. I went over to the door and saw Mum trying to run after him, but she kind of slipped on the dirt, and was left on the ground in Dad's dust cloud.

I ran out to help her. She was kind of like a crumpled-up piece of dirty paper, like something you'd find at the tip. She was crying too. Sobbing. A bit like when it was Jonny's funeral. I asked if she was OK but she didn't answer. She just got to her feet and walked slowly back into the house. Sissy was still at the dining-room table. Like she didn't dare move. She was staring straight ahead, and although she wasn't making any sound tears were running down her cheeks. Mum sat down next to her. I stood there for a minute, not knowing what to do, so I went back to my room.

I sat on my bed and wished I was somewhere with Jonny, just the two of us with the stars, far away from Timber Creek and Sissy's belly. I took out his cattle book, a handful of his soldiers, and his favorite dinky car—a Toyota, all chipped and worn. I slid on my back under the darkness of his bed and held Jonny's things tightly to my chest.

TWENTY-ONE

When I opened my eyes, it was dark. The house was quiet except for the whirr of the air con and every now and then something creaked. I'd forgotten where I was so when I tried to sit up, I smacked my head on the bottom of Jonny's bed. I yelped, half in pain, half confused. Once I'd remembered where I was, I swung my legs to the side and wriggled out from under the bed.

The footsteps I'd heard in my dream were real—they belonged to Dad. I opened the bedroom door a little and saw him and Mum sitting at the dining-room table. He must have calmed down and come home.

I watched Dad rub his face and shake his head. I dunno if he'd turned round before he got to the Smiths', or if he just couldn't find them. Mum was talking, real quietly, and she looked sad. I couldn't hear everything she was saying, but it had to be about Sissy and Gil. I felt my belly flip as I realized they looked a bit like when Jonny had the accident. After a while Dad said Gil Smith out loud, like he was trying to learn a new word. Mum sighed. Dad was just sitting there, with his mouth open. That's when Mum said, "People will talk."

Dad said, "Gil Smith?" Mum nodded and said it made sense. "The timing's right." Dad shook his head. Mum said people would gossip. Dad stared. Mum reckoned they'd have to tell people—she said the bush telegraph would work overtime when everyone found out. Dad didn't reply. They both just sat there, not looking at each other.

After a minute or two Dad said, "I can't have this feral baby under my roof, Sue. I can't. It'll have to go." Mum said that maybe we could all keep it a secret. She reckoned no one had to know the baby was a gin. She reckoned that because Gil was fair and had lighter skin than most of the other Blackfellas, the baby might be white. But Dad shook his head. He said he reckoned it didn't matter what color the baby was because him and Mum were probably the last to know the truth, and that he wouldn't be surprised if the rest of the Territory had already heard what Sissy had been up to with that mongrel bastard. He shook his head and said he couldn't believe Sissy could do such a thing. "Gil Smith," he said again, like it was a question.

After a minute or two, he said Mum should phone Aunty Ve in Alice and get her to have Sissy to stay until things had calmed down. Mum started to cry a bit then. I hated that. I didn't want Sissy to go to Aunty Ve's. Not really. Not forever, anyway. Just until she had the baby, maybe. Then she could leave it there and come home, like normal.

Dad stood up. He went toward Emily's room. I kept real quiet. He must have gone through Emily's room and opened Sissy's bedroom door because for a second I could hear her music. He came back out with Sissy waddling behind him. She didn't have any shoes on and her feet were real fat. He held a chair out for her to sit on.

I thought Sissy would blub again—but she didn't. Dad

spoke real quietly. He told her that there was no way he was having her and her gin baby living under his roof. He said she'd have to go to Aunty Ve's for a while. Sissy stared right back at him. Mum said, "Derek, please?" But Dad was having none of it. He said Mum should phone Aunty Ve straightaway and get things organized as quickly as possible. I saw him look at Sissy's big belly and then look away again. He looked at his hands and said Sissy would need to be in Alice for when the baby came anyway—this way she'd just be there a bit earlier than originally planned. That's all.

Mum twiddled a hanky round in her hands. Sissy didn't move. Mum blew her nose and her voice went funny when she said everyone would find out who the father was. I guess she reckoned Sissy would be embarrassed or sorry, or something. Sissy just shrugged, like she didn't care if the whole of the Territory knew she was a gin-jockey. I reckoned Dad would get angry about that—he hated it when we answered back or anything. But he didn't.

After what felt like ages, Dad said he still needed to go to see Mick and Gil. When Sissy heard that, she looked scared and said, "What for? If I'm not here, what does it matter?" I guess we all knew he wanted to beat the crap out of Gil. Sissy looked at Mum, like she wanted her to do something to make Dad change his mind. But Mum didn't say anything. I think she reckoned Gil deserved a hiding too—whatever the law said. Sissy must have known there was nothing she could do about it, so she looked at her big belly. She asked if she could get down from the table. Mum looked at Dad and he nodded, so she got up and waddled back to her room.

_____

When Aunty Veronica rolled up in her car at Timber Creek, it took her a few minutes to haul herself out from behind the steering wheel. She walked across the yard and grabbed the rail to pull herself up the steps to the door. Dad held the door open for her. He said g'day. She smiled, but he didn't. I guess he couldn't find one to give her. I was told to go out and play with Emily while they talked to Aunty Ve.

Emily sat like a crow on the fence eating an apple, while I hung around with Buzz wondering what was happening in the house. I knew Sissy was packing to go to Alice Springs.

After we'd all eaten lunch without anyone saying anything at all, Mum, Aunty Ve, and everyone else were busy washing up, so I went to Sissy's bedroom. I stood outside the door not knowing what to do. In the end I knocked on it, like the Pommie would. Sissy's voice came through real quietly asking who it was. I said it was me—Danny, and she asked what I wanted. I didn't know what I wanted—not exactly, anyway. I tried to think what to say. In the end I just asked if I could come in. I heard Sissy's feet get louder on the wooden floor inside, until they stopped on the other side of the door. After a second or two, the door opened and her face was there in front of me. "What?" she asked. She'd been crying. I shrugged and asked if she was OK. She shrugged back at me. Neither of us said anything. Then she said she still had a load of packing to do, so I nodded. She looked at me again. I dunno, I was going to say something about how I didn't want her to go or that I was sorry, or whatever. But I couldn't get it straight in my head. Instead I kind of half shrugged at her. We looked at each other again and then she closed the door, so I went outside to practice my bowling. I was still out there when the women all came out of the house like a flock of galahs at dusk.

Mum carried Sissy's bags for her. She and Aunty Ve loaded them into the back of her car. Aunty Ve began shoving her big body behind the steering wheel. Mum went round to the passenger side and helped Sissy in. She looked like a mirror to Aunty Ve at the other side. Mum stood there, fidgety and awkward, fussing around, flicking Sissy's hair off her forehead. She helped Sissy with the seat belt, and as she leaned over that big belly of hers they finally hugged. That's when Sissy really started to blub. She kept saying over and over again how she didn't want to go. "Don't make me. Please. Please, Mum. Don't make me go. I don't want to go. I'm scared. I'm so scared." Mum undid the seat belt again and helped Sissy out of the car. She rubbed her back and stroked her hair. Emily started wailing too, so Aunty Ve got out and picked her up while Mum whispered things in Sissy's ear I couldn't hear. Aunty Ve looked over at Dad and shook her head a little. Dad looked down at the ground when he saw her. I turned back to the car and Mum had got Sissy back into the front seat. She'd stopped sobbing.

Mum said Sissy had to call her when they got to Alice and as soon as anything happened. Dad watched from where he was working. Once he saw Mum let go of Sissy, he walked over to the car too. The door was already shut when he got there, so he tapped on Sissy's window and sort of waved at her. He didn't smile. Sissy looked at him, but she didn't wave. She had this weird, kind of blank face. Like she couldn't see or hear anything. When she opened the window as the car moved away, she leaned out a little bit with her hand waving like a broken wing.

As they left us behind we didn't shout, Bye! See ya soon! Drive carefully! like normal. That was how we always used to wave Sissy and Jonny off when Aunty Ve came over to take them back to boarding school after the holidays. I guess we couldn't pretend everything was normal any more. Nothing was normal. I guess it hadn't been normal for ages. I wondered if it would ever be normal again.

TWENTY-TWO

An hour or so after Sissy had left, Dad finished what he was doing with the generator, wiped his hands on his trousers, and walked toward the house. He stuck his head just inside the door and shouted to Mum, to let her know he was going to Warlawurru to see Mick. The fly screen twanged on its hinges like a rubber band when he let go of it. Mum came out and said he should just leave it. Dad looked at her and said he had to go and see them. Mum put her arm round him and said, "Let the dust settle, Derek. Let's just leave it until after we've finished the muster. Please. Sissy's not here, so let's just leave it for now." Dad looked like he'd been stung when Mum said about Sissy not being at the station. He stood still for a minute, rubbed his face with his hands, and thought about it. His eyes looked red when he nodded his head and said he was going to go to Wild Ridge to see the fellas and get the muster underway over there. Mum looked relieved and worried at the same time. She kissed his cheek. Dad got into his ute and it threw a dirty streak into the air as he left the station. Mum watched him go and then went inside.

When Mum and Dad gave me a list of chores—my punishment for running away—I couldn't believe how much I had to do. I'd hoped with Sissy leaving the station and everyone being so busy with the muster, they'd have forgotten about it, but it was like the opposite had happened. I reckoned they'd used the time to think of as many jobs as they could. When I saw the list, I shouted, "It's not fair!" I hadn't meant to, it just came out of my mouth without me thinking.

Dad held his finger up and said, "Don't. You. Dare." I kept quiet then and listened. I knew if I started blubbing or complaining I'd be in even more trouble. Dad reckoned there was nothing worse than a whinger. They went through the list with me. Dad said the sooner all the chores were done, the sooner I could stay out at stock camp with him and the fellas. But he said he'd be checking and if I didn't do the chores properly, he'd give me more to do. That's when Mum said I had to do them after school, which made me wonder when I'd get time to train Buzz. Dad said, "You should have thought about that before you ran away. All actions have consequences, Danny. That's something your sister's about to find out."

I had to sweep the shop, dust every room in the house, tidy the shelves in the cool room, clean my bedroom, and put my laundry away—neatly. I had to clean out the chook house, as well as repair the old pigpen ready for Mo's piglets being weaned. I had to help Liz feed all the poddies and the pigs and open the shop if any Blackfellas called by. I wanted to ask what to do if Mick or Gil called in, but I was afraid of what Dad would say, so I kept quiet.

Dad wanted me to clean out one of his sheds and tidy up the wood and sheets of metal that were inside it. He also said I had to go through all the jars and boxes of nuts, bolts, screws, washers, and things in another of the big sheds, and make sure they were tidy. There were hundreds of jars and boxes in there, all mixed up—screws thrown in with washers, big nails with drill bits, you name it. It was going to be hot and boring.

The next day Mum went to work as normal. She didn't seem very happy about it. She told me and Emily that if Aunty Ve or Sissy phoned we had to tell her straightaway. She kind of shouted the instructions at us, like we were already in trouble before we'd even forgotten what to do. She wrote the number of the clinic at Marlu Hill where she worked in big letters on a piece of paper and pinned it to the wall next to the phone, so we couldn't lose it. But the phone didn't ring that day and Mum spoke to Sissy and Aunty Ve that night when she got home. She hung up and said Sissy was fine but there was no news and then radioed Dad to tell him the same thing. I didn't get it. Why would you radio someone to say you had nothing to tell them?

For days I was stuck on the station. They felt like the longest of my life. Dad and the fellas were working all hours out at Wild Ridge. Some days they didn't even come home. I'd missed them rounding up the cattle there—that was the best bit. With Dad staying out some nights, dinnertime was strange. There were too many empty seats at the table. I didn't like it. It made me feel sad about Jonny and I wished Sissy would come home without the big belly. Like normal.

The only thing that was normal was Buzz. Even though I had all the chores to do, I made a deal that no matter what, I'd spend at least an hour a day with him. I dunno if he understood, but he seemed full of himself all week. He was a terrible rascal. He ran around, rearing up and kicking his legs like he was dancing, or something. Once or twice I thought I would have to get a stick, but after a few minutes he calmed down. It was like he'd get so excited about coming out of the pen and getting away from those dumb poddies, he wanted to jump up and down like he'd won a million bucks.

Liz saw us coming back into the yard one night after our training, and later at dinner she told everyone about how clever Buzz and me were. Dad and the fellas weren't there, though, they'd stayed out at stock camp at Simpson's Dam. They'd moved there after they'd finished at Wild Ridge. Bobbie said, "Just imagine what you could do if you put that much effort into your schoolwork, Danny." Then Mum said, "Or those chores." I dunno why grown-ups always had to ruin things. I thought about Dad and the fellas and wished I could just magically be with them instead of all the girls.

I'd heard Dad complaining about the dust. The ground was so dry that when the cattle were all together in the yards, they kicked up loads of dust. Dad reckoned it was a terrible storm. It got in the fellas' eyes and ears and their lungs when they breathed. Into everything. Normally they'd get a hose and pump water onto the ground in the yards to damp it down so there was less dust, but because of the drought Dad didn't like to do that much. But the dust was so bad he reckoned they'd have to do something because it was becoming impossible. I remembered the mark around Simpson's Dam where the water used to be, from when the Pommie and me were there looking at Arthur's stone. That was a while ago, though—I wondered how low the water had got now.

Mum said she hoped Sissy was OK. She said the baby's due day wasn't until a week after the muster was supposed to finish. She'd always said she'd go to Alice to be with Sissy once she started to have the baby. She'd said it would take hours for the baby to actually be born, so there'd be enough time to get there. She reckoned she'd spoken to her boss, Doctor Willis, at the clinic. He'd agreed to let her have more time off on compassionate grounds.

When I woke up on Jonny's bed, it wasn't even starting to get light. I must have been looking at the soldiers he'd painted when I fell asleep because in the morning I found a few hiding in the sheets. I counted them to make sure all forty-seven were there, taking care with my favorite. It was the soldier Jonny had worked on last. I recognised him easily because he only had trousers. Jonny must have had the accident before he'd got round to painting the rest of the uniform.

Once I knew they were all there, I carefully put them away and got dressed. I decided to finish off sorting out the jars in Dad's shed. As I walked into the dining room I saw the kitchen light was on, so I went to have a look to see who was in there. As I got to the doorway, I saw Dad sitting at the counter on the tall stool. He had his back to the door, and his hat was laid on the side, next to his cup of coffee. He was rubbing the sides of his head with his fingers. He hadn't heard me and I didn't want to spook him, so I made a little coughing sound in my throat to get his attention. He turned round and said, "Hey, Danny. What are you doing up so early?" His voice sounded weird, kind of croaky. Like his throat was sore, or something. I shrugged and said I just woke up. We looked at each other for a moment before Dad asked if I wanted some brekkie. I said I had some chores to do and so I'd get my brekkie later when everyone else was up. He nodded and said he was pleased I'd taken the right attitude to the chores. I guess that meant he was glad I was doing them.

It was starting to get light, but the sun hadn't arrived so everything was grey. There was enough light for me to find my way to the shed and open the door. Inside, the jars were all on the floor where I'd left them. I picked up each one in turn, unscrewed the lid to have a look inside to make sure there were only washers or nuts or bolts or nails inside each one. That was a bit tricky to start with because it wasn't really light enough to see, but after a while the sun poked its head over the desert and things got easier. I made sure all the jars went back on the shelves where they belonged and then closed the shed door behind me. I took out the list of chores Mum and Dad had given me and crossed that one off. As I looked at what I had left to do on the list, my stomach growled. I folded the piece of paper up and put it into my shirt pocket as the sun streaked the world orange.

I walked back to the house and Lloyd and Elliot were outside having a smoke. I heard Lloyd say something about Little Sissy with that gin. But Lloyd stopped speaking when Elliot said, "G'day, Danny, you're up early." I asked them why they weren't inside having their brekkie, and Elliot said the Pommie'd screwed up again, so they thought they'd have a smoke instead.

When I opened the door, the Pommie was inside waving a towel around. I soon realized why—she was trying to get rid of the smell of burnt toast. "Great start to the day," she said as I walked past. In the kitchen I saw six black slices of toast balanced on top of the pigs' slops. Bobbie was standing guard over the grill to make sure the next lot didn't go the same way. I went back into the dining room, where Mum was shaking her head at the smell while the Pommie opened more windows.

Eventually we sat down to eat the unburned toast Bobbie had made, while we pretended we couldn't smell smoke any more. The Pommie wasn't at the table—she was back in the kitchen watching the grill, like she had something to prove. By the time she brought the next lot of toast through, Mum had left the table to go to work, Bobbie had gone to the schoolroom to get things ready for us over there, and Dad and the fellas were probably halfway to Simpson's Dam. When the Pommie realized there was only Emily and me there, she sighed and put the plate on the table. I didn't want any more, but seeing as she'd gone to the trouble, I decided to take another slice. As the Pommie passed Emily the jam, she said she reckoned Sissy's baby would be a bit like everybody jam. I thought she'd totally lost it. I mean, why would the baby look like jam? But then she said that all babies had special powers, which meant everybody liked them—no matter what. I shrugged at her as I kept chewing. Emily said she'd like it, but only if it was a girl. The Pommie reckoned it wouldn't matter if the baby was a girl or a boy, everyone would still love it.

She said, "You'll see," as she carried the plate of uneaten toast back into the kitchen.

I reckoned she'd be in trouble if Mum saw how much bread had been wasted.

TWENTY-THREE

It was Sunday morning when things really started to go wrong.

The first bad thing that happened was when I got to the calf pen. Buzz was shouting his head off. I knew he was trying to tell me something, then I saw what was wrong. Elaine was dead. I dunno what killed her. She'd seemed like a pretty strong little poddy calf, but you couldn't always tell which ones would live and which ones would die. I felt bad for her. The others were staring at me—probably wondering where their food was.

I opened the gate and Buzz wandered into the yard. He waited there for me to get Elaine out of the pen. I grabbed her back legs and dragged her along the dirt, turning her pretty white hide orange. Her face fell over to one side, and her mouth was slightly open, so her tongue picked up the dirt too. She felt cold and heavy.

As I shut the gate and started to pull Elaine along the ground toward the Old Rover I saw Emily watching me. Once she realized what I'd got, she came running over and said, "Is Elaine dead?" I told her I didn't know why she'd died, but she was cold, so she'd been dead a good few hours.

I said I was going to take her to the carcass dump and Emily said she'd come too.

Buzz followed us to the house and I told him to stay outside. He didn't like that. When I went up the steps he tried to follow me, so I had to push his nose away so the fly screen would shut. Mum was in the kitchen on the phone. It was Bob, the road-train driver—he was real upset. Nine animals had perished in the trailers on the way to the slaughterhouse from Simpson's Dam. He said it was dehydration and the shock of being mustered. It happened sometimes. Dad and the fellas were out at Simpson's Dam taking down the yards. Mum reckoned she'd have to radio to let him know. I felt scared. While Mum took down the receiver and started radioing Dad, I ran through to the dining room and stood on my tiptoes to be taller than the photo of Jonny on top of the piano. I held the frame and gently ran my fingers over Jonny's face. It was the only thing I could think of to do.

I saw Liz and told her what had happened and how Emily and me were going to the carcass dump with Elaine. She sighed and said, "Oh no."

When we got to the carcass dump, Emily and me climbed into the back and pushed Elaine out into the desert. She landed on the ground like a couple of pairs of trousers that had fallen off the line. Her white hide stood out like a tooth amongst the dirty old bones of the other dead cattle and horses. She looked so new against the orange desert. It wouldn't be long until she was just a smaller version of the other old, empty, brown carcasses, picked over by the dingoes and crows. "Poor old Elaine," Emily said. She looked back at the white carcass as we drove away.

Dad was home when we got back to the station. He was on the phone, speaking to someone about the cattle that had died in Bob's road train. Dad wasn't happy, he reckoned it would get Timber Creek Station a bad name. He slammed the phone down and then slammed the door behind him as he went back out to Simpson's Dam. I knew not to ask if I could stay with him at stock camp.

It was less than an hour later when the radio fizzed and Greg Croft's voice came through. Seeing as I had my mouth full, the Pommie answered it. Greg asked her if Dad had been out to Cockatoo Creek Dam. That was the water hole on our land that was nearest to their station in the east. The Pommie didn't know, so she asked me. I wasn't sure, but I didn't think he'd been out there. Greg said he was real concerned. Gil Smith had shown up at Gold River, worried about Cockatoo Creek Dam. Greg reckoned Gil had been on a walkabout when he'd seen the dam was dry, so he'd run all the way to Gold River, the nearest place to the dam, to raise the alarm. Greg said it was a scorcher and that Gil looked wrung out, so Penny had made him some tucker and told him to have a shower. While Gil got cleaned up, Greg had been to check the dam out and said it was dry as a bone.

Liz looked at me and I felt the sandwich catch in my throat. I started to cough. I dunno if it was because of hearing about Gil or the fact the dam had gone dry. Liz told Greg she'd radio Dad straightaway, but she didn't have to. As soon as she said over and out, we heard Dad radio Greg. You can do that on the radio—listen in to what other people are saying if they're tuned to your frequency. Dad had heard everything Greg had told the Pommie and so he said he'd go to Cockatoo Creek straightaway.

To get from Simpson's Dam to Cockatoo Creek, you have to go through Timber Creek, so Dad said he'd pick me up at the station on his way. He radioed to tell me to make sure I had plenty of water and to have Jonny's gun ready. His ute tore into the station yard like it was in a race. He blew the horn as I ran down the steps with my water bottle, some bullets, and Jonny's gun. I'd made sure I touched Jonny's photo again too.

As we got closer to Cockatoo Creek Dam, Dad blew the horn at a wedge-tailed eagle that was ripping strips off a calf's carcass at the side of the road. The way it was tearing it to shreds made it look like the calf was made of paper. "That doesn't look good," he said. I knew what he meant. That calf had perished, and as we got farther away from the station and nearer Cockatoo Creek, we saw one or two more carcasses in the bush.

It was another scorcher of a day, but I didn't expect Cockatoo Creek to be as bad as it was. The water had gone and in its place was a big muddy mark on the desert.

With dead cattle dotted all over it—like freckles.

TWENTY-FOUR

It was a bit like we'd been beamed onto the moon, or had just wandered into a bomb blast. It didn't look like our station. The cattle were lying around, like rubbish blown by the wind. They were dead and dying, caught in the mud, desperate for water. They would have walked for miles to get to Cockatoo Creek for a drink. When they got there, they'd have been exhausted, but they would have smelled water and waded into the thick sludge. I guess they thought that if they went a bit further in they'd find something to drink, but the deeper it got, the weaker it made them. They died in the mud, too tired to carry on.

One cow was braying quietly as she lay in the mud. She looked mad. She seemed to be crying for something. Her legs were too tired to even stand up. The flies were probably already eating her. I was glad I had Jonny's gun with me. Dad always had a gun with him so he could deal with a sorry situation like that.

I couldn't stand to look at all the bloated carcasses any more. I hated the filthy stink coming from the mud—I could taste it, it was so strong. It smelled of stagnant water, like when the old wash-house drain blocked, but as well as that, I could smell rotten meat—and death. It made me feel sick. There were so many flies, it was like they'd beaten us to the muster. Every now and then I'd hear one of the cattle cry out. Sometimes I couldn't tell which ones were alive and which were already dead.

As we sat in the ute looking at the carcasses around us, Dad and me didn't speak much. I could tell he was thinking because his eyes were narrow and the tip of his tongue flicked from one side of his top lip to the other. We drove down closer to the dam. I pointed out a couple of carcasses as we went past them and he nodded. He didn't want to see them.

We hadn't thought about the shade from the trees and bushes, which were along the sides of the track on the way to Cockatoo Creek, until it was gone. When we left the trees behind, the sun came through the windscreen like a nasty surprise. It made my seat sticky and my eyes sting. On the bare part of the desert around the dam the ground shimmered, so the dead cattle appeared and disappeared like a magic trick. The drought had stopped being a chat about the weather. It wasn't even about water, or dead cattle. I guess Dad was scared we'd dry up too. His eyes darted around the dust in front of us and picked over the dead and dying cattle. He said, "Jesus," under his breath.

Dad stopped the ute and cut the engine. As he climbed out of the door he reached for his gun, which was on the backseat. "Right, Danny—shoot the worst. The fellas'll help shift the carcasses." We'd have to get rid of the dead cattle. If we didn't, it would mean that when the dam filled up with water again, it'd be poisoned. I asked Dad what we'd do with them. The carcass dump was too far away and too small for all the dead cattle at Cockatoo Creek. He said we'd burn them.

Dad started at one side of the dirty bit of earth that had been the dam and I went to the other. All you could hear was the buzz of flies, broken every now and then by a gunshot or a cow crying out. I shot a couple of cattle and then stopped to wipe my face and reload. I was concentrating on slotting the bullets into the barrel when Dad shouted, "Danny! Daniel! Watch out!" I turned round to see what was wrong, but before I could work it out, Dad had fired his gun. I felt my body jolt—the sound bounced off the desert into me. I looked to the other side, and out of the corner of my eye saw a cow flop over. It looked like it was wearing muddy trousers; a tide-mark of sludge clung to its belly. I looked back at Dad and he was running toward me. His face was hard as he grabbed me roughly by the arm and said, "This is too dangerous."

As we went back to the ute, he told me that the cow had seen me and had probably got spooked by the gunshots. He said it was crazed with dehydration, had scrambled onto its feet in the mud and for some reason was charging toward me. He said he had no choice but to shoot. "Even the live ones are no use," he said, like he'd lost already.

Instead of working on foot, we got in the ute. I drove and when Dad spotted a dying animal, he told me to stop. He'd load his gun and shoot at his target through the window. We'd been driving round shooting at the cattle for a while when we heard Reg's voice on the radio. He wanted to know how things were at Cockatoo Creek. "It's a bloody disaster—we'll be bust by the time the year's out at this rate," Dad said. Then he added, "A bloody disaster," again, but it was like he was talking to himself. I could tell things were real serious.

Reg said they'd almost finished taking the yards down at Simpson's Dam, so he'd send Rick with the tanker to Wild Ridge. Once it was full, he'd bring it over to Cockatoo Creek.

I knew that would take a while—it took hours for the tanker to fill and Wild Ridge was as far away from Cockatoo Creek as anywhere on the station. They wanted to know if there was anything we needed from Timber Creek because they'd be passing the station on their way through. Dad asked Reg to send Elliot over right away, and for him to bring the loader, chains, and some diesel from the station. "I've never seen it like this. Just get over here as fast as you can."

When Elliot arrived at Cockatoo Creek, he didn't bring the loader, he came in his ute with the chains and a few cans of diesel. When he saw the mess he pulled the neck of his shirt up over his nose to try to block the bad smells. He couldn't believe how quickly the dam had dried up. Elliot had checked the dams a few days before and he reckoned Cockatoo Creek had looked a lot better than Gum Tree Dam. Dad shook his head. When the loader growled down the track, I could tell it was Lloyd inside—no one else was as muscly as him. He stopped and climbed out of the cab. His mouth was open, and eventually he managed to find the word he wanted: "Jeez!"

Reg had told Elliot and Lloyd to come over to help Dad and me. He reckoned his mob could bring the tanker over when they brought the fencing, ready to build the yards. Elliot said that when Reg had the bit between his teeth, he worked faster than any fella he knew. Dad nodded and asked how long Elliot reckoned it'd be before they all got to Cockatoo Creek. Elliot looked at Lloyd, who shrugged. "It'll be later on tonight," Elliot guessed. It was a lot quicker to take down the yards than to build them up, but even so, it'd been real hot and the fellas were tired.

Dad turned his attention back to the carcass dump around us. We'd killed all the cattle we could see that needed to be shot. Dad told the fellas to start moving the dead ones over to a clearing a few hundred yards away from the dam. He was angry. Mainly with the weather, but all of us knew not to test him.

Elliot started off by tying the chains around the dead cattle. Then he attached the other end to his ute and dragged the carcasses away. He couldn't do that with the ones that had perished on the edge of the dam because the mud had dried solid and held them down like superglue. For the ones that had died in the dam, Lloyd used the loader. To get them he drove into the sticky dirt, then dropped the bucket into the mess and scooped up the carcass. Sometimes bits fell off into the desert when they were shaken by the loader bumping over an uneven bit of dry ground. Seeing a leg falling out of the sky was like being in a horror movie.

Lloyd carried the carcasses to where we were going to burn them. He dumped them on top of each other and then scooped up the dead ones Elliot had left there, to make them into a tidier pile for burning. From where I was, it looked just like fire wood, until you noticed a head or a hoof.

Dad and me were doing the same job as Elliot with our ute. Dad wouldn't let me tie the chains onto the cows, so I had to drive. It was hot inside the ute. My hands were sweaty and they slipped against the steering wheel. Every now and then Dad would swear when we accidentally ripped the legs off a carcass.

It was starting to get dark when Reg radioed to say he was on his way to Cockatoo Creek to help. He said him and Rick would drive over with the tanker while Jack and the Barron brothers finished off at Simpson's Dam. When Dad took the radio from me, his hand was brown and wet-looking from handling the rotten carcasses. He said, "Get over here as fast as you can, fellas, we need all the help we can get." Ron from Gold River came on the radio then.

Gum Tree and Cockatoo Creek were the two water holes nearest the station, and they were both fed from the same borehole.

Ron said he'd been to Gum Tree and the situation there was just as bad. He told Dad that him and Greg would be over to help as soon as they could. Normally Dad would have said it was OK, that we would manage. But this time he didn't. He just said, "Thanks, Ron."

When Mum and Liz arrived with some food for us, I realized I'd forgotten about eating. It was getting dark, but we'd been so busy scraping carcasses off the desert I hadn't thought about food. It was hard to feel hungry when there was such a bad smell everywhere. The Pommie looked like she did when she saw Dad and me butchering the killer. She'd gone real white and held her hand over her mouth and nose. After a minute or two she went round the other side of the ute where no one could see her. When she came back, wiping her mouth with a hanky, I guess we all knew she'd puked. She pretended to be OK, though. Mum just looked angry, like she was about to pick a fight with someone.

Mum and the Pommie lifted pots of chilli out of the ute. We all stopped what we were doing and sat down, as far away from the pile of stinking dead cows as we could. Mum rubbed Dad's back, and I could tell she was real worried. The Pommie dished the food up and we didn't speak until it was all gone.

Afterward Elliot asked Dad if he wanted him and Lloyd to go over to Gum Tree Dam to start cleaning up there. Dad said he couldn't decide what to do next. He said he thought the best thing would be to start burning the dead ones at Cockatoo Creek. As soon as the fire was lit, someone would have to stay with it until it had gone out. He was real concerned about the weather. It had been so dry, and if there was even the slightest breeze, it would take the fire and make it spread across the Territory. We didn't want a bushfire on our hands too.

While he and the fellas talked about what to do, Mum and the Pommie cleared the food away. We heard the tanker rumbling toward us before its headlights made our eyes water. When it roared into view and stopped, Reg leaned out of the truck window, like it was a nice, cool, sunny day, and shouted down to Dad, "Where d'you want it, Derek?"

Dad had his back to us and we couldn't hear what he said above the engine noise, but he pointed his arms to his right, at an area of flat ground farther over toward where the dam had been. Jack was behind, in the Toyota. He had a trailer on the back, full of fencing and some troughs, so we got up ready to unload them. Jack left the Toyota's headlights on so we could see where we were working. The fence panels felt twice as heavy in the dark.

The Crofts arrived. Even Dick came. He had his overalls on and his hat. I hadn't seen him dressed like that for ages. In the dark he looked like normal, but when his face caught in the headlights he looked old and empty, and if you were near enough you could hear his chest rattle. He walked straight over to Dad and Reg. He put his hand on Dad's shoulder. His voice was raspy because of whatever was inside him. He said, "We've seen worse than this, Derek." Dad shook his hand and said how glad he was to have Dick and his family there.

Dick reckoned the weather was about right for having a fire. He said he'd checked the forecast and thought we'd be as well getting the fire going as soon as we could. Dad explained we would have to go to Gum Tree Dam, to clear out the dead there too. We didn't want both water holes to become poisoned. Dick nodded and said Dad should leave him to see to the fire at Cockatoo Creek and take the fellas to Gum Tree.

Dad shook his head. He said he reckoned it would be better for them all to get some rest and tackle Gum Tree in the morning. Dick looked at Ron and Greg and they nodded at him, like they could read his mind. They said Dick would stay with the fire at Cockatoo Creek Dam while Greg and Ron went to Gum Tree to start cleaning up over there. "You take Danny home and get some rest," Dick said. I guess the sooner we'd dealt with the dead, the sooner we could get the live ones mustered. We needed to get them together into the yards where there would be water troughs.

Dad told me to get in the ute with Mum and the Pommie, who were going back to the station. I told him I wanted to stay with him and the fellas, to help.

But he rubbed his eyes as he squinted through the darkness and said, "There'll still be plenty to do tomorrow."

TWENTY-FIVE

In the morning Mum had to go to work, even though everything was going wrong at the station. Dad had stayed out all night with the fellas. Emily, Bobbie, the Pommie, and me were in the dining room eating our brekkie. The everybody jam didn't taste as sweet as normal.

When the phone rang, we all stopped what we were doing. We knew the only person who'd ring at that time was Aunty Ve. And if it was Aunty Ve, she'd only be calling about one thing—the baby. Bobbie answered it because she was the oldest. Emily, the Pommie, and me got up and went to the kitchen to listen. Bobbie said, "G'day, Timber Creek Station . . . It's on its way already? . . . Right. Yep . . . OK. I'll tell them . . . OK . . . Take care. Bye."

She gave us a quick look and then swapped the phone for the radio, to see if she could catch Mum before she got all the way to Marlu Hill. Bobbie said into the little black receiver, "Come in, Sue, Timber Creek to Sue. You read me? Over." There was nothing coming back except the crackly desert noises, so she tried again. Eventually Mum's voice fizzed and said, "Go ahead, Bobbie. Everything OK? Over."

Bobbie said, "You need to come home. Over." I guess Mum knew that was Bobbie's way of telling her Sissy's baby was coming early, without the rest of the Territory understanding what was going on.

The Pommie said something to Bobbie about getting some food together for Mum to take with her for the journey to Alice. That's when Emily asked what for, so Bobbie explained that Mum would have to go to Alice to be with Sissy because the baby was on its way. Emily looked confused. Bobbie said Sissy needed Mum with her when she went to the hospital to have the baby. She reckoned Mum would only be gone a few days or so. I was mad when I heard that. I couldn't help it—before I knew what I was doing I'd shouted out, "BUT IT'S THE MUSTER—WE NEED HER HERE!" That's when Emily started to blub. Bobbie rolled her eyes at me as she squatted down to give Emily a hug. Bobbie reckoned we both had to act real grown-up because we were going to have a niece or a nephew soon. She said we all had to pull together. It didn't feel like Sissy or her gin baby were pulling together.

Before we'd finished washing our breakfast plates, Mum got home. She burst through the door and ran into the kitchen. She grabbed the phone straight off the wall and rang Aunty Veronica without even speaking to us. She said the same things Bobbie had said to Aunty Ve a few minutes earlier, except Mum finished by saying, "Don't worry, love, I'm on my way."

We watched Mum run into the bathroom to get her toothbrush and a bottle of shampoo. She threw them in a bag. She dropped that by the door and went back into the kitchen. First she radioed Dad. When he answered she just said, "Derek, I've got to go to Alice. They're ready." There was a pause before Dad replied, "You're kidding?" Neither of them said anything for a moment, then at the same time as Dad asked if Sissy was OK, Mum said she was sorry, but she had to go. I guess we all knew Mum couldn't be in two places at once—I just couldn't believe she would leave the station when everything was going wrong. Dad said, "Drive carefully and phone later. Over and out."

Then Mum phoned the clinic at Marlu Hill. She said she wouldn't be going in because she had to go to Alice. She didn't need to explain anything else. Then she wiped the tears off Emily's cheeks with her thumb and said we had to listen to Bobbie and Liz and do what they told us to. We all went outside and watched Mum get in the Ford. She was still in her work clothes. The electric window zoomed down as she reversed. Once she was pointing in the right direction, she shouted out to us, "Look after each other. I'll call you tonight." The engine revved and her arm waved from the open window as she drove away through the dust cloud.

Long before we all got to Cockatoo Creek we knew the fire was still burning because we could see a big pile of brown smoke moving straight up into the sky—floating like a feather. It was already hot. I pointed at the smoke and said, "At least it's a still day." I watched the smoke get bigger and bigger until eventually, as we got nearer to Cockatoo Creek Dam, we could smell it. The Pommie closed her window and told me to do the same, but barbecue and bonfire smells still wafted into the ute. It got so strong, it made my eyes water.

No one had said much on the way over to Cockatoo Creek, but when we pulled into the yards and saw the pile of dead cattle waiting to be burned, it was like someone sucked the air out of the desert. I couldn't breathe. We got out of the ute, and I guess it was a bit like when Jonny died—no one knew what to say.

I'd never seen so many carcasses. They were piled up like horrible firewood—waiting to be burned. I knew Emily would blub. As soon as she did, Bobbie got back into the ute and sat with her on her knee. I guess on a day like that, the yards weren't really a place for a little kid like Emily. Not long afterward, Bobbie took Emily back to the station. I looked at the Pommie and she seemed whiter than normal. Her mouth was open and she looked a bit like when you can't catch your breath. I felt my chest tighten then, so I sucked on my inhaler as I studied the pile of carcasses. It looked like a horror movie—only it was real. The loader appeared then out of the bush, piled high with more dead.

I looked at the fire, and there was Dick, crawling round the edge like a little ant. He had a shovel in his hand. He was using it to manage the fire, to stoke the hot ashes and make sure it didn't get out of control. His hands were black and he had grey marks all over his shirt. He'd taken his overalls off at the top, so the arms were tied round his waist, but he still wore the blue legs. It was hot work standing in the sun poking a fire, and I wondered about his rattly chest.

Reg was putting the finishing touches to the yards. Everyone had the same look on their face. Water was getting warm in the line of troughs inside the fences. The tanker had gone. I went over to where Dad was. I asked him where the tanker was, and he said it would be at Wild Ridge, filling up again. He said they'd have to keep going back there to get more water to take to Gum Tree Dam too. He rubbed his face and said things were so bad on the eastern side of the station that he'd decided there was no way we could continue without a helicopter. He reckoned we could herd the cattle faster from the air than on the ground. They couldn't hide from us up there, so we'd spend less time looking for them and chasing after them. I guess the quicker it was, the less cattle we'd lose. Dad said it would be worth the money. I nodded so he knew I understood and then asked what he wanted us to do to help. He shrugged and said it was hard to know what to do for the best. That probably scared me more than anything. Dad always knew what to do.

Mary arrived then. She'd come to make sure her dad, Dick, was OK. He was holding a dirty hanky over his face when she arrived. Mary handed him a supply of tablets in a little box, which Penny had sent to keep him going. He started coughing and he sounded like his chest was trying to jump out of his throat. Mary looked worried and reckoned Dick had been working too hard. Dad agreed and said Dick should go home with Mary, or he'd have Penny to answer to. Dick looked at the hanky he'd been coughing into and then carefully folded it up. He didn't look too happy about it, but he went with Mary anyway.

Dad took the shovel Dick had been using and went to keep an eye on the fire. I saw another in the back of Elliot's ute, so I ran to get it. I followed him to the fire and asked again what we were going to do. He reckoned the only thing we could do was pin our hopes on the helicopter turning things around. He explained how some of the fellas were with the Crofts out at Gum Tree, clearing the dead out there. The Crofts had brought their tanker in from Gold River to make sure there was water at Gum Tree. I knew that was a real kind thing to do. If we were suffering on the eastern side of the station that meant the Crofts would be having a tough time on the west of theirs. I asked Dad if they were OK over there at Gold River and he shrugged. He reckoned it wasn't good, but they hadn't got the same problems as us—none of their water holes or dams had gone dry—yet.

The Pommie had come over with us to the fire. She'd tied a scarf round her face. She wouldn't look at the piles of carcasses around us. She said in a muffled voice how she'd really like to do something to help. Dad reckoned the best thing she could do would be to boil a kettle and get some tucker organized. He said, "An army marches on its stomach." I guess we were kind of at war.

Dad and me kept walking round and round that bonfire, making sure the dead were burned and we didn't start a bushfire. Every now and then, if I felt a slight breeze, I'd feel sick. I was scared we'd have no cattle left, but I couldn't even let myself think about what would happen if a bushfire started. Everything was so dry, I knew it would spread faster than the drought.

Lloyd kept appearing from the bush in the loader with more and more carcasses. With each load, I got more and more worried. I wondered if all our cattle out there had died.

Reg came over to tell us the Pommie reckoned smoko was ready. Dad told me to go and get myself some tucker. I told him he looked like he needed it more than me. I reckoned he hadn't slept all night. He smiled and told me he was OK. Someone had to stay with the fire at all times. Reg nodded, so I stuck my shovel in the ground and went to get some food.

It felt strange sitting there eating the food without everyone else. Dad and Reg had decided the best thing to do was to split the team up, so they could clear out both Gum Tree and Cockatoo Creek Dams at the same time. It was important we got rid of the dead and got water for the cattle that were left as quickly as possible. Reg said it was a race against time. So, as soon as most of the work was done at Cockatoo Creek, Dad had sent the fellas over to Gum Tree to get things sorted out over there. That meant there was only Reg, Dad, and Lloyd left at Cockatoo Creek, putting the finishing touches to the yards and burning the carcasses.

As we ate the sandwiches the Pommie had made, no one really said much. Lloyd reckoned there weren't too many more carcasses in the bush around Cockatoo Creek. I realized there wouldn't be many live ones, either—that made it hard to swallow my food. I guess we all knew there wouldn't be much to muster. Then Elliot's voice came through on the radio. Reg answered it. Elliot reckoned they needed Dad to go over to Gum Tree. They needed to know what he wanted them to do. Elliot said there were as many, if not more, dead over there. Reg swore when he heard that. Elliot said the Crofts reckoned that instead of burning the carcasses, it might be quicker to dig a pit in the desert, as far away from the dam as possible, and bury them. Reg took a deep breath and told Elliot he and Dad would be over at Gum Tree right away.

I felt like my eyes were going to burst out of my head. I looked up and saw the Pommie staring at me and I could tell she understood how serious things were. She looked as scared as I felt. I just hoped no one could see it on my face. Lloyd, Reg, and me went over to the fire to talk to Dad. When Dad heard what Reg had to say, his head dropped and he looked at the ground for a moment. I wondered if he'd decided there was no point. But then he said, "Right, well we'd better get over there." I saw his face had hardened. His jaw kind of jutted forward, like when he was angry. I guess he hadn't given up. He looked at me and said he was counting on me to look after the fire—"Do not take your eyes off it, you hear?" he said. I nodded. He told Lloyd to finish off moving the carcasses as quickly as he could because it sounded like they'd need the loader at Gum Tree Dam. Then he and Reg got in a bull catcher and sped off into the desert.

I was glad Dad had let me be in charge of the fire. It was a real important job. There was no way I was going to screw it up. I walked round and round, making sure not a single spark or a bit of hot ash got away. I made sure every hoof and horn, each tail, ear and eyeball, everything, was burned. I wanted to make sure there wasn't even the slightest trace of the drought left.

When Lloyd dumped the last load of the carcasses onto the fire, he jumped down from the loader and told me he was going to Gum Tree. I nodded. He looked at me and asked if I'd be OK with the fire on my own. I nodded again. I knew what I was doing. I told him it was hot, but that was all. He punched me gently on the shoulder and said I was a good kid.

I heard the noise of the loader grow quieter and quieter as he drove away, until I couldn't hear anything any more, except for the cracks and fizzes from the carcasses on the fire in front of me. As I looked at the pile of smoking legs, stinking bodies and breathed in the horrible, sweet smell of burning fur, I thought about Mum and wondered where she was now.

TWENTY-SIX

I looked up at the sky and the sun caught on my face and made my eyes sting even more than the smoke did. I hoped Jonny was paying attention and that he'd had a word with someone up there about getting us some rains—just because he was in heaven, it didn't mean he couldn't help.

Liz came over and picked up the second shovel. I kind of smiled at her. For a vegetarian, I reckoned she was pretty handy. The two of us didn't say much. We just kept an eye on the fire and tried not to think about what was on it. It was nearly dark when Bobbie's ute arrived back at the Dam. She'd brought some dinner for us. Emily was with her. She wouldn't get out of the ute, though. I guess after what she'd seen that morning she was too scared. Bobbie said Mum had called to let us know she'd got to Alice OK. The Pommie asked how Sissy was, and Bobbie told her there wasn't really much happening—yet.

I asked if Mum was coming home. I mean, if Sissy wasn't having the baby, she should just come home. Bobbie said she hadn't told Mum about how bad things were on the station— she said she didn't think there was much point in worrying her.

I didn't get it—if Mum knew, she'd definitely come home. I said that to Bobbie. She said, "Exactly—Sissy needs her there." Like that explained everything. She dropped the tucker for us and sped off to Gum Tree to take Dad and the fellas theirs, and tell him the news about Sissy. I reckoned Dad'd be real mad at her for not just getting on with it and having the baby so Mum could come back and help at the station.

Liz and me took it in turns to eat the food, so there was always one of us keeping an eye on the fire. It was more or less dark when I noticed in the light from the fire how dirty Liz had got. I don't think I'd ever seen her like that. She had black marks all over her face and clothes. Her hair was kind of wild and she looked tired. I guess we both smelled pretty bad too.

We were busy keeping an eye on the fire when through the darkness I heard a noise. Something moved. I realized my gun was in one of the utes at Gum Tree. I cursed myself as I wondered if I could tackle a crazed, dehydrated bull with just the spade I had in my hand.

Then I saw him.

It wasn't a bull. It was Gil Smith. "You need a hand?" he asked, like everything was fine. Like he hadn't been rooting with Sissy, or got her pregnant, or anything. I couldn't believe it. I was so shocked, I couldn't move. Because of him, Mum was stuck in Alice with Sissy when we were having the worst muster ever.

Everything exploded somewhere inside me.

I ran at him, and before he knew what was going on, I'd punched him real hard in the face. It felt good. I was about to go in for another, but Gil had got his balance and was ready for me. He was bigger than me, so he blocked me and grabbed my body and kind of pushed me onto the ground. I grabbed at his shirt and it ripped. Gil was on top of me then. Even in the dark I could see blood coming from his nose. We wrestled like that on the ground for what felt like ages. The Pommie was shouting at us to stop. I saw her try to grab Gil to pull him off me. He swung his arm backward to push her away and smacked her in the face. She staggered and fell onto the ground. I was mad as hell then. I kicked him a few times and managed to get a couple of good punches in—one to his eye and another to his side. He whacked my cheek twice and it felt like my whole face was going to burst.

Gil had my arm up behind my back and was pushing my face into the dirt. I was out of breath and my chest hurt as I tasted the dirt, all dry and gritty. I was wriggling around like that underneath him when all of a sudden there were lights and a load of people.

The weight on top of me lifted.

Dad and Elliot had come back from Gum Tree. Elliot pulled Gil off me, and Dad pulled me up off the ground. I was breathing real hard—but my chest couldn't suck in enough air. It felt like I was having an asthma attack.

As I reached for my inhaler I saw Dad had hold of Gil's neck in one hand and his other arm was high in the air, ready to punch him in the face. Elliot moved in then and started pulling Dad back away from Gil. I wanted Elliot to let Dad go, so he could beat the crap out of Gil, but my chest was so tight, I couldn't breathe, let alone speak.

The Pommie got between them then—so her back was to Gil and she was facing Dad, pleading with him to stop. She had her arms out as she tried to push Dad away. But Dad was real strong. Elliot's face was all twisted as he wrestled with Dad. He grabbed Dad's arm and somehow forced him backward. The Pommie was saying all this stuff about how Gil had only come to help—"He just wanted to help!" she said over and over again until eventually Dad seemed to hear what she was saying. He stopped what he was doing and let go of Gil.

Dad was breathing real hard and I could tell by the look on Gil's face he didn't know whether to run or stand his ground. The Pommie was babbling on and on, saying, "It was Danny—he started it. Gil just came to help. That's all." I was mad at the Pommie for dobbing me in. I shouted out, "He's a mongrel!" Dad looked at Gil for what felt like ages. Then, when he'd caught his breath a bit, he asked him if what the Pommie was saying was right. Gil didn't say anything. He just nodded his head. Dad slowly picked his hat up off the ground and knocked the dust off it. The headlights on the ute were still on and in the beam he noticed the blood coming from Liz's lip and asked if she was OK. She said it was an accident.

That's when Dad said, "Get in the ute, Danny. Now." He looked at Gil, then back at me and said Elliot was going to drive me and the Pommie back to the station. I was mad as hell then. I shouted all sorts of stuff about how Gil had been rooting with Sissy and that it wasn't fair. I wanted to stay at stock camp with him and the fellas.

Dad came over and dragged me by my shoulder out of the headlights away from the fire. When he let go of me, he told me to listen. He said he hadn't time to worry about me fighting with Gil on top of everything else. He said for once I had to do as I was told. He'd be relying on me the next day when the helicopter came. "Do you want to miss that?" he asked, eyeballing me. I shook my head. He kicked the ground and put one hand on his hip as he threw his head back and looked at the sky—like he was looking for something else to say. Then he turned round and saw Gil and said, "You still here? Go on—go. We don't need your help." But Elliot said to

Dad that if Gil hadn't raised the alarm about Cockatoo Creek, God knows what would have happened. Gil looked at Dad and said that he only wanted to help. I swallowed the lump in my throat. After a second or two, Dad looked back at me and said in a quieter voice, "You've done a good job here with the fire. But it's late. You need to go back to the station and get some rest." I knew not to argue.

As I walked to the ute, I looked over at Gil. He looked round too and we stared at each other. I heard Dad say to him, "OK well, as you're here, you might as well make yourself useful," and he handed him one of the spades. I still didn't like him. He was still a mongrel.

When I got in the ute, the Pommie said she was sorry. I knew she meant for dobbing me in. I didn't reply. She said she only told Dad the truth. "Gil just wanted to help." When I still didn't answer she gave up and asked Elliot how things were at Gum Tree. "Not good," he said. Liz asked how many he thought were dead. Elliot shrugged. I don't think anyone wanted to count them.

I can't remember going to sleep that night, I just remember waking up about a million times in the night, wondering if it was time to get up and go back to help the fellas. When I did get up, the Pommie was already in the kitchen. My face was sore from where Gil had hit me and so she got a tea towel with some ice inside it for me to put on my cheek. It felt real cold—or maybe it was my face that was hot. I couldn't tell. I noticed her top lip was lopsided. It was fatter at the right where Gil had hit her, and there was a little cut. I felt bad about that. She asked me if I was ever going to speak to her again. I shrugged and said, "Suppose so." She smiled then and handed me some toast.

When we got to Cockatoo Creek it was strange. The carcasses had burned down to nothing and the smoke had gone. It was a bit like everything we'd seen and smelled the day before had been a bad dream. If it wasn't for the black mark on the desert where the fire had been, I might have believed I'd just woken up after a nightmare. When we saw the fellas, though, I knew everything we'd seen the day before had been real. They looked feral. I guess none of them had slept. They smelled worse than some of the carcasses had and they were real dirty. I looked around, but Gil wasn't there. I didn't like to ask Dad about it in front of the fellas, but I reckoned he'd either sent Gil packing, or else Gil had stayed with Jack in the Blackfellas' camp. Seeing us arrive with some tucker cheered everyone up. I guess they were perishing because they made short work of the brekkie the Pommie had made for them.

And then we heard something buzzing in the sky.

We all looked up at the little silvery speck catching the sun against the blue sky. We watched it become a dot and eventually turn into a helicopter. Reg shouted, "The cavalry's here!" I'd heard about people mustering with a helicopter before. It was meant to be real quick, but it cost a lot of money. I couldn't believe Dad had hired one. I looked around and the fellas were all nodding at the sky, and I felt weird—scared, but like maybe, if we all worked real hard, we might be OK.

This guy called Jerry was the pilot. His clothes were real clean and his skin looked like the Pommie's. He wore these big sunnies and a pair of little gloves. He was a bit like someone on TV, all shiny, white teeth, and creases in his trousers. He shook hands with Dad, and the two of them and Reg had a chat about the muster. It looked a bit like someone had traveled back in time, or something. Dad and Reg looked like a couple of cavemen next to Jerry. Then we watched him climb back into the little machine and strap himself in. As the blades started turning, they threw dirt up from the desert, as well as a wind. The helicopter hovered upward off the ground, like it wasn't sure if it wanted to. It hung in the sky, unsteady, as though it was on a thin string. It looked like Jerry was waiting to get his balance, and then when he was happy, the helicopter began to move, dragging its tail like a dragonfly. When we looked up we could see Jerry in the glass bowl of the cockpit— he looked a bit like a goldfish when he gave us a wave.

I'd never seen a helicopter muster before. I didn't know how it worked. Dad asked if I wanted to watch, or if I wanted to go with him in his ute. I dunno. I felt strange about everything the night before with Gil, so I said I reckoned I'd watch the first one—just to get an idea of how it was done. He thought that was a good plan.

It was hard to keep an eye on the helicopter, though. There was a big heat haze and its blades flew round so fast it threw loads of dust into the air. Every now and then the sun caught against the helicopter's white metal and glass, so we could catch a glimpse of it rising out of the bush, dancing like a mosquito in a flash of light. It seemed to throw a tornado down on the ground, which sucked the cattle and dust out of the desert. Dad and the fellas were on the ground in their utes and bull catchers to help guide the animals out of the desert and into the yards. We couldn't see them, but we could hear them talking to each other on the radios.

I'd never seen anything like it. It worked like a magic trick. A bit like when you get a magnet and it picks up all those little metal-filing things. One minute there was just the hum of the helicopter and a dirty mark on the sky where it was dancing around, in and out of the bush. The next thing we knew, this mob of cattle started to snake out of the desert toward the yards. It made the desert and drought seem smaller somehow. Considering how dehydrated those cattle were, they moved real quick. I guess it was pretty terrifying for them. I wondered what the cattle thought the helicopter was, or if they just felt the tornado above them and heard the buzzing engine, like an annoying cloud.

Seeing the cattle moving along together made the knot in my belly loosen a bit and I felt like I could breathe more easily. After burning all the carcasses, I'd started to think there wouldn't be any live ones left. But there they were. Dawson cattle. They weren't the best-looking mob I'd ever seen—they looked like they'd had a fight with someone—all bruised and tired. I hoped they'd be OK. I looked at the Pommie and smiled. "You can do it!" she shouted. I guess that was how we all felt. We knew we had a long way to go, but it was the first sign that some of our cattle might survive—which meant we might too.

As Rick scrambled forward to close the gate after the cattle went into the yard, I saw him give a thumbs-up to Dad. Dad's fist came out of the window of the ute, and he held it high in the air like athletes do when they win a race. I knew we were getting somewhere. His hand then saluted the sky, to say thanks to Jerry too. Then they all circled the yards and headed off south, following the buzzing engine above them, to find the rest of the survivors.

The next mob looked about the same as the first—thin and tired. The fellas shut the cattle in the yards. We went over to see them. Reg shook Dad's hand. They were talking faster than before, like they were excited. They were talking about what to do next. They wanted to let the cattle at Cockatoo

Creek calm down, but the longer they were held in the yards, the more water they'd need to truck over from Wild Ridge. Reg looked at his watch and reckoned we could leave them there to calm down, while we all went to Gum Tree to muster the cattle there. That way Dad would only have to pay for the helicopter for half a day. Afterward we'd be able to come back and draft the ones at Cockatoo Creek, in time for when Bob, the road-train driver, arrived. Dad reckoned it was a good plan. He said the fellas were all bushed after working so hard, but if they could crack on and get things done they'd be able to have an early night. Reg nodded and went to tell his fellas what the plan was.

Bobbie and Emily showed up then. I guess Bobbie must have known the dead ones would have gone so Emily wouldn't be scared any more. Seeing the cattle in the yards, and watching Emily running over to have a look at them, made me feel better about things. Bobbie went over to Dad and I heard her say Mum had called, but there wasn't any news. Dad nodded and hauled Emily onto his shoulders. The three of us walked round the yards to look at our cattle. They weren't the best, but somehow that didn't matter. We'd saved them. Dad said it wouldn't take long to draft them because there wouldn't be many worth trucking. He reckoned it was better to keep them than risk trucking the weaker ones. That way, if they died, they did it in the desert where no one would see them. The last thing we needed was for Timber Creek to get a bad name. I guess everyone in the Territory would have heard about the nine that died on Bob's road train—bad news always seemed to spread like a bushfire. Dad said we'd need to bring water to Cockatoo Creek for as long as Wild Ridge could supply it. He reckoned it was the only way to try and make sure the cattle there survived.

As soon as we'd had a look at the cattle and made sure the pump was working so they'd have enough water, we all followed the helicopter to Gum Tree. When we got there, the yards were set up ready to welcome the cattle. When we looked past the metal grid drawn out in the dirt like noughts and crosses, we could see where Jerry was from the dusty mark in the sky. Me and the Pommie went with Dad in his ute. We fell in line behind Rick and all convoyed out into the desert.

———————

Normally when you muster on the ground, it's all about finding the cattle and sticking with them, so they go where you want them to go. This time it wasn't like that. Jerry had already found the cattle and herded them together, all we had to do was follow the helicopter and then flank the cattle, to stop any stragglers getting away. I couldn't believe how easy it was. It was much faster than normal and I guess that made it better for the cattle. I dunno how much that helicopter cost, but I reckoned it was worth every penny. As we watched the helicopter suck the cattle out of the desert, I punched the roof of the ute and shouted, "Wooohooo!"

Jerry made one last sweep of the desert to get a few more cattle for us to draft and once they were safely inside the yards, he landed the helicopter and came over to see Dad. Dad shook his hand and said he was a lifesaver. Jerry said, "Any time." Then he climbed back inside the helicopter and started the blades. We all watched Jerry leave in a cloud of dust, like a magic trick.

It wasn't like the drought had gone away, or everything was OK again. You only had to look at the cattle to know that. But we all felt better looking at the live ones. The fellas were chatting and laughing a bit again while we ate our tucker. We ate lunch at Gum Tree Dam so the fellas could check the water pumps were working properly before we went back to Cockatoo Creek to start drafting. Dad reckoned they'd have the cattle at Cockatoo Creek drafted in no time. There weren't many worth trucking, so it wouldn't take too long.

Ron and Greg came out of the bush driving the loaders they'd been using to bury the dead cattle. They looked real tired. When they jumped down from the cabs, Dad shook their hands and said, "I owe you fellas—big time." Greg smiled and said, "Thank God Gil Smith was on a walkabout, eh?" I saw one of Dad's eyebrows rise a little when he said that. My bruised cheek throbbed. Dad said he was serious—any time the Crofts needed a hand with anything, all they had to do was ask. Greg said, "No worries." He reckoned a couple of cold ones, once the muster was over, would cover it. Ron reckoned Greg would do anything for a couple of beers. Dad looked sad then and said, "Seriously—thanks. We couldn't have done it without you."

As we watched Ron and Greg head off back to Gold River, Dad realized there was no one at Timber Creek station. He reckoned he needed someone there just in case Mum phoned with more news about Sissy. I dunno what he was worried about—she had Mum and Aunty Ve there with her. The Pommie said she needed to go back to take the dirty pots and pans from lunch. Dad said, "Thanks, Liz," and then asked Bobbie to stay at Cockatoo Creek and help write the cattle numbers down while the fellas did the drafting. She agreed and Emily said she'd help too.

Dad was right, it didn't take long to draft the cattle at Cockatoo Creek. Afterward Dad sighed and said, "Well, they're a sorry bunch, but at least they're alive, I guess." Reg said that if we could truck a similar number at Gum Tree as what we'd got at Cockatoo Creek, then the station might break even. Elliot thought about that and said, "And we've still got to muster at Timber Creek too."

Dad looked at the sky and said, "Breaking even isn't exactly what I'd had in mind. But I guess as long as we don't go under, eh?"

Once the yards were down, Reg and his mob were going to go back to Gum Tree to set up camp there, ready to draft the cattle first thing in the morning. Dad said we'd have the best chance over there if we let the cattle have the night in the yards with the water. I felt taller than the Barron brothers when Reg said that if I wanted, I could go and stay at stock camp with them. He reckoned he could do with another set of eyes to keep watch on the cattle because the fellas were all bushed. I looked at Dad to make sure he reckoned it'd be OK too, and he smiled. I was so stoked.

Dad and me went back to the station so he could get a shower and I could get my things for stock camp. I'd got my swag ready for sleeping in. A swag's like an outdoor sleeping bag we use so you don't need a tent. My water bottle was full, I'd put Jonny's cattle book in my bag, and I'd been to see Buzz to explain I wouldn't be there to feed him in the morning. I was worried about him, but the Pommie said she'd look after him.

Eventually, Dad said he was ready to go—and as soon as the words were out of his mouth, the phone rang. We all knew it'd be Mum. Bloody Sissy! I was scared she was going to tell him something that meant we'd have to stay at the station. I reckoned I was never going to get to stay at stock camp with Dad and the fellas. I looked at the photo of Jonny on the piano. I wanted to touch it. But then Dad hung up the phone, and I guess he could see I was waiting to hear what was going on because he said, "Still no news." Then Dad grabbed his hat and said, "Ready?" I nodded, and so we went out into the yard, jumped into the ute and headed to Gum Tree.

When we got there I could tell the fellas hadn't been there too long. They hadn't even got the fire going. They'd got their utes and bull catchers parked round in a sort of circle, with the truck with all their supplies in the middle. They were just dragging boxes out of the truck to make some tucker when we pulled up. We jumped out and got our stuff from the back. I watched Dad dump his rolled-up swag on the ground near the others, so I did the same. Although it was getting dark, there was still enough light for the fellas to see what they were doing to build the fire.

Dad sent me to find some firewood, so I headed toward the thicker bush and started picking up any pieces I could find. When I got back with the first pile, Rick had already arranged some rocks on the ground to mark the place for the fire, and when he saw me with the pieces of wood stacked up in my arms, he said, "A few more loads like that should do it." When I got back with the third load, there was smoke billowing from the ground.

Reg was busy cutting up some meat and throwing it into this real black, metal pot, while Lloyd and Elliot peeled some potatoes. It looked weird watching them do that—I don't think I'd ever seen a fella doing kitchen work before. They chucked it all in together, and once the fire was going they put the pot on top of the flames and waited for it to cook. It was darker then, and so everyone came and sat round the fire to have a cuppa and a smoke while we waited for the tucker. In the red glow of the fire the fellas looked real feral. It looked like we were all in hell or something.

I sat down next to Elliot. The fire felt real warm on my bare arms as I poked at it with a stick. It was a real moon-lit night too. The nighttime desert noises were all around us, as well as the sound of the cattle braying in the yards. Even though they were a sorry-looking bunch, they were still pretty noisy.

Reg leaned forward to have a look inside the pot on the fire to see how his stew was coming along. I breathed in the stock-camp smells, and could almost taste the desert. I wanted to hold that breath in my chest forever so I'd always remember what it was like out there. I wanted to make sure that when I was at boarding school and the muster happened the year after, I could close my eyes and kind of imagine I was there with Dad and the fellas, even if I was two hundred miles away in Alice. Kind of like I did with Jonny's picture.

When Dad came back from checking the water pump he took a flask out of his bag and poured us both a cuppa. I didn't really like tea normally, but there, with the fellas at stock camp, I guess I felt differently about that. It was hot and sweet, and the plastic cup felt good in my hands. I watched how Dad held his, without using the handle, and copied him.

After a while, Reg took out this real dirty piece of cloth and carefully lifted the pot off the fire with it. Rick passed over a pile of dented metal plates as Reg said, "Grub's up," to no one in particular. He spooned the tucker out onto the plates and passed me the first one. It tasted good. Reg reck-oned we needed to get it down us while it was hot, to keep the cold off in the night. Even though it was real hot in the day, out there in the desert it got pretty nippy during the night. I knew that from when I ran away after Buzz went missing and how cold I'd felt when Mick had found me.

While we ate the steaming-hot tucker, Reg and Rick talked about a muster they'd done at a station as far south in the Territory as you could go, and how even down there they'd had problems with water. Dad listened to what they said, finished his mouthful of the stew, and said he reckoned it was a blip and that we'd weather the storm. Then he said he didn't want to talk about the weather any more. He reckoned he'd had enough of it. He looked at his watch soon after that and said it was time to turn in and everyone started rolling out their swags. I lay on my side and tried to sleep. The stars were so bright, though, and I couldn't stop thinking about Jonny and if he was up there somewhere, watching to see how I got on. I wanted to be the best stockman Timber Creek had ever had.

I dunno what time it was, but after what felt like hours and hours I decided to get up and have a walk round the yards—just to make sure everything was as it should be. I could hear Reg snoring under his swag and the other fellas all seemed to be sleeping too. I looked at Dad's swag, but he'd pulled it over his head, so I couldn't see if he was awake or not. It was strange being out there with them. Even though I wasn't on my own, I kind of felt more alone than ever before.

As I walked round the yards, with the moon shining down, it felt like my eyes could see as well as they could during the day. I was keeping an eye out for dingoes. I had a couple of rocks in my pockets just in case. If they got into the yards and started terrorising the calves I would throw the rocks at them—I was a pretty good shot. I'd been practising. That's when I caught a glimpse of something white in the yard.

TWENTY-SEVEN

At first I thought it was one of the wild horses and I was about to run back to the camp to get Jonny's gun. But as the cattle moved around, there between all the other brown cows I saw Casper, the white Brahman bull.

He'd been Jonny's poddy, named after the friendly ghost because he was white and so tame. He'd grown into a strong-looking bull—muscly and wide. As the others moved around and carried on mooing, pissing, and rearing up around him, Casper stayed still, his long ears floppy and friendly at the sides of his head. His eyes seemed almost black against his white hide as they watched me. He looked like an angel, or something. I turned and saw Dad and the other fellas in their swags on the ground. I didn't want to frighten Casper away, so I didn't shout to Dad to come and see who I'd found. I'd forgotten all about Casper. I couldn't remember seeing him for a couple of years, but there was no mistaking him—even in the dark. I didn't reckon we'd have another plain-white Brahman bull like him. But, there was something else too. The way he looked at me made me certain it was him. It was like we knew each other. None of the others looked at me like that. They weren't interested because they didn't know me.

Casper had been turned loose like all the poddies were once they were big enough. Some of them stayed around the house forever, too tame to make friends with the other cattle in the desert. But then there were others like Casper, who grew as wild as the rest, until we didn't recognise them any more. I guess because he was white, Casper stood out. I dunno why no one had spotted him when we'd mustered the cattle. Maybe Reg, or one of the other fellas, had seen him, but because there was only Dad and me who knew who Casper was, they'd just think he was another bull.

After a minute or two, Casper looked away and moved into the herd. I waited for a while and then walked back to my swag. Dad was awake. He asked where I'd been, so I said I'd been checking the yards. Dad nodded, like he approved. So I told him I'd seen Casper. He smiled and said we'd have a big decision to make in the morning, then.

———

I was awake before the sun came up. My nose was cold, but everything else was real warm inside the swag. I heard Rick coughing and so I sat up to see what was going on. Dad was already up, lighting the fire. No one else was awake, but I reckoned I should get up and help Dad.

We cooked sausages for brekkie, and man, they smelled good. All burnt and smoky. I had a cup of coffee afterward too—Dad reckoned it'd set me up for the day. As soon as the smell of sausages wafted over to the other swags, the rest of the fellas started to wake up. They were all scratching themselves and stretching, like the dogs did if they'd slept under the house.

Then the sun started to rise and the radio in Dad's ute fizzed. It sounded real loud out there in the desert. Liz's voice came through. She was radioing to tell Dad that Mum had called. We all heard her say Sissy's waters had broken. Reg looked at the ground and I could tell he was pretending he hadn't heard. Dad just said, "Right. Right. Righto, then. Well. Well, you'd better keep me posted then. Over." When I reckoned the fellas weren't listening any more I asked Dad what Liz meant about the water breaking and he said it meant they'd be taking Sissy back to the hospital and that this time she would be having the baby—for sure. Finally, Sissy was getting a move on with it, I thought. Dad seemed real fidgety. He said, "Not long now." I asked how long, but he didn't know. He said it was a waiting game.

Then we heard a rumbling in the desert and I thought the road train had come early but I was wrong. It was the Barron brothers. They'd been over at Wild Ridge all night, filling the water tanker. It rolled into the yards like a giant piece of tin foil.

Once we started drafting, everyone could see Casper. Reg laughed at him, he reckoned he was like a gin in a snowstorm. We all laughed at that, even Jack. I felt funny—it made me think of Sissy and the baby.

I wondered what would happen when Casper came into the yard. I didn't have to wait long. Rick opened the gate and Casper walked through. He looked real tall and proud compared with the handful of smaller Hereford cows that came through with him. They bucked, ran and jolted around, frightened of what we would do to them. Reg started off with them, choosing just one to go through to be trucked and releasing the rest into another yard to be sent back to the desert. When faced with Casper, Dad looked at me and

I could see he was unsure what to do. He forced a smile and beckoned me over. "Well? What should we do?" he asked. I shrugged. Dad put his hand on my shoulder and said that running a station was all about making decisions. I nodded so he knew I was listening. He then told me to think real hard. I looked at the ground. Thoughts of Jonny raced through my head. I wondered what he'd do. Then I thought of Buzz and I knew straightaway what the right thing to do was. I looked at Dad and said we should keep Casper.

Reg had come over to see what we wanted to do. Dad looked at me and said to Reg, "Danny reckons we should keep him." Reg turned the corners of his mouth down and nodded. Dad then asked me why. I dunno what was more important—the fact Casper had been Jonny's, or that he was such a good-looking bull, but it was the second reason I gave them. When they heard that, they both nodded. Dad patted my back and said, "Good decision."

Reg agreed, he said, "Good on you, Danny." He reckoned we needed a good, strong breeding bull.

Once the cattle were all drafted and the ones for trucking were waiting patiently in the holding yard, the road train rumbled into the yards. That's when Dad said he'd take me back to the house because he knew I wanted to see Buzz. I reckon the real reason was that he wanted to be there for when Mum called about Sissy.

When we got back to the house, Liz was cooking dinner. She said no one had called—even before Dad could ask. He looked real worried then, and went to the phone. I watched him dial the number for Aunty Ve's, pinned on the wall next to the one for the clinic where Mum worked.

He waited and waited for what felt like ages, before he slammed the phone down again and said, "No answer." He said he was going for a shower. When he came out, he still had the towel round him and he went back into the kitchen to use the phone again.

I guess there was still no answer because he slammed it down again and went to get dressed. When he was dressed he got the phone book out and started looking for the number for the hospital in Alice. He dialled the number there and asked to speak to someone who knew what was going on with Sissy Dawson. Whoever answered can't have known who Sissy was because that's when Dad said, "She's my daughter. She's having a baby." I guess they must have put him through to someone who did know who Sissy was because that's when I heard Dad say: "I see. Right. But she's going to be OK?"

When he finished on the phone he looked at us all staring at him and said, "No news yet." I didn't like it.

We were halfway through our food when the phone rang. Dad sprung up from his seat and almost ran into the kitchen. I could hear him breathing heavier than usual. "G'day, love, what's happening?" he asked, so we knew it must be Mum. Dad nodded a bit and said, "Right," then nodded again, more slowly like he was trying to understand something.

"Is she going to be OK?"

He looked at us all staring at him—"It's taking longer than expected," was all he said. I dunno why, but there was something about the way he looked that reminded me of how he'd been after Jonny died, and I felt sick. Real sick.

We all walked back to the table, but I couldn't finish my dinner. Everyone pushed the food round their plates in silence.

Afterward, Liz cleared the table and the rest of us watched TV. Dad was real jumpy. He kept flicking the channel over and he looked at his watch about a million times. He was real concerned about being able to hear the phone above the TV—even though it had never been a problem before. He didn't sit down all night—not really. He'd sit down and then jump up again. He'd pace around in the kitchen, and every now and then he'd pick the phone up, just to check it was still working, then put it down again real quick.

We watched all kinds of programs on the TV that we weren't usually allowed to. Then, at nearly midnight, Dad said we all had to go to bed. Emily was already asleep with her head on his knee. He picked her up and told me to switch the TV off. His face looked white and his eyes were real dark.

As I lay in bed I could hear voices in the dining room. It was Liz and Dad. Liz asked Dad if he was all right. I guess he must have nodded, or something because then Liz said, "I'm sure she'll be OK." Dad didn't answer for a minute. When he did he said, "If she comes through this, I won't give a damn who the father is. I've been a fool, Liz." Then there was a big silence, for ages, before Liz said Dad had done what he thought was the right thing at the time. He gave a big sigh then and said, "I don't know how much more we can take."

Hearing Dad say that made me real scared. I rolled over and looked at the empty bed next to mine and tried to remember what it looked like when Jonny was asleep in it.

TWENTY-EIGHT

When I woke up, I was full of panic. I wanted to know what was going on with Sissy and the baby. I was in such a rush to get ready, I was still doing my flies up as I burst through my bedroom door into the dining room. Seeing Dad there made me jump. I felt sick. But then he smiled and said, "Morning, Uncle Danny."

Sissy had had a baby boy in the night. Dad said he was a healthy little fella, just like all us Dawsons. Mum and Sissy had to stay in Alice for a couple of days because Sissy had to stay in the hospital—but not because she was crook. He said it was just what happened after having a baby. I didn't know what he meant. If the baby was out of her belly, I reckoned they should just come home. When the pigs or the cattle had babies, they just went back to normal after an hour or two. Dad reckoned it was a bit different for humans.

He said Mum wouldn't come home until Sissy and the baby were ready. I said Aunty Veronica could bring Sissy out to Timber Creek once she'd finished in the hospital, that way Mum could come straight home. Dad shook his head and said that wasn't going to happen. I didn't say anything else. I just ate my breakfast.

"Don't you want to know what your nephew's called?" Dad asked. I didn't—not really. I didn't get it. I thought we were meant to hate the baby—because of Sissy rooting with Gil. I was kind of sick of it all, especially with it happening during the worst muster ever. Anyway, I didn't answer, I just shrugged, like I didn't give a damn. That annoyed Dad just about as much as the weather forecast. He slapped his hand down on the table, which made my plate jump. He said, "Stop being a selfish little brat, Daniel. There's other people in the world apart from you. Sissy needs Mum a lot more than we do. You're an uncle now—so grow up!" He stared right at me and I felt my heart beating against my chest.

I'd finished eating, but I didn't ask to get down from the table. I had a lump in my throat, which meant that if I tried to say anything I might blub. After a few minutes with us both just sitting there, Dad got up. As he reached for his hat he told me to brush my teeth. He opened the door and added, "And your nephew's called Alexander James—after your grand-dads. Now get a move on." I waited to hear the door slam shut before I got up and touched the picture of Jonny.

When I came out of the bathroom, I could hear Dad in the kitchen on the radio to Reg. Reg said everything was fine at Gum Tree. They'd finished there and were on the way to Timber Creek for the last part of the muster. Just before Dad could say over and out, Reg remembered to ask about the baby. "So, was it a girl or a boy—Granddad?" That made Dad laugh a bit, but not like it was funny—if you know what I mean? He said, "As of four thirty this morning, I have a grandson. Healthy little fella—Alexander James—and Sissy's doing OK too. Over." Reg laughed and said congratulations. "The Dawson dynasty continues."

Just after Dad put the radio back on top of the fridge, it fizzed and old Dick Croft's voice came through. He must have heard Dad talking to Reg because he said, "Come in, Timber Creek. Congratulations—great news about little Alexander James. Over." Dad lifted the receiver down again and said: "G'day, Dick, and thanks. Over." He didn't need to explain to Dick why Sissy had called the baby Alexander James. I could almost hear Dick's grin when he said, "Old Alex'll be strutting around up there in heaven with a smile from here to Alice Springs." Dick said it was a good, strong name and that he and his boys looked forward to wetting the baby's head. I couldn't work out why any of them would be bothered about washing Alex. I was thinking about that when I heard Dad say, "Sue reckons Alex looks just like his Uncle Danny." My mouth fell open as Dick's laughter came through the radio. I lifted my hand up to my face to feel the smile I was wearing—like it suddenly belonged to someone else.

I went back to the dunny. I didn't need to go—I just wanted to look at myself in the bathroom mirror. I looked real hard at my face, turning my head from side to side, so I could see it from all angles. I tried to imagine what a baby with my face would look like, but I couldn't. All of a sudden I wanted to see Alex. I needed to know if he really did look like me.

Dad and me drove to the yards at Timber Creek to meet the fellas. They'd finished taking down the yards at Gum Tree and were real near the station—getting ready for the last place they'd muster. Reg and the fellas were waiting for us. The yards at Timber Creek were permanent ones, which Dad and Granddad had built about fifteen years before. It meant we didn't need to build the fences—they were already there. Dad looked at me and said, "Well, we'd better get cracking, I guess." It was the last part of the muster—I was going to make the most of it.

Reg threw the last of his coffee out of his cup onto the ground. He reckoned we'd have a real big mob from Timber Creek because he'd seen some healthy-looking steers. Dad nodded and said he hoped Reg was right.

Lloyd had already started pumping water from the tanker into the troughs in the yards, and the Barron brothers were unloading the motorbikes from the back of a trailer. Jack walked over and tipped his hat at Dad and me. There was a bit of breeze and Jack looked around at the sky and said, "It's changing." Dad shrugged and said he hoped a bit of breeze might help cool things down. Jack said: "Drought won't last forever." Dad said he hoped he was right about that.

Before I knew it, everyone was ready to go. I was real excited. Reg asked if I wanted to go with Dad or him. Knowing I'd be in school in Alice Springs when Reg and his fellas came back the year after made my excitement slip down into my belly—like when you realize you've forgotten to do something.

I told Reg it was OK—I was going to go with Dad.

TWENTY-NINE

Dad tapped me on the shoulder and asked, "Ready to go?" I laughed and went to give him a dead arm, but he saw me coming and dodged it. I couldn't wait to get out into the desert to find the cattle—I guess Dad felt the same because he turned the stereo up real loud and shouted, "Wooohooo! Here we go!" The music blasted out into the desert.

As we crashed over witchetty bushes and big tufts of dry spinifex, we woke everything up—cockatoos flew out of the gum trees and there were a couple of flocks of galahs, as well as the usual crows. Twice we were fooled by a bunch of big reds. We saw a cloud of dust and went after it—hoping it was a mob of cattle. Dad laughed when he realized we were tailing a couple of kangaroos—he reckoned that if it came to it, we might have to truck them. He said we could live off them, like the Blackfellas did.

When we hadn't seen a single cow, I felt a bit worried. I wondered where they were hiding. As soon as I'd thought that, we bounced down a small ravine and, on the other side of some bushes at the bottom, found a cow and her calf. When it saw us the calf got up and followed its mum as she tried to get away. We got behind them and moved west in the direction of the yards. It wasn't much of a mob, but Dad reckoned it was a start. As we went toward the yards, we found a couple more Herefords and Dad drove round to herd them together—that made four, including the calf. I said they didn't look too bad. Dad agreed. He said he hoped the fellas were having more luck.

Dad radioed Reg and said, "I dunno about you fellas, but we haven't found much other than a few big reds. Over." Lloyd replied to say he'd got a mob of about fifteen, which Elliot was helping him to bring in, and Reg reckoned he had around twenty. For a second I wished I'd gone with Reg, and then felt bad for even thinking it.

When we got to the yards, our four cattle got lost in among the ones Reg was taking in at the same time. I didn't mind—it was a bit embarrassing only having four. Dad picked up the radio and told the fellas we'd try going northeast of the yards next. I asked if he'd let me drive. I'd never driven during the muster before. Dad looked me in the eye, and I could tell he was thinking about it. He put the ute into neutral and said, "OK—we'll see how you go." I couldn't believe he'd said yes. Dad walked round to the passenger side, while I quickly climbed across into the driver's seat—just in case he changed his mind. As he got back in he said, "Now remember—it's not about speed. We could outrun any cow. Just concentrate, keep an eye on the terrain ahead and try not to completely wreck the suspension." He switched the stereo off, and when he saw the look on my face he said, "You need to concentrate." I didn't argue—I knew it was my chance to show him what I could do.

Dad didn't say anything as we followed the fellas into the desert. He held onto the handle above the door and looked out the window. I dunno if he was pretending not to be interested in my driving or if he really was thinking about the desert, but as soon as we were off-road, he didn't shut up. Look out for that bush . . . This bit's always full of holes . . . Careful . . . What's that over there? Left. Go left . . . Go round the trees over there . . . There's usually a mob of them in this area . . . Slow down . . . It's not a race . . . That's it, now change down a gear . . . I wished he'd be quiet and just let me do it. But then I spotted a cloud of dust and pointed to it, so he shouted, "Go on, Danny, get after them!" My first mob.

My heart raced as I dropped down a gear, ready to accelerate to get ahead of them and make them turn round. I went wide and steered round a couple of bushes, before turning hard right and blocking their path. "Nice one," Dad said, as I eased the ute into second and flanked the cattle, carefully herding them back in the direction of the yards. There were about eight of them. I was watching them and thinking that, apart from one old-looking cow, they weren't bad. A little thinner than we would have liked, but much better than the ones we'd seen at Cockatoo Creek and Gum Tree Dam. Dad shouted, "Don't let that one get away," pointing at a young bull, which was starting to break away to the left. I accelerated forward and got round the side of him. That bull didn't care that the ute was made of metal and weighed a couple of tons—I guess he must have had as much to prove as I did. He kept coming and as he clipped the front wing with his back leg, the ute jolted and the sound went right through me. "Watch it," Dad said, "he'll write the ute off." I backed off a little but kept up with the bull's pace so he knew I was still there. He couldn't get away. After driving along like that for about half a mile, I guess that bull got the message because he went back into the mob. "Nice work," Dad said.

Nearer the yard, we met up with Elliot who had a small mob like ours, so we joined up and brought them all in together. Dad kept on with his instructions all the way back. Keep an eye on that one . . . Watch out for the ravine to the right here . . . Now into third . . . That's it . . . Like I'd never changed gear before. Once we'd herded them past Jack into the yard with the others, we waited for Reg and Rick to get back. As Dad picked up the radio to find out where they were, Reg's voice came through. He said they had a big mob and could do with a hand to bring them in. I'd turned round and was heading north of the yards before Dad could reply.

I accelerated up through the gears quickly. The faster we got there, the more chance we had to bring all the cattle in. As we crashed over bushes and bounced out of the cracks in the desert, Dad shook his head. "Not so fast," he complained. He drove just as fast when he was mustering.

It wasn't long before I spotted a dirty mark in the sky to the west. Dad wound his window down to make sure and then he said, "I reckon you're right—that's it. Let's go!" I pushed my foot down and the ute sped forward after the dust cloud.

A tiny white bull catcher appeared from behind some bushes. It looked like one of Jonny's toy cars against the big mob it was bringing in. The cattle kicked up so much dust, it looked like a brown wave was rolling along the desert. Dad told me to pull alongside the mob, behind Reg. We'd flank the back while Reg and Rick took care of each side until the others arrived. We didn't have to wait long. The Barron brothers were soon there on the motorbikes. It felt like a long time since I'd seen a big mob like that. Dad smiled and nodded slowly to himself. I dunno how many were worth trucking—probably not a lot. But I guess that wasn't the point any more. Knowing there were cattle out there was enough. I felt real proud of them. They might not have been the greatest cattle the station had ever produced—but they were Dawson cattle.

When we were at the yards and we stopped to watch the last mob thunder past the gates, Dad clapped his hands. Jack and Rick shut the gates behind the cattle and we jumped out of the ute. The smile I had felt like it was bursting off my face. A hot wind had kicked up out of nowhere and it took my breath away. Grit flew around like sharp mosquitoes, so I pulled my hat down to protect my eyes. It was hard to hear anything with that wind and the noise from all the cattle— but there was no mistaking Lloyd's WOOOOHOOOOO! as he ran round the yards punching the air. Dad laughed at him. Reg came over and, as the two of them watched Lloyd acting like a crazy chook, Reg said, "Well, it's definitely worth celebrating." I looked round and watched the other fellas shaking hands and clenching their fists in the air, like a footie team that's just scored a goal. Man, it felt good. We'd done it. We'd mustered the Dawson cattle!

Bobbie, Emily, and the Pommie showed up with our lunch. They'd come down to let Dad know Sissy would be allowed home later that day, so she'd stay at Aunty Ve's for the night and get on the road with Mum in the morning—in time for the end-of-muster party. Aunty Ve was coming too, in her car, to help bring everything home. Dad smiled and said, "That's music to my ears!" He asked if they wanted to stick around to watch us draft the cattle. They said they would. I looked round and realized the only person missing was Buzz. I reckoned seeing the cattle in the yards would be real good for his training. He needed to get used to being around them if we were going to muster together one day. After lunch I set off back to the station to get him.

When he saw me he shouted, as though to say, about time—where the hell have you been?

We set off in a different direction to normal. We went out into the desert to the north of the station—which confused Buzz. He wasn't sure where we were, so he didn't run off as soon as I opened the gate. But when we went round the side of the house and set off down the track to the yards, he shook his head from side to side, like the athletes do when they're limbering up at the Olympics. Then he started to kick his legs and we were off.

When Buzz saw the yards, all the cattle, the utes, and the fellas, he didn't know which way to turn. He got all jumpy and scared. I panicked a little then. I didn't want him to hurt anyone. I called to him. He didn't know where he was meant to go, so he ran back and forth. Before I could grab him, Reg had run forward and Buzz reared up at him.

I went over as fast as I could, but it was OK, Reg wasn't frightened of the toughest of bulls, so he wasn't scared of Buzz. He held Buzz's neck in his big hands and was whispering something in his ear. Buzz's ears had gone back—flat to his head and his eyes were so wide, I could see some white. Dad had seen what was going on and before I knew it he was shouting, "What the hell's that camel doing here? This isn't a bloody playground, Danny . . ." I tried to explain it was all part of Buzz's training, but Dad wasn't interested. He reckoned he didn't have time to worry about a camel getting loose in the yards. I felt sick. I didn't want him to be mad at me. We'd had such a great morning. I tried to get Buzz to come with me— but he was spooked. All the noise from the cattle, the dust and wind—as well as Dad shouting—had made him jumpy.

The Pommie got down from the back of the ute where she was sitting with Bobbie and Emily to help me with him. I told her I could do it myself.

The road train arrived, like a clap of thunder. Buzz's eyes widened and so I kept talking to him and held his neck until I felt him relax again.

I was watching the fellas working when I noticed Lloyd scrambling to lift his legs up from where he was sat on top of the fence panels. A young bull was going crazy in there and I guess Lloyd was making sure his legs didn't get in the way. But then, that bull kicked the fence panel or something, because I saw Lloyd's body jerk back and then suddenly forward and he fell off into the yard.

As soon as that happened, we all heard a weird sort of a scream.

The fellas all ran toward where Lloyd had been working. Bobbie was on her feet trying to see what was going on. I jumped down from the tailgate and ran across.

I climbed onto the fence panel opposite where Lloyd had been. I looked over into the yard, just as Jack and Rick got the wild bull into the race, so I could see Lloyd. He looked like an old bloody piece of cloth on the ground. There was a lot of blood. I guess he'd been trampled. Dad and Reg lifted Lloyd out of the yard. They each had one of his shoulders over theirs. The worst of his injuries seemed to be his right leg—that was where the blood was coming from. Dad cut Lloyd's trousers open and Reg wrapped a bandage round his leg. It didn't take long for it to turn red. Bobbie drove over and they helped Lloyd onto the backseat of her ute. He had his hand over his face, which was all twisted up in pain. They shut the door and I heard Dad tell Bobbie to get him to the clinic where Mum worked in Marlu Hill—as fast as you can. As we watched the ute speed off down the track, I saw Emily wave from the passenger seat. Dad shook his head and asked Reg if he thought he should have gone with them. Reg shrugged and said he reckoned Lloyd was in safe hands with Bobbie.

Then, I dunno what made me look into the yards, but when I did, I saw some of those damned wild horses in there. There was this real dark stallion, throwing his ragged mane back, rearing up, trying to clear the fence, but he didn't have enough space in there to get a proper run at it. His back legs caught against the metal and he brought down the fence panel. Then suddenly the sound of hooves on metal was deafening as horse after horse and then the cattle ran out of the yards. Before I could tell Dad what was going on, I realized they'd taken down almost a whole side of the yard. It was like everything was against us. I turned round to get Dad and saw Reg run to his bull catcher. I reckoned he'd seen what was happening and was going to head the cattle off. I started to wave and shout at the fellas, but they didn't seem to hear me.

As Reg started the engine of his bull catcher, it coughed and spluttered. That's when I remembered Buzz. I must have let go of him when I ran across to see what had happened to Lloyd. I quickly looked round. He wasn't with the Pommie— she was standing on her own next to Elliot's ute. I was scared Buzz was going to get run down in all the chaos around us, but I couldn't see him—he'd gone. I had a terrible feeling in my belly when I saw a tornado of dirt kicked into the air where the cattle were escaping. They were stampeding back out into the desert, like sand in a real big egg timer.

I shouted Buzz's name, but against the wind, the noise from the cattle and the engines, it was useless. Then I saw him—he was in among the mob outside the fence. I only saw him for a second and then he was gone—like he'd been swept away by the tide. I ran over to the nearest vehicle—it was Elliot's ute. The Pommie was in the way, I shouted at her to move as I got in the driver's seat. The keys were in the ignition, so I started the engine. The ute was moving when the Pommie grabbed the door handle, it swung open and hit her leg. She screamed a little—a bit like that noise dogs make when you accidentally stand on them. I braked—scared I'd really hurt her—but then she jumped into the ute and shut the door. I had no business taking Elliot's ute—I hadn't asked him, so I knew I'd be in trouble for it, but I didn't care. Buzz was the only thing on my mind.

I skidded in the dirt as I accelerated—that was when the Pommie screamed for a second time. "It's Buzz!" I shouted, like that would make her stop. I wondered how I'd find him among all the cattle and dust. I punched the steering wheel, slammed on the brakes and shouted, "DAMNED HORSES!" I swore I'd take Jonny's gun and shoot every last one of them.

I slipped the ute back into first gear and I decided to pull away from the mob, out into the open desert. I went back on myself and headed round the other side of the yards, accelerating quickly through the gears. The Pommie didn't say anything, but I could tell by the way she was gripping the side of her seat, she thought I was gonna kill us both. I was driving so fast that we shot over witchetty bushes like they were blades of grass. As I got into top gear I saw Dad's face flash by—he had his hand in the air. I kept my eye on the dust cloud ahead. Buzz was inside it somewhere—I had to find him.

As we got closer to the mob I tried to wind my window down. The glass was stiff and the handle was awkward. It screeched a bit and then the glass fell down inside the door panel. With the window nowhere to be seen, I looked through the gap where it had been and tried to search the mob for Buzz. It was real hard looking for him and driving at the same time. I could see cattle everywhere—ears, horns, udders, brown and white hides . . . But no Buzz. "Where is he?" I asked out loud.

I told the Pommie to take the wheel, so I could concentrate on looking for Buzz while she steered. As she reached for the wheel, our hands touched. I don't think I'd ever touched a girl's hand before—except for Mum's, or Grandma's, and that was when I was a little kid, so it didn't count. The Pommie stared straight ahead as I glanced back at her. I forgot Buzz for a second—Liz's mouth had taken over my thoughts. Her lips were pushed together because she was concentrating so hard on driving. She had a little wrinkle on her forehead between her eyes and when the sun caught against the sweat on her face, she kind of sparkled. I dunno—it looked a bit like that glitter stuff Emily stuck on everything.

Just then I heard the word DANNY! belch out of the radio. Dad must have really shouted it because his voice was loud, even against the drumming of the hooves outside. He said, "Get out of there—you're in the mob!" I shouted to Liz to ignore him. Dad didn't know Buzz was lost and I didn't have time to explain it to him. I was too busy leaning out of the window shouting for Buzz.

The cattle were all around jostling against us, kicking clouds of dust into the ute. Liz begged me to slow down as she did her best to steer us through. That's when she said she should do the driving so I could concentrate on finding Buzz. I slowed down so Liz could swing her legs into the driver's side of the ute. She moved her right foot to the accelerator and put her boot lightly on mine, so I knew she was there, ready to take over. I lifted mine away and although the

engine lurched a little, it was a pretty smooth changeover—
we didn't stall, or anything.

The engine strained again. There wasn't enough room for
the Pommie to change gear with me stood there, so I pushed
my hand onto the dashboard and pulled myself over to the
other seat. She changed up a gear and smiled at me before
attempting to close the broken window. I felt kind of dumb
then because I didn't know what we should do next. I didn't
even really know where we were. I shrugged my shoulders
and carefully opened the window at the other side. I stood on
the seat and leaned out to get a better view, over the top of
the cattle. I still couldn't tell where we were other than being
in the middle of the mob, so I decided I'd be better off in the
back of the ute, standing against the cab. I'd see more from
up there. I told the Pommie to keep her eye on the road—she
laughed and said, "What bloody road?"

The radio crackled again and Dad's voice shouted, "Daniel! What the hell are you playing at?" I knew I was in big
trouble—no one called me Daniel unless something serious
was wrong. I imagined Dad wringing his hands together and
his eyes all narrow like they were whenever he was angry, so I
didn't reply. I reckoned it'd be best to find Buzz because whatever happened, I'd still be in trouble.

I squeezed out of the window backward and lifted my left
foot up to the sill and held onto the roof. Once I felt like I had
my balance, I counted to three and pushed up, so I was standing on the windowsill—kind of crouching, but on the outside.
It was real bumpy and I was so close to the cattle that I could
feel the heat off them. If I slipped, I reckoned I'd either be
trampled to death or run over by the ute. That's when Jonny
came into my head. I could see him clear as anything. He
looked real serious. It was weird because sometimes, when I

wanted to think about Jonny, I couldn't remember what he looked like. But then at other times, when he just kind of arrived in my head without me thinking about it, I could see him so clearly—like he was sitting right beside me. I had to concentrate. I needed to get into the back of the ute, and it wasn't easy.

I reached for the back of the cab and found a bar to hold onto. I pulled on that bar as hard as I could. At the same time I threw my right leg up toward the back of the ute. I pushed off the windowsill with my left foot too. Everything happened at once. As my right foot reached into the back, the left one dangled behind me and smashed against the metal ridge on the side of the ute, then it swung backward and I kicked a cow. I imagined ending up like Reg's road-train driver—the one who got crushed by the cattle in the trailer—that gave me the strength to pull my body into the back.

As the ute bounced through the desert, I lay face down in the back on the ridged metal, which felt hard against my ribs each time I breathed. I gasped for air and waited for the pain in my leg and chest to stop. As I listened to my heart thump, I noticed a tapping sound. I realized it was the Pommie knocking on the glass at the back of the cab. I got to my knees and looked through the dirty window. Her face was reflected in the rear-view mirror. She was asking if I was all right. I nodded and pulled myself up properly, so I was standing against the cab. I looked around at the mob and realized we were some way from the front. Behind us I could see the yards. Dad's ute was a way back. I was glad I couldn't hear the radio any more. Sometimes, I guess, when you're in that much trouble, you can only keep going forward. I had to find Buzz.

It wasn't easy, though. We were trapped between all the cattle—it was like being in a great big cattle sandwich—only we were the filling. The Pommie did her best to move through the mob. She used the horn a lot and she almost ran one steer down when he refused to move for us. But we needed to pull away from the cattle. We had to go round them to get nearer the front.

I tapped on the window again to tell the Pommie to pull away, out of the mob. She didn't get it, so I said go left. She mouthed back, "What?" We did that a few more times until she eventually understood and gave me a quick thumbs-up. Then the Pommie turned and it knocked me off balance. I fell and gashed my knee on the bottom of the ute. I stayed down for a moment, to catch my breath. I had tears in my eyes but the last thing I needed was to start blubbing like a baby.

I heard the Pommie change down a gear and accelerate. I was surprised—she'd never been much of a driver, so I reckoned she must have learned a thing or two while she'd been at the station. Anyway, we were racing along the side of the mob. I pulled myself up and started to look for Buzz. The dust and the pain from my knee meant I could hardly breathe. I needed my inhaler, but I didn't dare let go of the ute to fish it out of my pocket. If I'd used it, I'd probably have ended up swallowing it, the way the Pommie was driving.

As we flew along, I strained to keep the dust out of my eyes, so I dipped my head down a little. That's when my hat blew clean off. I turned and watched it disappear into the cloud of dust behind us. My hat! It was my good one—the one Greg bought me. The sun was in my eyes then, and it was hot on my neck and head, so that made everything worse.

I tried to look for Buzz and sometimes I thought I saw him, but everything was moving so fast, including us, that when I'd look again, it had all changed—all I'd see was cattle. I wanted to see his long neck lifting his head above the mob, so he could see me with his big, brown eyes. I began to think it was useless. I reckoned he'd probably already been trampled to death. That's when the tears came again. I couldn't stop them. It felt like there was a big mob of them, running down through the dirt on my face. I was too scared to let go of the ute to wipe them away—even with one hand. The snot was heavy and salty on my top lip. I stared ahead into the desert. I couldn't look at the cattle any more. It was no use. I bent my knees and crouched down in the back. My backbone bounced like an old bike chain against the cab as I wrapped my arms around my knees and cried—hard.

When the banging started on the window again, I thought the Pommie was wondering what I was doing. I felt like telling her to mind her own business, but then she'd see I'd been crying. Instead I wiped my wet face on my sweaty arms—hoping no one would be able to tell I'd blubbed.

When I heard her shout, "Look, Danny! LOOK!" I looked at her in the rear-view mirror and saw her hand pointing out of the window to the right.

"It's Buzz—THERE!"

I looked back to where she was pointing and moved to the right side of the ute, to try and see where she meant. There were Herefords and a couple of Brahman, but I couldn't see a camel. I thought she'd mistaken a Brahman hump for Buzz's. Then it felt like everything was in slow motion because he was there—right there in front of us. His long, thin legs were working like pistons to make sure he kept up with the mob. He took long strides and his neck was moving—stretching forward and backward. Then he disappeared. I jumped up and stared as hard as I could. I wanted to see him again to be sure it was really him. A couple of seconds passed and I began to think he wasn't real. But then he appeared and I was sure it was him, so I shouted as loud as I could "BUZZ! OVER HERE, BUZZ! BUZZ—HERE!" One minute I could see him, the next he was hidden behind a bigger heifer or steer. Each time he disappeared I got scared he'd fallen. I told the Pommie to go right. She turned suddenly, and I fell down again. I didn't have a chance to be annoyed—I needed to get up and find Buzz.

It took me a few seconds to get my balance, but then, once I was up, I couldn't believe it—Buzz was just ten metres or so from me. I shouted for him as loud as I could and that's when he saw me. Our eyes seemed to lock and he opened his mouth like he was shouting my name back at me. I kept calling him until eventually there was a gap between a cow and her tired little calf. That's when Buzz made his move out of the mob toward me. He kicked so hard—he was better than any Melbourne Cup winner. I waved my arms and shouted again as we flew over a bump. I hung onto the side and tried not to fall down so I could make sure Buzz stayed with me. But it was OK, he was stronger than I thought. He stayed there, right by my side. He ran with me, just like we'd practiced in our training. I didn't want to take my eyes off him. Even though he looked OK, I was scared he'd fall or the cattle were so crazy they'd trample him.

The Pommie drove us out of the mob. She cleared a path for Buzz to follow. If I'd still had my hat, I'd have thrown it into the air—I was so happy. That's when I needed to touch Buzz, kind of like with the photo of Jonny—to make him real. As I reached out, Buzz's face came closer with each of his strides. Then I felt his breath on my hand as he snorted. I reached up and touched the fur on the top of his bony head and closed my eyes. He was back. Buzz was back!

I banged on the window to tell the Pommie to slow down

a bit. I reckoned we should give Buzz a break—he'd been running for a while. She smiled so hard back at me, it made my cheeks burn. When I looked behind to check on Buzz, I noticed a mob of cattle following him. I thought I might be wrong—but I was right, some of those dumb cattle had got confused and were following Buzz. I told the Pommie to slow down a bit more, to see if we could get Buzz and the mob to go all the way back to the yards. She nodded. As I turned round and looked at Buzz and the mob he had with him I started to laugh harder than I'd laughed in ages. I couldn't stop. I tapped on the window to get Liz's attention and shouted, "We did it! WE DID IT!" Like the three of us were the greatest muster team the Territory had ever seen.

We went past Dad's ute. He'd stopped and was watching us take that mob in. He looked serious, but I couldn't tell how annoyed he was. I put my hand up, but I dunno if he saw. Then I turned to watch Buzz leading the mob. I knew he could do it. His legs never gave up.

Elliot and Spike were putting the finishing touches to the broken part of the fence when we cruised past. Elliot looked up at us. I didn't know what to do—I had sort of stolen his ute. For some reason, I waved at him. He didn't wave back, though—I couldn't blame him. I looked at Buzz and it made me feel better. I shouted for him to keep going. The Pommie drove to the yard gates, which was where Jack was waiting for us. When we stopped I jumped out to help him shut the gates as Buzz ran through with the mob. There were more cattle than I'd thought—they kicked up quite a dust cloud. As soon as they were all in the yard, Jack and I pushed the gates shut. That's when he stopped me. For a minute I was afraid I was in trouble with him—as well as Dad and Elliot. But he nodded and his smile was brighter than the sunset behind him. He said, "A decent mob. That camel's pretty handy, eh?" I don't think Jack had ever really spoken to me before, not like that—man to man. I didn't get a chance to say anything back because Dad grabbed me by my arm and dragged me away.

His hand was hurting me, so I shouted for him to get off, but that just made it worse. His eyes were wide and he had a wild look about him when he threw me down on the ground. I wriggled backward through the dirt, trying to get away from him, but he was too quick. He grabbed me again and made me stand up. I started to shake—I dunno why. It wasn't like I was trying to do it—my body just shook all on its own. When Dad lifted his hand and slapped me hard in the face, the shaking stopped. I dunno if he knocked me down or if I was so shocked that I fell down. One thing's for sure—when I looked up I was scared of him. But then I saw his face twist, like Mum's had at Jonny's funeral. He seemed to choke when he said, "You stupid boy—d'you want to end up like your brother?" Dad's legs seemed to give up and he was on his knees in the dirt next to me. His whole body shook and he gasped for breath. He grabbed me and kind of held me against him. I didn't know what to do, so I kept real still.

After a few minutes Dad let go. He wiped his mouth on the back of his hand and he pinched the top of his nose. He sighed real hard and whispered, "Don't ever do that again." I was still afraid of him so I didn't say anything. "You hear me?" he asked, his voice louder than before. He lifted his head to look at me. His eyes were red like Emily's were when she'd been crying. I felt my chest heave and I nodded once before a tear rolled from both my eyes, down my cheeks.

Dad grabbed me then and gave me a big hug. He said everything was OK and then put his hand on my shoulder.

He said, "You did a great job out there. I dunno if you've done a better job of training that camel or the Pommie." That made us both smile. He picked his hat off the ground, stood up, and knocked the dirt off his trousers. Then he gave me his hand and pulled me up off the ground and said, "Come on, let's go home."

THIRTY

The radio in the kitchen fizzed when Mum's voice came through, it felt like the rains had come. She said they'd be back at Timber Creek before we knew it.

Knowing Alex was so close to the station made us fidgety and nervous when we waited for them to arrive. Dad was the worst. He couldn't sit still. He kept getting up and down, looking at the clock, opening and shutting the fridge without taking anything out. When we finally heard the cars pull into the station, for a moment we all went quiet, so we could listen again, to make sure we hadn't imagined it. Once we were certain, Emily and me ran out of the kitchen toward the back door, like it was a race. I wondered what Mum and Sissy thought seeing us running toward them. It must have looked like something in the house was about to explode.

The doors on the car opened like Brahman ears twitching a fly away. Sissy looked tired and happy, and Mum looked exhausted, but clean as well. She had on a different shirt—one I'd never seen before—and she'd had her hair cut. Dad arrived at the car last of all. He hugged Mum and kissed her cheek. They walked toward Sissy. Dad and her kind of looked at each other for a bit before he asked her if she was OK. Sissy nodded. She looked as awkward as I felt.

Aunty Ve was struggling to get out of her car, as usual. Mum was hugging Emily and she came over and put her hand on my neck. It felt warm, but nice, not sweaty. She said, "How are you, Danny boy?" I said I was OK. I could hear Buzz braying in the distance and felt bad that he was stuck with the poddies, so he couldn't join in.

Even though it was nice to see Mum and it felt good her being home—and Sissy too, I suppose—we were all really waiting to see Alex. Dad had opened the back door and I heard him say, "So here he is then?" Mum and Sissy both smiled and then shushed him. "You'll wake him," Mum said. Dad asked how you undid the little seat thing Alex was in—it looked like it was all tangled up in the seat belt. Sissy leaned in and easily undid the straps so Dad could lift the car seat out. He held it all wrong, but seemed too scared of dropping it to change where his hands were. I could see a bit of white poking out of the seat, but that was all.

Mum said, "Come here, will you, Derek?" And took the seat off him. She lowered it down almost onto the dirty ground so we could all bend over and have a look.

I didn't know what Alex's skin would be like—whether he'd be more black or white, but it wasn't either. It looked real pink. He was much smaller than I'd expected and he looked like someone had accidentally sat on him. His hands were all squashed into his chest and his eyes looked like they'd never open. He had this thin layer of fluff on his head too. It made me wonder if there was something wrong with him because I couldn't see how anything that weird looking would ever grow up to be a normal person.

When we all went toward the house, Alex's hands suddenly

moved, like someone had flicked a switch to turn them on. One hand opened wide, but it was sudden and mechanical, like he was a robot. Then his mouth twitched and he wiggled a foot inside the miniature overalls he was wearing. Sissy wanted to take him inside then, she reckoned it was time for a feed. Bobbie said she'd make everyone a cuppa and Dad said me and Emily should go outside and help him unload Mum and Aunty Ve's cars.

We finished bringing everything into the house, so I went to get Buzz. I reckoned he'd been left out for long enough. I let him go in the garden, so he could hear what was happening inside the house. Sissy came out of her room with Alex and sat with Mum on the sofa. She held Alex on her knee, but he was all floppy and useless, like he couldn't even move his arms in the direction he wanted them to go in. She rubbed his back until he puked.

"D'you wanna hold him, Danny?" Sissy said after she'd cleaned him up. I didn't know if I did or I didn't. Emily said she did though, so Mum made her sit next to Sissy on the sofa. Mum carefully laid him on Emily, so his head was propped up against her belly. Once he was there, it was like no one knew what to do next. After a minute or two, with Emily just staring at her belly, I sat next to her and said I wanted to hold him. Mum told me to bend my arm a bit, so I did and she laid him sideways on my knees, with his head balanced on the inside of my arm. He felt warm, which I hadn't expected, and for someone so small, he seemed very alive. I was scared to move in case I hurt him, so I stayed very still.

Dad came back in from putting things away in the cool room and stood behind the sofa. When Sissy realized he was there, she scooped Alex up from my knees and walked round to where Dad was. She asked him if he wanted to hold his grandson. Dad didn't say anything, he just nodded. She laid him in Dad's big arms and he stroked Alex's little hand with his giant thumb.

"Is that camel eating my plants?" Mum screeched, as she looked out of the glass doors. "He is!" She answered her own question as she flung the doors open and shouted, "Who put the camel in my garden?" Even though I was in trouble, I quite liked it. I raced past her to grab Buzz. I needed to get him before she could get a clothes prop and flog us. As we ran together out of the garden I looked back as I shut the gate and I could see Mum smiling in the doorway. I guess we were all too happy to get angry. I reckoned the end-of-muster party was going to be the best we'd ever had.

I was out in the yard with Buzz when Reg pulled up in his bull catcher. He'd come to get some diesel, but when he saw me with Buzz he shouted, "He sure is a beauty!" When he saw Reg, Buzz forgot about everything else and ran over to say g'day. I guess he could tell Reg was a decent fella and wanted to get to know him. Reg held his hand up to Buzz and said something quietly to him. I strolled over to see what he thought. He nodded at me and said I'd done a real good job— he could see I'd be riding Buzz in no time.

Dad came out of the house then. He said Dr. Willis had called to say Lloyd was well enough to come home. "How's his leg?" Reg asked. Dad said he'd be scarred, but he'd live. Reg reckoned Lloyd had been lucky. Dad nodded and then asked what he thought of Buzz. "He's done a fine job with him," Reg said. That's when I told them I'd like to muster with Buzz one day. That made them laugh. Dad reckoned it'd be like going back sixty years. Reg agreed, but added, "Hell, it'd be wild though, wouldn't it?" He shook Dad's hand and then turned to me and held his big, rough hand out for me to shake too. I'd never really shaken hands with anyone before. I put mine in his and felt him take a firm grip and give my hand a couple of shakes. I felt so good about that, I almost forgot to let go.

As we said see you later to Reg, Mum came out. She said I was meant to be helping get things ready for the muster party. I was going to explain I'd been talking to Reg, but I knew she wasn't interested. Mum was too busy getting all crazy about the party. She said my job was to get the tables lined up outside, so when she put the tablecloths over them, it made it look like one big table. Then I had to find enough chairs for everyone to sit on.

It took a while to find enough chairs for everyone, and moving the tables was pretty hot work. Once it was done, I was real thirsty, so I went inside to get a drink. No one was around except Aunty Ve—I could hear her singing to herself as she folded the laundry in the lounge. I went into the kitchen and was just putting my glass back on the draining board when I heard Mum and Dad. They were in the dining room, and it sounded like they were having a bluey. Mum said she reckoned Dad never kept a close-enough eye on us kids— that he let us run wild like the Blackfellas. Dad said something back about how he should have known better than to have told her about what had happened at the yards with Danny— because he knew what she'd think. That was when Mum said, "What I'd think? What d'you mean—what I'd think? What is it I think, Derek?" Dad didn't reply. "SAY IT!" she shouted. "SAY IT—DAMN IT!" Mum never swore.

Dad's voice sounded small when he said, "You reckon Jonny . . . You think it was my fault, don't you?"

Mum's voice was real small when she said, "I just don't want to lose any more children, Derek." She said she was scared they were going to lose Sissy and Alex too, if they weren't careful. She reckoned Gil was a good kid. He'd tried to call Sissy when they were in Alice to make sure she was OK. Mum started to cry then. I heard her sniff a bit.

Aunty Ve came through with the laundry basket, so I couldn't eavesdrop any more. I told her I was going to see Buzz and ran outside. My heart was beating faster than normal and I had to stop and use my inhaler. I hated it when Mum and Dad rowed. Knowing it was because of what I'd done at the yards made it even worse.

I was with Buzz in the calf pen when Emily came to get me. She said Aunty Ve had brought her camera and wanted me and Buzz to go to the garden to be in the family photo. I heard Aunty Ve shouting, "Yoo-hoo, Danny! Come on. I want a photo of everyone . . . Come on—you can bring Buzz too . . ."

We all lined up in the back garden. Aunty Veronica had put three plastic chairs in a row, for Mum, Dad, and Sissy to sit on. When I looked at Mum, I reckoned she'd been crying. Dad kept his hand round her shoulder the whole time, like he was trying to keep his balance, or something. Mum saw me staring and kind of smiled at me. I didn't know what to do so I smiled back and then looked at my boots. Sissy had Alex in her arms. She looked different too. I dunno how to explain it, but it was like she'd got older.

Liz looked out of the window then and said she'd take a picture of us all if we wanted. Mum thought that was a good idea. She sat down on the front row with Dad and Sissy, while

Aunty Ve stood at the back with me, Buzz, and Emily. Aunty Ve said we should get a move on, or we'd never be ready for the party. We all smiled while Liz took our picture. Once she'd finished, it was funny because Mum said, "I wish Jonny was here." Then she stopped and looked round like she hadn't meant to say it out loud. Even though it made everyone feel weird and we didn't know what to say back, I liked it. Mum didn't talk about Jonny very often—no one did, so it made me feel like it was OK to think about Jonny and to touch his picture every day. But Dad got up and walked away. He didn't look at anyone or say anything. I felt kind of empty again then. Like I was wrong to think about Jonny after all.

THIRTY-ONE

When Dad brought Lloyd home, we all got to have a look at the dressing on his leg. It was real big, but you couldn't really see any blood or anything. As he rolled his trouser leg back down, Lloyd said I could watch when Mum changed the bandage, if I wanted. Sissy said we were all gross.

After that Aunty Ve told Emily not to bother Mum and Dad. They were getting ready for the muster party. She went to find Emily a big piece of wallpaper to draw a picture of the poddies on and Emily took it outside. She was leaning over the little table in the shady area outside the front door where the fellas were drinking coffee and smoking. Elliot pointed at the sky of her picture and asked her what she'd drawn. Emily stopped what she was doing and looked at Elliot like he was dumb. She said, "That's Elaine." Elliot laughed and said he'd heard pigs could fly, but not cattle. I guess he didn't know Elaine was at the carcass dump.

We all heard Alex start screaming again inside and Lloyd looked like the sound made his head hurt even more than his leg did. Elliot got up then and said, "I'm going for a lie down." He slung the last bit of coffee out of his cup onto the ground. I guess everyone was bushed after the muster.

When Emily heard the crying, she got straight up to go and help Sissy with Alex. It was like she had a new poddy calf, or something. She left her picture and ran inside. The wallpaper curled in on itself and the wind caught it, so it rolled off the table onto the ground. Lloyd bent down to pick it up. He uncurled it and looked at the picture she'd drawn. I could tell he didn't get it either. He put the paper down on the table and pushed the tin of crayons on top of it. We both looked up when we heard a car pull into the yard. It was Mick and Gil Smith. That's when Lloyd said, "The in-laws!" I watched the car pull up and could see Gil staring at me. Lloyd said I'd better get Mum and Dad, so I went inside.

Mum and Dad were both in the dining room with Sissy. I told them that Mick and Gil were outside. Dad looked at Mum and then they looked at Sissy. She looked at the tablecloth. Dad put his hat on and said, "Come on then." Mum looked at Sissy and said, "You wait in here with Alex." Sissy nodded. The two of them went outside to see Mick and Gil. Aunty Ve asked Emily to help her in the kitchen and Sissy went into her room with Alex.

I hadn't had a chance until then to touch Jonny's picture, so I went over to the piano. I held the sides of the picture and then before I put it back down again, I touched his face with my nose. The glass felt cold and it steamed up with my breath. When I put my thumb on Jonny's face, it made a clear mark in the wet condensation, bringing him back into focus. When I turned round Aunty Ve was there. She said. "D'you miss him, Danny?" I didn't answer. I looked at her and then at the floor. She said, "Because I do."

I dunno why, but part of me was glad she'd caught me touching the picture, but I felt embarrassed too, hearing her talk about Jonny like that. I shrugged at Aunty Ve and said, "Yeah, he was real good at stuff, like remembering birthdays and the numbers on the cattle tags."

Aunty Ve laughed and sat down. She pulled another of the chairs out and patted it, so I'd sit down with her. She was laughing about the time Jonny fell into one of the dams and accidentally caught a yabby in his hat. Then we both sat there for a while, saying nothing. I guess we were both just thinking about Jonny. Remembering. That was when Aunty Ve smiled and said it was nice to talk about Jonny. I told her no one else did and she nodded. She reckoned it was because everyone was so sad about him dying. I guess it was because no one had ever really said Jonny was dead to me before, but hearing those words made me blub. A red-hot tear burned a streak down my right cheek and then my chest heaved and I didn't think I'd ever breathe again. Aunty Ve pulled me to her and I felt small and cold against her big, warm body. After a few minutes she took a hanky out from her sleeve and handed it to me. It felt warm when I wiped my eyes on it and blew my nose. "D'you need your inhaler, love?" she asked. I shook my head and said I was OK.

"You're not the only one who misses him, you know? How d'you think I feel—and Gil?" Sissy had overheard everything we'd been saying. I shouted at her to rack off—I didn't want to hear about her and Gil, and I didn't want her to know I'd been blubbing either. That's when Aunty Ve held her hands up and said, "Enough," and that we had to call a truce. She put her soft, warm, fat hand over mine and said I had to listen to her, so I did. She looked into my eyes and smiled right at me. She said that if ever I wanted to talk about Jonny, I should just say whatever was in my head. I said I wanted to, but it was hard. No one else ever really talked about him—especially Dad. Sissy nodded, like she knew exactly what I was talking about. Aunty Ve paused, like she was thinking and then said, "Well that's just Dad's way. It doesn't mean it has to be your way." She said the three of us should all make a deal. She said that I should talk to Sissy or we could call her on the phone and talk to her about Jonny because she liked talking about him too. Aunty Ve held out her hand for me to shake, like we were making a deal. As I shook it, I felt different. I dunno why, but it felt good. Like when you've got a secret. I smiled at them both.

Mum came into the house then and asked Sissy to get Alex. Sissy didn't say anything, she just went to get Alex and took him outside in his basket. As Mum held the door open for her, Sissy turned round and smiled at Aunty Ve and me, so I smiled back.

I went to my bedroom to see what was happening from my window. Mum, Dad, and Mick were all leaning against Mick's car, with the empty basket on the bonnet. Sissy was standing opposite them, watching as Gil held Alex in his arms. They were out there for ages, talking and handing Alex from one person to the next, until eventually he started to cry, so they gave him back to Sissy.

Mum, Dad, and Sissy came back into the house. Dad said me and him were going to have a talk—man to man. Mum went with Sissy and Alex into the kitchen. As Dad shut the door, I wondered what it was I'd done wrong. When he sat back down he looked at his hands for a minute. Then he looked right at me and said, "Like it or not, Daniel, Gil is Alex's dad. We all have to accept that."

I stared back at him, waiting to hear what else he had to say. Dad breathed in and then said, "We've known the Smiths a long, long time. Mick's been a mate of mine for years and Gil was mates with Jonny." Dad hardly ever said Jonny's name.

Almost never. Then Dad said something about how he reckoned Sissy and Gil were both far too young to have a baby, but there was no point in thinking about that because Alex was here and we all had to do our best to help him. He reckoned Alex was just like me when I was little and that he deserved just as many chances as I'd had. He said, "He's your nephew, Daniel. Remember that."

Mum came in. Dad looked at her and then back at me and said how they'd talked about it with Mick and they reckoned me and Gil needed to shake hands and put things behind us. I said there was no way I was shaking his hand. He was Jonny's mate and he'd been rooting with Sissy. I dunno why the two things were important, but somehow I knew they were. I said it wasn't my fault. That's when Mum said sometimes it didn't matter whose fault things were. She said sometimes things happened that were no one's fault and that we had to find a way to move forward. Dad put his arm round her then and they said I had to go out and see Gil. I didn't want to. I said I'd do it another day. Dad said, "No, Daniel, now."

He followed me outside. The sun was real hot and I didn't want to look at Gil. He was leaning against Mick's car, with his arms folded. When I got to where they were, I didn't look him in the eye—not straightaway. I stared at his yellow T-shirt instead. Dad said something about how he reckoned me and Gil should let bygones be bygones. Mick nodded. Gil and me just stood there. No one said anything for a bit and then Dad said, "Well we haven't got all day, so come on, you two, just shake on it, will you?" Gil held his hand out then and I heard him say, "Fair dos." I didn't want to, but I took his hand and shook it a bit harder than I'd shaken Reg's a few hours earlier.

Mick kind of laughed and said, "Good. Let's go." Him and Gil got in the car and Dad and me went back inside.

THIRTY-TWO

Mum was going crazy in the kitchen, trying to get everything ready. She said I had to feed all the animals because everyone else was too busy getting ready for the party. She looked at her watch and said she'd never have it all done in time. Aunty Ve shook her head and winked at me. I decided I'd be better off outside feeding the animals—starting with the chooks. By the time I'd got to the poddies pen, fed Buzz, and shut them all in for the night, it was getting dark. When I went back to the house, there was music spurting out into the garden in bursts. I went round the side of the house to see what was happening—hoping I'd avoid Mum. I found Dad wrestling with the old hi-fi speakers and an extension cable. I asked what he was doing and he said, "A party's not a party without music." He'd got a dodgy connection, though, and until he found it, all we heard was the odd cough and splutter from Willie Nelson. Then Lloyd and Elliot showed up. They were both all scrubbed and clean, like new.

When Dad fixed the dodgy connection everyone cheered. Aunty Ve came out then with piles of cutlery and plates, which the fellas helped her put down on the table. She told me I needed a shower and that I'd better get a move on before Mum blew a gasket. As I went through to the bathroom, Emily ran past me flicking her wet hair in my face.

After I'd had my shower and I'd washed out a whole week's worth of knots, smoke, sweat, and dirt from my hair, I heard the Crofts' horn shouting their arrival, so I ran outside to see them.

Greg carried two whole crates of beer with him from the car, while Mary and Ron carried the food they'd brought. Penny had come too. She was with Dick, who just wheezed along with them—I guess carrying that chest of his must have been enough. I dunno what was inside it, but it sounded heavy. Mum and Dad stood outside the house to let them in. Penny, Mary, and Ron followed Mum into the kitchen with the food, while Dick and Greg went with Dad round the back to get a beer. They came back out and talked nonstop about the muster. It was almost dark, the sky was inky blue and Dad was standing in a white pool thrown into the garden by the outside light. As moths and mozzies danced around him, Dick and Greg asked how Dad thought we'd done out of the muster. He said he hoped we'd made enough to keep us from going under. Dick slapped Dad's back and said, "Sure you will—we've seen worse, you know?"

When I looked behind me, I saw Bobbie and the Pommie. They both looked real clean, sort of shinier than they usually did. Bobbie's hair was tied back in this silvery thing, but she'd made a bit of a mess of it—she'd missed a load of bits, which dangled down in her eyes like curly spaghetti. Her face wasn't like it normally was either. Her lips looked wet and her eyes were all dark. They looked like they couldn't open properly. I'd never seen her look like that before, and I guess I was staring at her because she said, "What are you looking at?" I felt dumb then, so I looked away and said, "Nothing."

The Pommie had her hair down round her shoulders, but her face was all weird too. Her eyes seemed real big and sparkly, she just seemed shinier than normal somehow. I looked round and saw Greg was staring too. When he saw me looking at him, he started studying the bottle of beer he was holding, like he'd noticed something real interesting on the label. When he looked up he saw Bobbie and the Pommie chatting with Lloyd. Greg got up and dragged his chair over to where they were sitting.

Not long after that Mum, Aunty Ve, and Penny started bringing some of the salads out to the table. The barbecue had been lit and Dad threw a few of his burgers on the hot plate. They hissed and Mum reckoned they smelled real good. They smiled at each other. I hoped they wouldn't kiss. They didn't get a chance, though, because that was when Reg and his mob rumbled into the yard.

Seeing them was the strangest of all. I dunno what they'd done to themselves, but it was a bit like when you dipped a paintbrush in turpentine. All the bits of desert, which had got stuck in the sweat on their skin and on the wind in their hair were gone. The bloodstains on their clothes had disappeared and even their boots looked clean. Aunty Ve whistled at them and shouted, "Look, girls—it's the bloody Chippendales!" Reg laughed, and lifted his cap off toward Aunty Veronica, and said in a voice a bit like the Pommie's, "Good evening, ladies."

Dad was laughing and said, "Jesus, Ve! Let the fella get a beer before you start hitting on him, will you?" Aunty Ve laughed. Dad handed all the fellas some beers and then held his in the air in front of him. He said, "Thanks again—we couldn't have done it without you fellas." Everyone said,

"Cheers!" and then they took a big drink from the bottles. That was when Reg said, "And here's to Danny—the Camel Man—for saving the day." Dad smiled at me and I heard his voice clearer than anyone else's when they all said, "To Danny!" I don't think I'd ever felt as tall as I did then.

The voices around me hummed. Everyone was talking about the food, the home-brew, or where the fellas would be working next. I was too busy thinking about what Reg had said to join in with them. But then I heard the Pommie say something to Greg and Elliot about getting everything ready for when she left tomorrow. I didn't know she was leaving. I asked what she meant, and she said Mum had told her that Aunty Ve was going to be staying at Timber Creek for a while to help Sissy with the baby and things, so we didn't need Liz to work for us any more. She reckoned it was all organized— Liz was going to get a lift back to Alice with Reg and his mob when they left in the morning after the party. I felt funny about that. I didn't know what to say. My face felt hot. I looked at Liz and she looked at me. I dunno why, but she said, "We can write to each other, if you like. I know it can be lonely out here sometimes, but you'll be at boarding school soon." I told her I was OK. I had Buzz. I dunno why, but I couldn't say anything else after that. My throat kind of closed up and Liz looked a bit sad, or something.

Greg said Liz would be back in civilization soon, as I walked away. I dunno what made me do it, but as I walked past the table I picked up one of the bottles of home-brew and hid it behind my back. I went round the side of the house and took a big gulp of it. It tasted bad. I still didn't like it and that made me mad. I wanted to be like Dad and the others.

When I heard Mum say the meat was ready, I went back round into the garden. Dad went over to the barbie and loaded the burgers, ribs, and sausages onto a couple of plates. Aunty Ve put them on the table and shouted, "Get started." When everyone sat down and started eating, it was quiet enough to hear the crickets croaking. Bobbie said, with her mouth half-full: "That's shut us up!" And Dick nodded, he said, "Bloody good tucker as usual, Sue and Ve," and Reg raised his bottle of beer and said, "Hear! Hear!"

After we'd eaten, Mum and the girls cleared the table and us fellas stayed outside and talked about the cattle. Greg and Elliot didn't join in. They were talking about the Pommie. Greg wanted to know what Elliot's game was. Elliot wasn't happy about that—I could tell because his face was red and he looked at the ground, like he didn't know what to say. "Well? You making a move or what?" Greg asked. By then Dad and everyone else was listening too. Elliot looked at Greg and said, "What's it to you?" And Greg laughed and said, "I just want to know the lie of the land, mate . . ." Everyone laughed then—even Elliot. I dunno why they talked like that about Liz. I didn't like it. I wanted to talk about the cattle, or cricket. I hated all that stuff. It made me want to puke. I noticed a half-empty bottle of beer on the ground and got up and pretended to move it out of the way. No one noticed me take it and put it round the side of the house with the empty one I'd had earlier. I took a quick drink of it and even though it was warm and tasted worse than the first one I didn't throw up.

Liz came out to collect the last few plates from the table, so the fellas stopped talking about her. She asked, "What's going on out here?" Dad and Greg both said, "Nothing," at the same time, so Liz looked at them like they were crazy and went back inside.

Soon after that I noticed the music had gone off. I went round the side of the house with another half-empty bottle of the home-brew, had a gulp of the beer and went inside to change the CD. Then I went outside, round the side of the house to where my empties were. I drank the last of the dregs out of the bottles and sat on the ground. I dunno why, but all of a sudden I wished Jonny was with me.

When I went back into the garden where everyone else was, the Crofts said they had to get back—because it was late. Dick yawned. I said I didn't want them to go. Dick smiled and said we'd do it all again next year, when Reg and the fellas came back to muster. I said I wouldn't be around the next year because I'd be at school in Alice. I don't think Dick knew what to say, so he rubbed his bony hand in my hair.

While everyone else waved the Crofts off, I took another bottle of the home-brew—a full one this time—and went round the other side of the house and necked it, just like I'd seen Dad and the fellas do. It didn't taste as bad as the other bottles I'd tried. I reckoned it must have been a different batch. My belly felt like it was going to burst, though, and then I did the biggest burp I'd ever done. As I swigged from the bottle, I thought about Liz. I didn't want her to leave the station. After everything with Buzz and the muster, it felt like we were mates, or something.

As I went back round to where the party was happening, I noticed a light was on in the shop. I thought someone must have left it on by accident, so I went over to turn it off. Walking was kind of strange though—the ground kept moving and everything looked a bit blurred. I reckoned it was just because it was dark. When I got nearer I thought I could hear voices. I tried to remember how much of the beer I'd drunk, but then I saw Sissy and knew what I was seeing was real. She was in the shop with Gil and little Alex. They were kissing. I didn't even think about what I was doing, I just threw the door wide open and shouted, "What d'you think you're doing?" But the words didn't come out right. Sissy turned round and said, "What?" like she hadn't heard me. I swallowed and told them they'd be in big trouble if Dad found them. That's when Gil said, "I only wanted to see Alex again. I don't want trouble." He had his hands in the air. I pointed at him, but it looked like the room was moving. I felt crook. I swallowed some spit and had to bend over to steady myself. That was when Sissy said, "Are you drunk?" at the same time as I threw up all over the floor. "Aww! Gross!" she shouted, then picked Alex up and carried him outside. Gil tried to get hold of my arm, but I shrugged him off and fell over. As he held out his hand to me I told him he was a mongrel. I heard Sissy say, "Jesus, Danny. He's trying to help you." Then I heard them laughing, and that made me real angry. I got to my feet and said I was going to kill him. I don't remember things too well after that. Sissy grabbed my arm and called me an idiot. She kind of marched me across the yard to the house. I remember thinking she seemed real mad with me. She must have taken me into my bedroom because I can kind of remember lying in bed and her pulling my boots off. But that's it. Nothing else.

THIRTY-THREE

Alex was screaming his head off when I woke up the next day. It made my head hurt. I'd slept in my clothes and I felt real hot. I sat up and threw the doona off. I felt weird. After a minute or two I decided to get out of bed and went into the dining room. Sissy was sitting at the table having a cup of coffee. I said, "Can't you make him quieter?" Sissy stared at me. She had the same look on her face as she'd had the night before when she'd walked me back to the house. "Sore head?" she asked and then carried on drinking her coffee.

Aunty Ve came through from the kitchen wearing a dressing gown, with her flabby feet tucked into a pair of little pink slippers. Her hair was stuck straight up at one side and she looked like her eyes had just opened for the first time. Aunty Ve said, "If only God made babies with a volume control, eh, Siss?" Sissy looked away and didn't say anything.

Aunty Ve picked Alex up and rocked him for a bit before putting him back in his seat. She told me to talk to him, to see if that might calm him down. She told me to sit with Alex while her and Sissy made us all some bacon sandwiches.

Emily came out of her room, rubbing her face and

scratching her leg. "He's noisy," she said. I couldn't be bothered to speak to her, so we sat in silence while Alex screamed at us. Bacon smells came from the kitchen and my stomach rumbled. I was perishing.

Everyone was there for brekkie, except Mum, Dad, and the Pommie. She was packing, and Mum and Dad were still in bed. Aunty Ve reckoned that considering how late some of them had stayed up, she was very surprised to see them before lunchtime. Elliot, Lloyd, and Bobbie just grunted. They looked a lot like I felt.

As Aunty Ve put the plates of bacon sandwiches down on the table and swapped them for Alex, it felt like years since we'd had anything like that for brekkie. After she'd set fire to the kitchen, the Pommie had only ever made us toast and everybody jam. When I thought about the fire it seemed like a long time ago.

Mum and Dad got up while we were eating our brekkie. Mum reckoned the smell of bacon worked better than any alarm clock. Elliot reckoned it was the best hangover cure too, and everyone laughed a little. Aunty Ve went back into the kitchen and cooked us a load more.

Not long after we'd all finished eating, we heard the roar of a truck in the yard. It was Reg's mob. They'd come to the house to say good-bye. We all went out to see them and I went to get Buzz. That was when I saw the Pommie. She looked tired, her eyes seemed real small compared to normal. She waved when she saw me, so I smiled back.

She had her bag on her back like a little snail. She was saying good-bye to Mum and Dad. She said she'd had the best time ever at the station, and Mum and Dad reckoned she should come and visit again—next time she was in Australia. The Pommie hugged Bobbie and said she'd keep in touch. She nodded and smiled at Elliot and Lloyd and said, "Thanks for putting up with me." Aunty Ve gave her a real big hug—so big, the Pommie nearly disappeared. Emily gave the Pommie the picture she'd drawn of Elaine flying in the sky. That made the Pommie blub. Emily asked her if she liked it and the Pommie coughed and said, "Very much." She rubbed Sissy's arm and told her to take care, as she kissed her little finger and touched Alex's head with it.

When it was my turn to say good-bye to her, we just stood there.

I couldn't think what to say.

Liz said she'd miss me and Buzz most of all. I nodded, but I didn't say anything. We stood there looking at each other for what felt like ages. Then I held my hand out for her to shake. She took it. Her hand felt warm and small, but it was a pretty good handshake for a girl. That made me smile—and she smiled back.

When Liz climbed into Reg's bull catcher, he was already in it waiting for her. "See you all next year," he said and waved. He revved the engine and led the others out of the yard. As they passed through the gates Reg's horn belched and Alex woke up again. Sissy sighed and shut her eyes, so Mum picked him up and gently rocked him from side to side.

I watched the Pommie go. She waved at me, so I lifted my hand to wave back, but Buzz wanted to run along with them, so I had to grab him and hold him still.

I dunno if she saw me wave or not.

Everyone walked back to the house then, but I stayed where I was with Buzz, until the dust cloud Reg and the fellas had left behind them had settled and I knew the Pommie had really gone. That's when a fat drop of water hit my head making me look up at the sky. Then another hit me on the cheek. It felt cold. I wiped it off and looked at the wet on my fingers. More drops peppered the ground around me like slow machine-gun fire.

I reckoned Jonny must have been in the heaven above Timber Creek, after all, so I looked up again and smiled at him.

Acknowledgments

This book would not have been written except for a chance meeting with my old friend, Michael Wilson, in Alice Springs. He introduced me to the Martin family when they were looking to hire a house girl. As a result, I spent an incredible month working at their cattle station during the annual muster. The way of life and the vast beauty of the desert left a lasting impression. So thank you to you all.

I am very grateful to my parents, Ian and Janet, for their unwavering support. Without it I would have given up on all of this a long time ago. My brothers, Rob and Matt, have unwittingly provided inspiration—I cannot imagine who Danny Dawson would be without them. I would also like to say thank you to my gran, Joyce, as well as my sisters-in-law, Heidi and Katy, for their support.

I am indebted to my agents, Christine Green and Claire Anderson-Wheeler, as well as Charlie Sheppard at Andersen Press. I will always be grateful for their belief in me and *Timber Creek Station*.

I must also pay tribute to the patience of my friends Emma Ward and Hayley Jones. Not once did they fail to respond to my many requests for help and advice. I would also like to say thanks to Barbara Smith, Steve Jones, Zoe Boynton-Gonzalez, Richard Barker, Sheraz Ahmad, Nick Morrison, Nigel Whitfield, and Sarah Caldecott. Whether they know it or not, they all helped to get this book published.

About the Author

Ali Lewis was born in rural North Yorkshire, England. After graduating from university, she went into journalism. In 2002 she took a break from reporting to travel the world. It was in Australia, working on an outback cattle station, that she found the inspiration for her first novel, *Timber Creek Station*, which was shortlisted for Britain's prestigious Carnegie Medal.